HEAVEN'S PAVEMENT

A Novel By

Juarez Roberts

This book is a work of fiction. Any
resemblance to actual persons living
or dead is coincidental.

ISBN 1453647910

 For even in heaven his look
and thoughts
 Were always downward bent,
admiring more
 The riches of heaven's pavement,
trodden gold,
Than ought divine or holy.

     Milton, <u>Paradise Lost</u>

Juarez Roberts is kneeling on the lower left.

FORWARD

This is the story of three paratroopers from a fictitious Parachute Infantry Regiment, the 705th. Having jumped in Normandy and fought in The Bulge, the regiment was old and battlewise. Their roster of veterans was one quarter old time original members of the Regiment, one quarter replacements from the Normandy jump and one half replacements from The Bulge.

Now, on the nineteenth of March 1945, the Regiment with its mix of old and new troopers was revving up for another combat jump. Instead of plunging right into the middle of it, I have purposely chosen to start this story at the beginning of the preparations for this combat mission. I wanted the reader to experience the rising tide of tension that culminated in the unbelievable violence and excitement of an airborne assault across the Rhine River onto defended ground in Germany. The jump was at 10:30 in the morning and it was a bloody day.

In Heaven's Pavement I have compressed my own combat experience with the 507th Parachute Infantry in Normandy, the Bulge and over the Rhine into one fictional jump. The combat in Heaven's Pavement is real. These events either happened to me or I personally saw them happen to others. The 705th Regiment, the characters, and the story are all fiction, made up as a way of showing, at both the spiritual and physical levels, the impact of combat on human lives and everything surrounding them.

When the surviving paratroopers came home from World War II, we were thought of by some as heroes. We thought of ourselves as no more than good troopers. The real heroes were those who died over there. Heaven's Pavement is a salute to those who will never come home and who will be a sacred part of the soil of Europe forever.

Chapter 1

The 705th Parachute Infantry Regiment's combat record was one of blood-spattered valor. They had jumped three thousand troopers deep into Normandy on the night of 5 June 1944. Thirty-four days later the Regiment was down to four hundred and fifty men who were withdrawn from combat and returned to their home base in England.

There the survivors were awarded Bronze Stars and the regiment was given the Distinguished Unit Citation. The 705th was billeted in British army barracks near the southern end of the Salisbury Plain. By winter they had acquired replacements and were back to full strength.

24 December 1944. At noon the 705th was alerted, and nightfall found them loading onto C47's in the midst of snow flurries. They were in full battle gear, weapons, ammo, grenades, high explosives. The 705th was on their way to help turn back the German advance in the Ardennes forest.

After a short flight they arrived over a location on the French side of the Meuse River. A jump had been ruled out due to unfriendly terrain and the difficulty of night reassembly. There were three separate landing sites for the regiment. One by one, planes landed between two rows of gasoline burning in the snow. After disgorging its cargo of paratroopers, the plane would take off and another plane would land. It was slow, but by Christmas morning the regiment was down and fighting. Merry Christmas, 705th!

Thirty-six days later they had lost almost half of their men, one thousand three hundred and seventy nine killed, wounded, and missing in action. But the combined efforts of American units had not only stopped the Germans but had pushed them back to the Rhine.

By 19 March 1945 they had once more been brought up to full strength and were quartered in pyramid tents near Chalons sur Marne. Right after noon chow on the 19th they were alerted. As the men returned to the tent area, they were buzzing with excitement. The regiment was to make another combat jump!

In the army everything was alphabetized. Shortreed, Sanford and Sellers had come over with the regiment in 1943. Now they were the last of the demolition platoon's original S's. Shortreed and Sanford were buddies. Sellers hung out with them a lot because it polished his image as an old-timer, but he was only tolerated by them. As they returned to the tent area, they theorized about the alert.

"We won't jump. It's just a false alarm," Sanford wished aloud.

"We're going to jump all right," Sellers told them. "We're going deep into Germany to liberate the death camps."

"You know how the army fucks around." Shortreed laughed. "There'll be a dozen alerts before anything happens."

"If it ain't death camps, it'll be across the Rhine." Sellers was always sure he knew everything.

As they entered the company area, Sellers spotted a trooper he wanted to see.

"Hey Smitty!" he called. He left them and ran after him.

"What's with Sellers?" Sanford asked.

Shortreed laughed. "Smitty owes him money."

"That's all he ever thinks about." Sanford spat contemptuously.

They turned away and continued to their tent. On each of the bunks lay a mimeographed list of what to take with them when they left for the staging area. To the rookies this list validated their secret misgivings. What a lousy break! The war was almost over and here they were, getting ready to make a combat jump!

Sellers entered the tent while Shortreed and Sanford were packing their gear. He sat on his bunk and began counting a fistful of francs onto the bunk. Shortreed finished with his gear and stacked it on his bunk. "You know where to find me," he told Stanford.

"At that house near the bridge?"

Shortreed nodded. "My mark will be on the window."

Sellers stopped counting his money to listen to this exchange.

"What'll I do if they issue ammo?" Sellers wanted to know.

"Draw mine."

Sanford objected."But they won't give it to me."

"Kramer will."

"But—"

Shortreed overrode him. "Tell him I'm getting laid."

"Oh, you going to see your true love?" Sellers kidded.

Shortreed bristled angrily for a moment, then relaxed slightly. "I wish," he said bitterly, then turned and lifted the bottom of the tent and slipped out under it.

"What's eating him?" Sanford asked.

"When we came back from Normandy there was a Dear John waiting for him."

"His girl friend left him?"

"His wife," Sellers corrected and returned to counting his money.

At regimental communications Perine, the switchboard operator, was busy switching calls and listening in on all calls from Division to Colonel Breit, the CO of the 705th There was a sound and he looked up to find Shortreed had come in quietly.

"What's up, Shortreed?"

"When're we moving out?" Shortreed asked.

Perine lowered his voice conspiratorially. "I just heard General Hobart tell Colonel Breit to be ready at 2200 hours, but we won't load onto transport until after 2400 hours."

"Is that another bullshit alarm?" Shortreed wanted to know.

Perine shrugged. "Could be. But they got the MP's patrolling all the roads."

"Why?"

"We're restricted to the regimental area."

"Then it might be real." Shortreed shrugged. "But either way, whatever happens, we're going to be part of it."

Both laughed.

"See you later," Shortreed said and left.

It was dusking as he moved quickly through the back row of tents and out onto a narrow road that led to a small village a quarter of a mile distant. The village was strictly off limits to the 705th, by orders of the Regimental CO, Colonel Wheatley C. Breit.

A jeep turned onto the road from the village and Shortreed ducked into the underbrush. While he gave the jeep time to move past him, his mind was on Cecile, the French girl who was waiting for him in the village. She was pretty, but she sure as hell wasn't any true love. He didn't believe in that crap anymore.

It was nearly dark and he was still almost a hundred yards from her house at the outskirts of the village. He listened for a moment to see if he could hear a jeep motor, then sprinted the remaining distance in the gathering gloom.

He stopped before the second house beyond the bridge, and rapped at the shuttered window. As he waited, he took chalk from his pocket and quickly scrawled a crude pair of parachute wings and the letter "S" on the shutter. If Sanford had to come for him, this would help.

He rapped again. "It's me."

There was a rustle inside the room. The shutter opened and he climbed quickly in the window.

In the tent area, when darkness fell the replacements, most of whom had never been to combat, were seized by a sudden manic excitement. Their gear was packed and with the darkness, trucks began arriving on the road outside company headquarters. The first thing that happened was that Kelly took a jerry can full of gasoline and poured it in a long thin line down the middle of the company street, then struck a match to it. The graveled street wicked up the whole jerry can and a line of flaming gasoline blazed down the middle of the street for two hundred feet. Amid cheers and urging from the company, Kelly mounted the message center bicycle and rode it down the length of the street, weaving in and out of the ribbon of flame, while there arose a big argument over who would take the next ride. Someone from I Company fired off a clip from a tommy gun into the air. Then things began to accelerate. The entire regiment buzzed with pent-up energy, Demolition set off a couple of pounds of C2 down by the creek. They were all sharp-set, peeling off layers of civilization, reducing themselves to basic combat mind-set as the clock wore away toward the time of departure.

At 2100 hours, orders came from Division rescinding the 2400-hour departure time and ordering the regiment to be loaded on trucks and standing by to move out in convoy at 2200 hours.

Immediately Sanford slipped away to get Shortreed. As he left the glare of burning gasoline behind, he could see easily in the bright moonlight. Since time was short he ran the quarter mile or so to the village, no big feat, since the whole regiment as part of their conditioning was running four miles every other day.

As he ran across the bridge at the edge of the village, he slowed to a fast walk. He could hear the sound of a jeep motor at the other end of the village. He hurried along until he found the window shutter that had been marked with parachute wings by Shortreed.

He rapped at the window, shattering the quiet, and called out in a loud whisper, "Shortreed. Shortreed, it's me, Sanford."

The sound of the jeep got louder. More urgently he rapped again and after a moment someone unlatched the shutter. The jeep continued to approach, but finally the shutter opened and the French girl Cecile appeared in the window in a hastily pulled on negligee. It was flimsy and brief and did little to hide her well-endowed body. Embarrassed, Sanford tried hard not to stare.

She scolded him in a heavy accent, "Shush! Do you wish to awaken the dead?"

"I've got to talk to my buddy Shortreed," he told her urgently.

"Why?"

"It's important."

"You can tell him tomorrow." Cecile shrugged, doing little to lessen his discomfiture. She started to close the shutters, but Sanford grabbed them.

"The regiment's moving out!"

'Wait." She ducked back into the room, pulling the shutters closed behind her.

Sanford waited nervously, listening for the sound of the approaching jeep. It had become increasingly clear that if he didn't get inside fast, the MP patrol would be upon him. He began to pound on the shutters.

"Hey, Shortreed!" he called urgently. "The MP's are coming! What'll I do?"

Suddenly the shutters flew open and Cecile beckoned to him. He crawled quickly through the window, closing the shutters behind him. It was none too soon, for the MP patrol passed by seconds later.

Inside the house where he could see her more clearly, Sanford found Cecile even more toothsome and he gawked at her openly. She brushed her hair and ignored him.

Shortreed was nowhere in evidence, but his jump jacket was hanging over the back of a chair and his dog tags and a money clip lay on the dressing table. The tags were on top of the money clip. Cecile looked furtively at the money clip. She would have liked to grab it, but Sanford was still gawking at her and gave her no opportunity.

After a moment, Shortreed entered from the bathroom, trailing bootlaces and buttoning his pants.

"What's up, Sanford?"

"We're going to combat!"

"Is this another rumor?" Shortreed wanted to know.

"Perine's on the switchboard. He heard the General tell Colonel Breit."

"I bet." Shortreed was skeptical.

"Honest! The company's already lined up on the company street by now."

"Perine told me the plan was for 2400 hours -"

"It was moved up," Sanford said. "We're moving out at 2200 hours."

Quickly, Shortreed wrapped his bootlaces around his boots and tied them. He could lace them later. He grabbed his dog tags and put them around his neck and slipped on his jump jacket.

"If we really hurry we can make it," Sanford told him urgently.

"Check the road."

Sanford opened the shutters and peered out.

Cecile put her arms around Shortreed and bellied up to him. "Please, Blondi, you stay here?"

"Sorry," Shortreed said. "We're moving out."

She kissed him warmly. But as they kissed, her hand went to and lifted the money clip from the table.

Sanford turned from the window and Shortreed, breaking from the embrace, looked at him questioningly.

"The road's clear," Sanford reported.

"Okay. Just a second."

With Shortreed's attention apparently distracted, Cecile took advantage of the moment to back away from him and stuff the money clip quickly into the front of her negligee. But now he was looking at her again and advancing with hand outstretched.

"Hand it over, baby."

"But Blondi-"she protested as Shortreed made a grab for her. "What do you want?"

She ran across the room to where Sanford stood nervously by the window.

"Don't let her get out the window!" Shortreed shouted.

She took refuge behind Sanford, pleading, "Please don't let him hurt me."

Sanford squared his shoulders and blocked Shortreed, who told him, "Get out of the way!"

Sanford stood his ground. "Why are you bothering her? Leave her alone!" he demanded.

Shortreed pushed Sanford aside. "She stole my money clip!"

He grabbed Cecile who struggled silently. Shortreed pinioned her arms and Sanford cocked his fist for a punch, warning," Shortreed, I don't want to fight with you-"

"Then don't!"

In civilian life, Sanford had been a heavyweight boxer. In a fight with Shortreed, he would get a few lumps, but Shortreed would get his ass kicked.

"You ain't going to shove no lady around while I'm in the room!" Sanford told him angrily.

"She's no lady!" Shortreed protested.

Sanford glowered. "If you don't turn her loose, I'm going to hit you!"

"Didn't you hear me?" said Shortreed, outraged' "She stole my money clip!"

For the first time, doubt began to assail Sanford. He relaxed his combat stance slightly and asked Cecile, "Do you have his money?"

"No!" she protested. "He lies!"

"Turn her loose," Sanford ordered.

"It's in the front of her negligee."

"I don't believe you."

"Reach in and get it!"

Taking advantage of their confrontation, Cecile made another effort to escape. Sanford wasn't sure how to take this. Assailed by uncertainty, his glance went shyly from Cecile's face to the front of her negligee. Should he?

Tentatively he reached toward the lacy cleavage, muttering in embarrassment, "I'm warning you, Shortreed-"

"Go on!" Shortreed told him. "Get it!"

"It better be there," Sanford said.

"If it's not, I'll give you a free punch at me," Shortreed invited.

Sanford took a deep breath and steeled himself to reach into the front of Cecile's negligee. Her struggling grew more frantic, but Shortreed was able to hold her fast.

"Excuse me, mam'selle," Sanford said almost pleadingly, his face a study in conflicting emotions. Embarrassed, angry at Shortreed, he was at the same time pleasantly aroused at the prospect of putting his hand into the top of Cecile's negligee.

Mumbling again "Excuse me," he reached down past all that lace and there it was. With an accusing glance at Cecile, he handed the money clip back to its owner.

"I told you,' Shortreed said.

"Well she acted like a lady." Sanford was apologetic. "She sure had me fooled."

Shortreed shoved the money clip into his pocket. "You're catching on."

"To what?" Sanford asked, bemused.

"They're all like that."

Sanford looked doubtful.

"Pigs!" Cecile shouted. "*Cochon*, get out!" She began throwing things at them from the dressing table.

Prudently Shortreed beat a hasty retreat through the window. But Sanford lingered long enough to lecture her reproachfully, "You ought to be ashamed of yourself. I believed you."

In retort she hurled a box of face powder at him. It opened, spattering Sanford with a cloud of powder. A jar of cold cream followed, and Sanford dove quickly out the window after Shortreed.

At the company area a line of army troop trucks waited on the road with motors idling. The drivers stood near their trucks, smoking and talking quietly. In the background, Headquarters Headquarters Company was lined up in formation. Behind the lines of men, the ribbon of flame still burned here and there, and the company dogs wandered aimlessly around in the empty area.

First Sergeant Whitson and Lieutenant Best stood before the demolition platoon who stood easy with their packs on the ground before them. Whitson held a flashlight for Best, who was calling the roll, fast and snappily. The men were young, vigorous and athletic looking, and wore and carried all of their combat gear, except ammo, explosives, and parachutes. Nearby other platoons had lined up and were beginning to respond to roll call.

In the back row of the demolitions platoon, Sellers stood at one side of a gap in the line. He was stocky but somehow managed to look dapper and stood out as the only man present in a jump suit with creases ironed into the legs and sleeves.

The gap in the line had two packs lying on the ground. Sanford's BAR and Shortreed's tommy gun were propped against them. On the other side of the gap, the replacement, Skidmore, was determined to do his best to cover for Shortreed and Sanford. They were from the original cadre of the 705th and demigods to him.

"Oglethorpe, William H."

"Here sir."

"Perine, Robert M."

"Here sir."

As the roll call approached the "S's", Sellers looked at the two packs lying on the ground and thought, I knew they were going to get caught.

"Sanford, Augustine M."

"Here, sir," Skidmore answered.

Sellers shook his head. "Assholes."

"Sellers, John T."

Sellers answered. "Here, sir."

"Shortreed, Leroy T."

"Here, sir" Again the answer came from Skidmore, trying to cover for them.

Together Best and Whitson strode through the ranks of men until they came to the two packs lying on the ground.

"All right! Who's answering for the AWOL's?" Best demanded..

Nobody spoke. He turned to Sellers. "How about you?"

"I don't know anything about them, sir," Sellers protested.

Best turned to Skidmore. "Did you answer for Shortreed and Sanford?"

"They'll be here, sir," said Skidmore. "I know it."

Best spoke over his shoulder to Whitson. "Sergeant, put Skidmore's name on the shit list. And list Shortreed and Sanford as absent without leave."

"Sir." Skidmore asked. "Couldn't you wait a little?"

Best shook his head and, with Whitson, started toward the front of the formation. There was a sudden commotion and they turned to see Shortreed and Sanford, racing through the ranks of the other platoons. They went to their position and just as Whitson and Best strode back to confront them, took up their packs

"Where the hell have you been?" Best demanded.

"Shooting craps with some guys from A Company." It was Shortreed who answered.

"A Company was the advance party. They left two hours ago, " Best informed him.

"Sir, actually we were shooting craps with their cooks," Shortreed said glibly. "They're all non-jumpers."

The lieutenant moved closer to study Cecile's face powder, still clinging to the front of Sanford's jumpsuit.

"Were you shooting craps with a powder puff?"

"No sir." Sanford hung his head, embarrassed.

"Sergeant."

"Yes sir."

"Both of these men are to get extra duty at the earliest opportunity," Best ordered and returned to the front of the formation.

Whitson scribbled in his notebook, finished, then lingered to wrinkle his nose at Sanford in mock disgust.

"If you don't smell sweet!" He went to rejoin the lieutenant.

Skidmore was grinning. "I knew you guys would make it!"

"Skidmore, Harold A." The roll call had resumed.

"Here sir."

"Stoyle, Gerald T."

"Here sir."

"Turk, Michael R."

"Here sir."

"Watkins, Robert C."

"Here sir."

"Tenshut!"

The platoon came to attention.

"Fall out and follow Sergeant Whitson to the trucks."

Breaking ranks, the platoon followed Whitson through a break in the line of tents toward the sound of truck engines. The other elements of Headquarters Headquarters Company were also in motion from the tent area to the road and the waiting trucks. Looking down the company street, there were a few places where the gasoline still burned. The flickering flames showed the tents with their sides rolled up and the company street deserted except for the half dozen or so dogs, part of Headquarters Headquarters Company, but they had to be left behind. It was an empty, lonely sight.

On the road both squads of the demo platoon were boarding trucks. Elsewhere the rest of the company was also loading. Shortreed and Sanford stood at the tailgate, helping the others into their truck. With the last man aboard, they climbed in behind him.

The driver raised the tailgate, fastened it with a chain, and climbed into the cab. He pulled his truck onto the road behind another truck and, moments later, the convoy rolled away into the night. As the last truck left, the company dogs put their noses in the air and howled mournfully.

Through sleeping villages, over bridges, past kilometer markers, the convoy rolled through the night. Submerged in this faceless, characterless convoy were the personalities of Shortreed, Sanford, Sellers and some 3000 other paratroopers, soldiers now in the most basic definition of the word.

End of Chapter 1

Chapter 2

The regiment arrived at a military airfield right after sunrise. It was near Chartres, France, and the entrance was alive with pacing guards, barbed wire entanglements and other such military security. In the fields outside the airbase there were a multitude of anti-aircraft emplacements with uplifted muzzles menacing the empty sky. The gun crews gawked at the paratroop convoy as MP's shepherded it away toward the distant hangars. Background to this, row after row of C47's were lined up on the hard stand on both sides of the runways.

Headquarter Headquarters Company unloaded before a hangar that was surrounded by barbed wire. There was only one way in and out, and that was through a gate guarded by two MP's armed with tommy-guns. A chow truck waited inside the barbed wire enclosure. While the company lined up for chow, mess personnel supervised three large drums of boiling water that would be used to wash the mess kits.

To one side of the hangar, a work crew of riggers was unloading packed parachutes from a truck, main packs in one pile, reserves in another. Very quickly there were two large growing piles, and another big truck waiting to unload.

As the first troopers began lining up to wash their mess kits, Sergeant Whitson blew his whistle and all fell silent.

"Give me your attention, men." Whitson spoke in his official voice. "Captain Farlow has something to tell us."

Farlow was the CO of Headquarter Headquarters Company and without exception despised by his men.

"Take-off time in the morning will be at 0600 hours. All officers and non-coms will be briefed at 1300 hours today. When you have finished eating, draw your parachutes from Sergeant Davidson, and follow your sergeant to your bunk area. Any questions?"

"What about letters, sir?" Oglethorpe asked.

"Write all you want," Captain Farlow told him. "But don't mention the mission. Any more questions?"

"Yes sir. When do we draw ammunition?"

"The orders for that will come from Division. Anyone else?"

No one spoke.

"As you were."

The men went back to eating and cleaning their mess gear. Shortreed washed out his mess kit, then joined Sanford who had been waiting for him. Together they walked to the pile of parachutes where Sergeant Davidson and a division packer were issuing the chutes. Davidson handed each of them a backpack, and the packer gave them a reserve. Examining his reserve closely, Shortreed found that a bit of silk had worked past one of the end covers.

"Give me another reserve," he demanded.

"What's wrong with that one?" the packer wanted to know.

"It's bleeding silk."

The packer was unimpressed. "Shove it back in."

"I'll shove it all right!" Shortreed said angrily.

The Sergeant hurried to join them. "What's going on here?"

"I want another reserve," Shortreed told him. He held the reserve out for Davidson to inspect.

"That's not going to hurt anything," the packer complained.

Davidson looked and said, "It is kind of small."

Shortreed was unconvinced. "Suppose it catches on something and pulls out at the wrong time?"

Davidson shrugged. "Give him another one, " and returned to his pile of main chutes.

The packer took back Shortreed's reserve and gave him another. "First jump?" he asked arrogantly.

In a flash Shortreed grabbed the packer by the front of his jumpsuit and waved a fist angrily in his face.

"How'd you like for me to pound your fucking head in?"

"I was kidding! Just kidding!" the packer protested.

It would not have ended there but for Sanford who pulled him off, telling him, "Forget it, Shortreed. He's nobody." He handed him the parachute he had dropped when he went for the packer. "Come on. Let's go."

They left together and went on to the hangar which was filled with cots in tight, neat rows. Each trooper has his equipment piled on or near his bunk. Near the entrance, a detail from demolition was finishing with the packing of the equipment bundles that would ride in para-racks on the outside of the plane.

The rest of the troopers were gambling, writing letters, sleeping. They were a bunch of guys with something heavy hanging over them, killing time. Writing letters home and gambling were the two main diversions.

Shortreed and Sanford made their way through the crowded hangar to their bunks. They found Sellers sitting on his bunk next to theirs. He was totally focused on giving his M1 rifle a good cleaning and oiling. Sanford lay down on his bunk and closed his eyes.

Sellers was in a talking mood. "This is going to be the last jump of the war," he told Shortreed.

"How do you figure?"

"The Krauts are folding up."

"You're dreaming."

"There's nothing left but a bunch of *volkstrummers*."

Skidmore hurried over to them from the front of the crowded hangar. "Hey, we're not going to be demolition after the jump."

"Who says?" Sellers asked.

"The Lieutenant.."

Sanford opened his eyes. "If we're not going to be demolition, what will we be doing?"

"The Lieutenant said we're going to be an anti-tank squad."

Sanford sat up on his bunk, the better to figure out this change in demo's assignment,

"How the hell are we going to stop a tank?" he demanded.

"Gammon grenades."

"Oh boy." Shortreed was skeptical. "Sounds like real fun."

"Everyone gets two apiece," Sellers told them.

"And after we throw them two grenades, then what?"

"Dunno," said Skidmore. "The Lieutenant didn't say."

"I know," Shortreed said glumly. "Then we'll do the patrolling for the regiment."

There was silence as the three combat veterans retreated into themselves. Skidmore saw this and wondered. He sat down on the bunk between Shortreed and Sellers and asked, "How do you know?"

"That's how it was in Normandy," Shortreed said. "As soon as we ran out of demo work, we started patrolling."

"Yeah," Sellers corroborated. "And that's how we lost everybody."

This wasn't the first time he had messed with Skidmore's mind about the coming jump. Skidmore was an easy target. He was apprehensive and openly trying to get some idea of what to expect.

"So you think it's going to be as bad as Normandy?"

"Worse," Sellers assured him.

"Why worse?"

"It's going to be a daylight jump."

"I never thought of that," Skidmore said.

"We'll be jumping right down their throats!"

"Hey, Sellers, knock it off!"

Ignoring the warning from Shortreed, Sellers moved his arm like a machine gun pointed upward, imitating at the same time its staccato burst.

"Achtung! Falschirmjaeger!"

Once more Sellers imitated the sound of a machine gun firing. "And as soon as we hit the ground, the 88's will start coming in."

He made the sound of a shell screaming toward them. Suddenly Sanford sprang from his bunk and jerked Sellers to his feet. There was a brief struggle and Sanford dropped Sellers with a left hook.

"I told you before, lay off the recruits!"

Sellers rolled over and came up with an M-1 rifle in his hands and suddenly the hangar was in an uproar. With cries of "Fight! Fight!", the troopers crowded around the two men. Those whose view was blocked climbed on their bunks in an effort to see the fight.

Sellers swung, trying to brain Sanford with the rifle, but Sanford sidestepped, then closed with him. In most situations, Seller would have been no match for Sanford, but his level of anger and the fact that he had the M-1 made him a dangerous adversary. Sanford had all he could do to keep from getting hit by the rifle. Finally he succeeded in feinting Sellers out of position, grabbed the rifle and threw it aside. He took a boxer's stance and with the watching crowd of troopers roaring their approval, began to close on Sellers.

Pushing his way through the onlookers, Lieutenant Best came between the two men.

"What's the matter with you two?" he demanded.

There was no answer.

"Who started the fight?"

"We weren't fighting, sir, " Sanford said.

"Just scuffling, huh." Best was sarcastic. "Save that shit for the Germans!"

Disappointed that there was not going to be a fight after all, the crowd began to disperse.

It was time for the demolitions bundles to go to the plane, and Best had come into the hangar to pick up a work detail. The bundles were cumbersome and heavy and he would need four strapping troopers for the job. Now, seeking out Sergeant Burns, he ordered him, "Give me four guys to load the demo bundles."

"Where do you want them, sir?"

"I'll be at the pile of equipment bundles by the hangar door."

"I'll have them there right away, sir."

Best turned and left. Sergeant Burns considered the work detail and ordered, "Sanford, Skidmore, Shortreed, Oglethorpe. Bring your gloves and come with me."

"Where are we going, sergeant?"

"To the plane,"

"How come?" Shortreed wanted to know.

"We're going to load the demo bundles," Burns said. "Come on, let's get moving!"

Together, but not in formation, they threaded their way through the labyrinth of cots and equipment that filled the hangar.

Right outside the hangar, they found Lieutenant Best waiting near a large truck, parked beside several piles of equipment bundles.

"Men, be careful you load these in the exact order I give you," he instructed them. "That way we can off-load in the proper sequence at the plane. First will be two communication bundles for the para-racks. Find them and get them on the truck."

The men divided up, with two men in the truck and two on the ground, allowing them to lift the bundles to the truck with relative ease. Next were demolition's own two bundles, both identified by lengths of attached red ribbon as containing explosives. The explosives were mostly C-2 and gun cotton booster charges. The detonating caps, being unstable, were packed separately.

As they loaded the bundles, it came to Shortreed that there was enough C-2 here to blow up the hangar. "And I'm getting ready to fly into combat riding on top of all that C-2 and gun cotton." He shook his head in wonderment. He was going to be glad when this was over. Assuming he survived.

Most of the other bundles contained ammo or medical supplies. After about twenty minutes of work, they had all been loaded into the truck and it took off for the flight line. Lieutenant Best and his men piled onto a jeep and led the truck to the planes. As they moved along the taxi strip, they could see a great multitude of C-47's occupying every bit of space on the airfield.

"Sir, how many planes does it take for a regimental jump?" Shortreed asked.

"There they are. Count them." The Lieutenant said and laughed.

"Where will we be in the flight, sir?"

"The Colonel and his staff will be in the first plane and we'll be on their right wing."

"Fuck!" said Sergeant Burns. "We're going to be in the front of the attack!"

"What's new about that?" Shortreed asked as they pulled up before their plane.

"Nothing," Burns said, and they all laughed.

As they dismounted from the jeep, Best ordered them, "I want you to go from plane to plane and set off the para-bundles for each plane. The planes are numbered and the bundles are numbered. Match them up and you've got it," he said, adding, "Shortreed, you'll be the pusher on the work detail. When you're finished, report to Sergeant Burns."

"Yes sir."

The Lieutenant and the Sergeant watched for a while, then Best told him, "When they're finished, I want you to check that the numbers match for each plane."

"I'll do that, sir,"

"Yeah, when you open a demolition bundle and it's full of radios, it's a bad time to find out that somebody fucked up."

Burns grimaced agreement and Best added, "Also you'll be in charge of hooking the bundles to the para-racks and double-checking that the static lines are securely fastened."

"Sir, how do we know that these systems that are part of the plane are in good order?" Burns questioned.

"It's on the Air Corps check list and we have to take their word for it."

"Sergeant Burns!" Shortreed called out. "We're finished."

"I'll check those numbers now, sir."

Burns moved to where the work detail waited beside the now empty truck. Two equipment bundles complete with cargo chute, stood before each of the seven planes.

After the bundles had been checked by the sergeant for matching numbers, the men lifted them to the para-racks that were between the front landing gear. The work progressed rapidly, with Lieutenant Best carefully inspecting each hook up when it was finished.

As they worked Shortreed found himself looking up at the demolition bundles beneath the plane. He felt the twitch of his adrenal glands as he realized that he would be seeing those bundles at the same angle tomorrow when he jumped, and he allowed himself the luxury of playing the mind-game from then until the work detail returned to the hangar.

The mind game was different each time. This time he wondered about the interval between leaving the plane and the opening shock. That moment when he was still close enough to hear his pack cover hit the side of the plane. That moment, was it somehow special to the mind as well as to the body? Did doors open and special, perhaps even noble thoughts enter his mind? Or was it more prosaically involved with survival, with such thoughts as "Will this fucking chute open?"

He and Burns had talked about this very thing once before. If that moment bestowed some special awareness, what were the tokens? This thinking proved nothing, it went in useless circles and discovered no new thoughts. But the mind chatter distracted him from the realities of tomorrow's jump. Shortreed was fully aware that this was its purpose, to keep himself from thinking bad, troublesome thoughts about the jump tomorrow.

Way back, when the regiment was getting ready for the Normandy jump, Sergeant Burns had advised him, "Keep your gear in good order and your mind free of worry till we get there. By then you'll be too busy to worry."

He and Burns had been friends since the regiment was forming up in the Frying Pan Area at Fort Benning back in '42. Now, many battles and many dead friends later, they were still in the game and still friends.

Sanford spoke quietly to Shortreed. "Skidmore hero-worships you."

"I know it."

"Then why won't you let him be your friend?"

"I'm friendly,"

"But not friends."

There was a pause in the conversation as both men considered this. Then Shortreed spoke.

"You know why."

After a long moment Sanford nodded, then crossed himself. Long-term combat survivors could look over a bunch of replacements and pick out the ones who would die first. This wasn't a hundred percent of the time, but it happened often enough that many took it as a truth.

"I hope we're wrong."

After chow was over, the men played cards or went over their equipment for the tenth time. When the officers and noncoms went for a final briefing, the tension levels were still climbing.

Things changed abruptly when they returned. The news spread like wildfire. The regiment was going to jump over the Rhine in front of an attack across the river by ground troops on the following day! A great clamor of excited voices filled the hangar briefly, then was quiet as a voice barked a command: "Tenshut!"

Everyone popped to attention and shut up instantly. The voice continued:

"This is Colonel Breit, your commanding officer, speaking. Here are the orders of the day. Lights out in thirty minutes. Sleep well, for you will turn out for roll call tomorrow at 0400 hours. After roll call will be chow call at 0500 hours. You will turn out in full battle gear and wearing main and reserve parachutes. You will then draw ammunition, grenades and one block of composition C-2. From there you will go directly to your assigned planes. Takeoff will begin at 0600 hours. The forward elements will be over the Rhine at 1025 hours and over the DZ five minutes later. Together we will strike the enemy's flank. We'll give those bastards hell! At ease."

There was a babble of voices as the men reacted to the news. The P.A. came to life again and another voice announced:

"Give me your attention, men! Please give me your attention."

The hangar fell silent and the voice went on:

"There will be religious services near the hangar door. Catholics to the right, Protestants to the left. Go now, for the services will stop at lights out. As you were!"

The babble of voices began again as many of the troopers started moving toward the hangar door and the religious observances there.

Skidmore asked Shortreed, "Aren't you going to services?"

"I'm not a Christian."

"What are you then?" Skidmore wanted to know.

"I'm not anything," Shortreed said tersely.

"You mean you don't believe in God?"

"I didn't say that," Shortreed said. "I know damn well there's a God, and I'm on pretty good terms with him."

"But you won't go to services?"

"The churches don't own God," Shortreed told him flatly.

Skidmore had been about to leave for the services, but now he sat back down on his bunk, and Shortreed felt a twinge of guilt for the part he had played in this decision.

"Skidmore, what goes on between you and God is your personal choice. I don't need anyone to validate my attitude toward God and you don't need anyone to validate yours."

Skidmore was confused. "What does that mean?"

"It means, get up off your ass and go to services." He grabbed Skidmore, pulled him from his bunk and, with a shove, aimed him toward the front of the hangar. Skidmore took a few steps, then abruptly returned to Shortreed with outstretched hand. As they shook hands, Shortreed could see tears welling up in Skidmore's eyes. But he said only, "Thanks, Shortreed", turned away and hurried toward the religious services.

Shortreed watched him go. "He's got a hunch he's going to die," Shortreed thought. "And he knows that I know."

There was a poker game going on a few bunks from Shortreed but, as much as he liked to play poker, he ignored the game. This was his moment of introspection, the moment when he faced tomorrow and God squarely and without self-delusion. Tomorrow was going to be a bloody day and he was going to be right in the middle of it. The lights in the hangar blinked once. It was only five minutes till lights out.

Shortreed concluded his moment with God with a short, silent prayer." Dear God, I pray that You are enjoying Your creation and that You will guide me in the coming battle. If I must die, I pray that I will die gamely. Either way, I've had a good life, and I thank You for it."

A little later as the men were returning to their bunks, the lights dimmed, then without further ceremony went out. The hangar was left in total darkness, except for a few low lights so that the men could find their way to the latrine, and Shortreed slipped quickly into a deep sleep. Had this been known, he would have been envied by many.

As was usual with Shortreed, some inner clock roused him before the appointed 0400 hours. He made a leisurely trip to the latrine where he did his morning ablutions, then went to the front of the hangar. He went outside, lit a cigarette and searched the early morning sky for a sign of the dawn. Except for Orion laying over on his side and almost touching the horizon, there was none.

Lieutenant Best came from the hangar and also lit a cigarette. He looked up at the sky with its ocean of stars for a moment before he became aware of the other man's presence.

"What's the matter, Shortreed? Can't sleep?'

"I slept fine, sir."

"I did too."

They were silent, then Shortreed said. "This is the hardest part for me."

"This?" Best was surprised.

"Look at those planes, sir."

For a moment, both took in the multitude of planes in the distance. At intervals armed guards paced back and forth, while on the far horizon the day was showing the first signs of dawn.

"They're setting there waiting," Shortreed said. He pointed back into the hangar. "They're waiting. We're waiting too. I don't like it."

Best checked his watch and laughed. "Well it won't be for long. In a few minutes the day's going to start."

"I'm ready," Shortreed said. And he was.

Best hesitated only briefly, then said, "Shortreed, I got a letter today from my wife. We've agreed to name our first son Leroy."

Shortreed looked at him questioningly.

"It's the only way we can thank you for dragging me to safety when I was hit and those tanks had us pinned down in the snow."

"Thank you, sir," Shortreed said, "It's a good name."

Inside the hangar the lights came on and whistles began to blow. The sergeants were beginning to turn out the troops. From within the hangar, a stentorian voice bellowed, "Drop your cocks and grab your socks!"

"Your wailing's over, Shortreed." Best stuck out his hand. They shook hands and he continued, "Good luck."

"Thank you, sir, "Shortreed said, meaning it. "Good luck to you."

They turned and went back into the hangar just as the sergeants began calling roll call, and briefly the hangar was filled with the sounds of men answering "Here" to the roll call while dressing. It added a sense of further urgency to what was already an urgent day. After roll call, they went on piss call. It turned out that the latrine space was inadequate, and long lines formed at all of the plumbing. More than one trooper showed his contempt, his impatience or both by going outside and pissing against the hangar.

With all this, by the 0500 chow call the hangar was ready to go, with the bedding rolled on each cot in such a way to leave room for both parachutes and gear to be placed there. The men were in combat fatigues, and many of them had already applied camouflage paint to their faces and to the back of their hands.

Breakfast was hearty, bacon and eggs (fresh, not powdered) ham and eggs, shit on a shingle, or less descriptively creamed chipped beef on toast, and eggs. The fried eggs were the star of the menu. They had been eating powdered eggs too long. This was a real gladiators' breakfast that had been laid on by the cooks and bakers of Headquarters Headquarters Company. It was the traditional hot meal sendoff to combat. The welcome home meal would be smaller, but just as lavish.

The mess sergeant, Vickers, had welcomed Headquarters Headquarters Company back from Normandy with a meal for 240 men. The company could only muster 37. Vickers had stayed drunk for weeks, then started the tradition of the gargantuan sendoff.

But even as they ate this breakfast that Vickers and his crew had put out for them, the men were being urged by their noncoms to hurry, and hurry they did. As soon as the mess gear had been washed, the men went to their bunks and donned their packs and their parachutes. The chutes were put on, but not fastened up in jump position. This made walking easier and would allow them to distribute grenades and ammo about their persons later.

During the night, grenades and ammo had been offloaded before each company area. Now the men of Headquarters Headquarters Company filed past this pile and were given their basic combat load: two bandoliers of M-1 ammo, two fragmentation grenades, two gammon grenades and for some, one white phosphorus grenade.

When Sellers came for his issue, Lieutenant Best handed him a grenade launcher.

"Put this on your rifle," Best instructed him.

"Yes sir."

"You'll be our mobile artillery."

"Yes sir."

The line moved quickly and reformed by planeloads before trucks waiting to take them to the airplanes. The dawn sky was getting lighter in color. There was a clamor of discordant noise as aircrews energized the engines, and the air was filled with the sounds of one hundred and fifty twin-engine planes being warmed and run up. As each engine turned slowly in the energizing process it made a whining sound, then it would catch with a ragged roar and finally settle into a steady idle. Up and down the flight line the planes were acquiring their aircrews. The cacophony of all this military enterprise heightened yet again as the paratroopers arrived at their planes by planeloads. The men looked bulky in field pack and parachutes. As they arrived at their planes, they began making a final securing of their parachutes to their bodies.

When Demolitions got to their plane, they found Lieutenant Best and Sergeant Burns waiting for them. The men of the demo platoon now wore or carried everything that was going to combat with them. Shortreed had his tommygun slung over his shoulder, and Sellers had an M-1 rifle. These weapons were slung over their shoulders in a way that would not interfere with the wearing or function of their chutes. Each man wore a parachute assembly, complete with a twenty-eight foot main chute and twenty-two foot reserve.

There was a first-aid kit fastened to the camouflage netting that covered their helmets, and their leg pockets were stuffed to capacity. As members of the Demolition platoon, some of them also carried leg packs of explosives. Festooned with grenades and ammo and wearing their parachutes, they seemed bigger than life in the still, meager light of early dawn. Throughout all of this there was a steadily increasing flurry of activity along the flight line, and the mounting prop whine of this mighty concourse of C-47's screamed menacingly like a nest of angry hornets.

Sergeant Burns and Lieutenant Best stood in the cargo door of the plane, and the crew stood outside on the ground. Strapped to the sergeant's waist was the .45 revolver that his father had carried all through World War I. It was Burns' good luck charm, and he had carried it through Normandy and the Bulge.

They began loading the platoon, with the lieutenant seeing to it that they were placed into the plane in reverse jump sequence. As he called a name, the man would come forward and stop on the entrance steps, where Best and Burns would reach down to help the heavily laden trooper aboard.

"Number 20, Turk."

Hines went to the steps and was helped into the plane.

"Even numbers on the right and odd numbers on the left," Best told him. The loading went quickly as he continued to call the names in reverse jumping order.

"19, Cooper."

"18, Shepherd."

"17, Stoyle."

"16, Murray,"

"15, Tippet."

"14, Shortreed."

"13, Oglethorpe."

"12, Skidmore."

"11, Sellers."

"10, Sanford."

As Sanford was helped into the plane, the Lieutenant ordered him, "Sanford, as you go out of the door, hit the switch for the equipment bundles."

"Yes, sir."

"So we're sure what we're talking about," Best said, "show me the switch."

"It's the red switch in the panel by the door." Sanford pointed. "Right there, sir."

"Don't forget."

"No sir. My BAR's in the demo bundle."

Best went on, "9, Melrose."

"8, Kelly."

"7, Riley."

"6, Gill."

"5, Peringian."

"4, Forgetti."

"3, Corporal Martinez."

"2, Sergeant Burns. And I'll be number 1."

He turned to Burns."Tell them we're loaded."

As Sergeant Burns made his way forward toward the pilot's compartment, Best turned back to his men and spoke loudly so all could hear.

"Here's how it is. We'll have P-51 fighters over us at 20,000 feet. We'll have P-51's flying on both sides of us. In front, more P-51's will strafe ground positions ahead of us. As we approach the DZ, bombing, strafing and artillery will cease and the airborne assault will begin."

Best went on, "We'll be coming under ground fire before we're over the Rhine, meaning we'll be under fire for six or seven minutes before we reach the DZ. If anyone gets hit, leave them in the plane. They'll get better medical attention back at base."

The sergeant returned and the engine noise mounted. Shortly, the ground outside began to move as Plane Number 3 of the airborne assault began to taxi. The view through the cargo door was one of ordered movement as the rest of the planes began to line up on runways for the takeoff. The C'47 was a tail-dragger that had been strongly built for rough and damaged landing strips. In common with the other tail-draggers, it had one fault. Until the tail came up into a level position, it would taxi fast but would not get off the ground.

Thus it was that when Plane Number 3 with its cargo door open was in take off position, the paratroopers were ordered to move forward and place their full combined weight over the wing. The heavily loaded plane shuddered as the pilot ran his engines up to begin their take off roll.

After a long minute of engine roar and moving forward on the runway, the tail rotated to flying position and Plane Number 3 was airborne. The troopers returned to their bucket seats.

"Well, here we go again," Shortreed said to no one in particular.

<u>End of Chapter 2</u>

.

<u>Chapter 3</u>

At 1015 hours the airborne assault had formed up in the skies over France and Belgium, and the armada of C47's now flew on station in giant circles. The on station position for the 705th was only ten minutes flying time from the Rhine.

The regiment existed now as three serials of fifty planes each. The first fifty carried Headquarters Headquarters Company and the First Battalion. The Second and Third Battalions were turning their own circles behind them. Overhead, fighter planes at various altitudes patrolled the skies aggressively. Ahead of them, low-flying fighters bombed and strafed along the path of the approach. Somewhere below on the British side of the river, General Eisenhower and Field Marshal Montgomery, along with the other generals, watched this beginning of the airborne assault. The ground troops would begin crossing at 0600 hours the next day.

In Plane Number 3 some of the men were starting to get twitchy. It was getting close to time to stand up and hook up, and after that the shit was going to hit the fan. Lieutenant Best rose from his seat by the cargo door and commanded loudly over the noise of the engines, "Give me your attention, men."

He continued, "There may be too much noise later, so I want you to get this straight now. When I stand in the door, that is a command for you to stand in the door when your turn comes. When I jump out that door, that is a command for you to follow me when your turn comes. Any questions?"

There were none. Best went on, "I remind you, that if anyone gets hit, unhook them and leave them in the plane. They'll get better medical attention at base. That's an order."

He paused and glanced down the two rows of paratroopers before him. "Men, the time is now. Stand up and hook up."

The men got to their feet and hooked up rapidly, the odd numbers meshing with the evens to place the stick in jump sequence.

"Check equipment," Best ordered.

Each man began to check the equipment of the trooper in front of him. This was a ritualized but legitimate safety check that assured that back pack, snap fasteners, static line, and the rest were in good order.

"Sound off for equipment check."

"Number 20, okay."

"Number 19, okay."

"Number 18, okay." This continued until Lieutenant Best, at the front of the line, got patted on the back by Sergeant Burns, and said, "Number 1 okay."

A red light came on, on the light panel over the door. Oglethorpe complained, "I don't like being Number 13. I was 13 on the stick on the last jump, and nothing ever went right for me."

"You're still alive, aren't you," someone said,

Oglethorpe shook his head emphatically. "I've got a hunch."

"Don't worry about it. You'll be okay,' Shortreed told him.

Oglethorpe ignored him and called out loudly, "Does anyone want to trade places?"

When there were no takers, he turned frantically to Shortreed. "I'm scared of 13. What'll I do?"

"Quit calling it 13 and start calling it 12B," Shortreed suggested.

"Come on, Shortreed," he pleaded. "Trade with me."

"I don't know about that."

"It's a step closer to the door," Oglethorpe wheedled.

Shortreed shrugged. "Check with the lieutenant. If it's okay with him, it's okay with me."

"Lieutenant Best, sir," Oglethorpe called loudly.

"What's the problem, Oglethorpe?"

"Is it okay if me and Shortreed swap places in the stick?"

"Why?" Best wanted to know.

Oglethorpe admitted reluctantly, "I'm superstitious about number 13."

"Go ahead."

The two men unhooked their static lines and changed places, then hooked up again quickly in the new order. As number 14, Oglethorpe was now one position further from the only door in the plane from which the troopers could jump. But a burden of fear had lifted, and he was visibly elated as he patted Shortreed on the shoulder and told him, "Thanks, Shortreed. I owe you a favor."

"Forget it," Shortreed said.

An Air Force sergeant came from the pilot's compartment. He tried to make his way back to the jump door and Lieutenant Best, but the narrow aisle was too crowded with paratroopers for him to get by. Giving up, he shouted instead, "Lieutenant sir!"

"What do you want?"

"We'll begin our approach in two minutes," the sergeant told him. "We'll start taking ground fire in three or four minutes. Your DZ is five minutes away."

"Okay, I got it," Best shouted over the noise and the Air Force sergeant disappeared back into the front of the plane. The red light over the jump door started to blink.

The outside view suddenly changed as the circles at the front of the giant formation began to uncoil. Like a whip being cracked, the one hundred and fifty planes carrying the 705th Parachute Infantry peeled off and slanted down to jumping altitudes. The front of the formation was at five hundred feet, with the rest of the formation stair-stepped up to the rear. With this accomplished and with the regiment lined up along the bombed and strafed corridor, they took off at full throttle for their objective beyond the Rhine.

A heavily loaded C47 makes strange sounds as it is flogged through the air at full throttle. But these sounds would soon be lost in the din as flak and small arms fire began to pelt against the planes like deadly hail on a tin roof.

In Plane Number Three, Lieutenant Best stood before the jump door and addressed his men.

"Sanford, don't forget the switch for the bundles."

"Yes sir."

"Stand in the door and follow me!" Best shouted as he moved to the door, he addressed Sergeant Burns. "You know what to do if I'm hit."

"Yes sir."

The stick closed up tight behind the Lieutenant as he stood in the door. They shoved their static line snap-fasteners along the static line with their left hands until they reached the door. It was a little early, they knew, to stand in the door. But being in the front of the formation and low to the ground, every second could count if they had to get out before they reached the DZ.

Turning to the back of the plane, Sergeant Burns yelled out, 'Hey Shortreed."

"What do you want?"

"If I don't make it, you can have my revolver."

"You'll be showing it to your grandkids," Shortreed yelled back.

All of a sudden the plane gave a lurch. It was taking multiple shrapnel hits from close ack-ack aerial bursts. After that, there was an almost continuous rattle of small fragments hitting the plane, punctuated by the occasional "Thump!" of a much larger piece of shrapnel. Then a large fragment came through the side of the plane.

It tore a great, gaping hole in Skidmore's chest. He gasped, "Save me, Shortreed," and fell to the floor of the plane, where he convulsed and died. Quickly Shortreed unhooked Skidmore's static line and tossed it to the floor.

Then there was a loud "Bang" up front in the pilot's compartment. The plane gave an abrupt lurch and a voice could be heard screaming.

"Get his leg!" another voice urged. "Pull him out of the way!"

The screaming stopped and the plane righted itself. At the door, Best peered out at the smoke and debris blowing back from the burning engine on the jump side of the plane

"The engine's on fire, " he said. "So's the gas in the wing."

"Think we'll make the DZ?" Burns asked.

"No!" He shouted the command, "Follow me!"

"So long Shortreed, I'll see you in hell!" Burns yelled, as he went out the door behind the Lieutenant. In rapid sequence the stick followed them. The German gunners were still hitting the plane.

Back in the stick, Shortreed, Sellers and Sanford, as if by silent agreement, put their shoulders down and charged the door. This surge of power from behind literally shoved out Number 9 in the stick and those in front of him. Shortreed was charging so hard when he hit the door that there was a gap between him and the men behind him.

He was aware of two things when he left the plane, first, that the plane was quickly losing altitude, and second, that the burning wing was crumpling away. Then his chute opened, and he was momentarily stunned by the opening shock.

Inside the plane, frantic men were still clawing their way toward the door when the wing collapsed and Plane Number 3 whipped over into a sickening spin. As the ground rushed up to meet them, someone cried out in an anguished voice, "Oh God, we'll never make it!"

The plane hit the ground and disintegrated. So died Numbers 14 through 20 in the jump stick, all good men.

Shortreed was so low when his chute opened, that the chute oscillated only once and he hit the ground hard. He lay there until Sellers found him.

"You okay, Shortreed?"

Sellers activated Shortreed's point release system and helped him out of his harness.

"Where's Sanford?"

The question answered itself as Sanford went by, crouched low and running, shouting "Come on!" at them as he passed. Shortreed got to his feet, and he and Sellers ran after him. Above them the middle of the formation, flying higher than Plane Number 3 had, before it went down, continued toward the Drop Zone under heavy Ack- ack fire from the ground.

They caught up with Sanford at the wreckage of Plane Number 3. It was burning fiercely and so twisted by the impact that it was barely recognizable as an airplane. Sanford was very agitated and unable to accept the reality of all those dead troopers.

"We've got to get them out of there!"

He tried to approach the plane, but Shortreed restrained him. "The wing came off just as I left the plane."

"That's right," Sellers agreed.

Sanford stopped struggling and shook his head as if trying to clear this from his mind.

"They're all dead, Sanford," Shortreed told him. "Let's get going."

"The Krauts are going to be looking for us!" Sellers said urgently and took off.

But Sanford turned back with drooping shoulders to stand looking at the burning plane. Shortreed touched him gently on the shoulder.

"Their grenades will be going off any minute."

Sanford crossed himself, then followed Shortreed and they ran after Sellers, who was headed for the cover of a nearby copse of wood. Near at hand a battery of ack-ack guns was pumping rounds into the formation of C47's. Further away, a battery of 88's was concentrating its fire on a burning C47 that faltered, then dropped out of formation and began losing altitude. The 88 rounds were exploding in puffs of black smoke all around the burning plane as it disgorged a few paratroopers. Then, while the troopers were still jumping, the burning wing collapsed and the plane went in nose first from about 500 feet.

"We've got to get those fucking 88's!" Sanford said vehemently.

"We'll get them," Shortreed told him.

From back where Plane Number 3 was still burning, they could now hear the sound of exploding grenades and the shrill whine of shrapnel. So distracted were they by the aerial armada and the guns that harried it, that they were almost surprised by a German patrol, double-timing toward the crash site of Plane Number 3.

With instincts honed to an edge by a thousand close calls, they spread out and took advantage of cover. They were close enough to communicate, but spread out enough that a single artillery shell or grenade could not get them all. Sanford had his BAR on its tripod. But when he looked to Shortreed for approval, Shortreed signaled him to lay back. Wait.

When Sanford started to object, Shortreed pointed in the direction of the ack-ack guns that were still firing into the formation. He got the picture and nodded. On the other side, Sellers was drawing a bead on some Germans when Shortreed made a squeaking sound to stop him. He looked to Shortreed, who shook his head and the three of them watched as the German patrol disappeared in the direction of the smoke rising from the crash of Plane Number 3.

"What's wrong with you, Shortreed?" Sellers was pissed off. "We could have got a bunch of them!"

"While we were after them, those ack-ack guns would still be shooting more planes down!"

"We could have wiped out that patrol." Sellers lingered stubbornly on the thought.

"Fuck the Goddamn patrol, "said Shortreed. "Let's get those guns!"

He turned and took off at a trot in the direction of the guns. Sellers still hesitated.

"Get moving," Sanford told him and they both ran to catch up with Shortreed, who signaled for them to be quiet. When he spoke he kept his voice low. They were so close to the gun emplacement that they could hear a non-com as he called out cadenced commands in German to the crew of the clip-fed 30mm. ack-ack gun.

They quickly assessed the situation and planned their attack. Apparently the German patrol they had seen was most of the infantry complement guarding the gun emplacement. A sniper was also concealed in the tree at the edge of the forest, and there was a machine gun dug in so that it could sweep the open space with machine gun fire. These seemed to be the only guard troops present.

"You see that guy in the tree?' Shortreed asked.

"Yeah," Sellers said.

"Can you get him?"

"Yeah," he answered,

"Sanford, do you see that machine gun over there?"

"I see it."

"See the gunner?"

"Where?"

"There in the shade."

"Okay."

"Now listen to those gunnery commands." They listened for a moment. "He's saying something like load, lock, fire."

"So?"

"I'll count and the two of you will fire on my signal. That'll bury the sound of our guns in the sound of their ack-ack."

Sanford shook out the bipod on his BAR and took a bead on the distant gunner. Sellers slipped into his sling and got into position, and Shortreed began removing the safety tape from his grenades.

"What's up, Shortreed?" Sanford asked.

"When you guys are shooting at your targets, I'll run close enough to throw grenades in the emplacement. And keep a sharp eye that we didn't overlook a German somewhere."

With that he began counting with the German sergeant, "Load, lock, fire! Load, lock, fire! This time, load, lock, fire!"

Sellers squeezed off a round, and Sanford fired a short burst. The sounds were completely lost in the uproar of the ack-ack gun firing a clip and the German gun crew, totally focused on shooting at the formation, was oblivious to what was going on.

The sniper turned loose and fell the thirty or forty feet to the ground. The machine gunner spasmed briefly, then lay still.

Sprinting to the edge of the gun emplacement, Shortreed pulled the pin on a grenade and let the safety lever fly. He counted to himself, one thousand, two thousand, then threw it into the gun pit. The counting used up two seconds of the grenade's fuse time, and it would explode before it could be thrown back. Shortreed sent a second grenade after the first.

"Look out, Shortreed!" Sanford yelled, and Shortreed hit the dirt. While he was still on the way down, he could hear the sound of a short high-pitched burst from a Schmeiser machine pistol. Bullets hit all around him, and then the overlapping sound of Sanford's BAR silenced the machine pistol.

"Okay!" Sanford called. He and Sellers rose from their positions and raced to join Shortreed, who by now had leapt onto the sandbagging that protected the gun crew and was raking the survivors with bursts of fire from his tommy gun.

Overhead a burning C47 took a near miss from an 88 round fired by a gun that was no more than a quarter of a mile from where they watched. Undaunted, the burning plane held position in spite of more close misses as the formation continued inexorably toward the DZ.

Sanford let out a bellow of rage. "Let's get that fucking 88!" He started along the trail in the direction of the 88. but Shortreed stopped him.

"We'll go through the woods."

"Why?"

"If they've got any troops left, they'll be watching the trail."

Suddenly a firefight developed at the site of the distant 88. There was a fierce two or three minutes of small arms fire, followed by the sound of a hand grenade and the whine of shrapnel. The gun fell silent, and moments later they could hear the sound of a half a block of C-2 going off. The attackers were blowing the breechblock off the 88, thereby putting it permanently out of action.

"Hey!" Sanford enthused, "They got it!"

Shortreed turned to Sellers. "We'll stand guard. Go put a charge on that loading gate and take the gun apart,"

Sellers jumped into the gun pit and molded a fist-sized blob of C-2 into the loading gate, then primed it with a booster charge and a fuse lighter.

Meanwhile, the tail end of the 705th Regiment were going over above. They were under sporadic small arms fire and ack-ack fire. The sky was briefly empty, then the crippled planes began flying over. First was a C47 limping along on a single engine, with its pilot wondering if after the troopers jumped his crippled plane would have enough left to get him home. The next crippled plane was shot all to hell. It was still flying on two engines, but one of them was smoking, and the rudder and tail assembly had great holes shot in them.

As it passed over, the smoking engine burst into flames. The plane continued toward the DZ for almost half a mile before the troopers started jumping. Shortreed counted 15 parachutes. They must have wounded still in the plane, he concluded. The thought caused him to flash back to his own recent experience, and to see again Skidmore's face as he stepped over him to get to the door. In that brief unguarded moment, Shortreed grieved for Skidmore and felt guilty because he had been unable to help him. The words "Save me, Shortreed" would be imprinted into his memory forever.

"Get down! That's got a short fuse!" Sellers yelled in warning, and they all dropped behind the sandbagging. The explosion destroyed the backpack gun and brought Shortreed back to the moment.

After the flight went over, the tempo of the fight changed as the Germans targeted instead the small groups of paratroopers who had survived by jumping before they got to the DZ. There was a rash of small encounters and one sharp but brief firefight that ended in a flurry of hand grenades followed by silence.

"What do we do now, Shortreed?" Sellers asked.

Shortreed pointed. "The DZ is that way, about five miles."

"There's a lot of Krauts between here and there," Sanford said. He removed the nearly empty clip from his BAR and replaced it with a full one. "Are we going to sneak or fight?"

"We'll do whatever it takes," Shortreed told them. "For now we're going to sneak." He slung his tommy gun over his shoulder and moved into the woods, followed closely by the other two men.

They got near enough to the DZ that they could hear the sounds of battle coming from where the paratroopers were already assembling and hammering hard on the German defenders. It looked like they could make a quick dash to another clump of woods and from there to the regiment. But at the last minute a company of Germans filed out of the woods and divided into two sections. One section began a sweep of the approach corridor in the direction of the DZ. The other began their sweep in the opposite direction.

Wisely the three troopers left the corridor and, with no other choice, went deeper into German territory. It was clear that the enemy felt that their sweep along the attack route would take care of any patches of stragglers. They were on general alert, but the further they got from the path the planes took, the more the Germans seemed to be preoccupied with things other than stray troopers.

Shortreed, Sanford and Sellers had little difficulty in avoiding any groups of Germans that were moving about. If the group was too large for them to fight, they hid. If it was small enough, they would shoot it up and keep moving.

The Germans were frustrated and confused by the airborne invasion which had isolated those units that were down by the edge of the Rhine. These would bear the shock of the British river crossing and could no longer be resupplied with ammunition or receive reinforcements. The 705th had landed across the main supply route and all access roads had been sealed. The German units could get nothing. They had no chance whatsoever of preventing the British crossing tomorrow.

The three American paratroopers had unwittingly strayed from the flight path of the attack to the path of return for the now-empty planes. After dropping their load of paratroopers, each C47 would make a steep turn as soon as possible and head back for the British side of the Rhine.

The steady stream of C47's racing back to relative safety gave Shortreed his first realization of where they were. The planes with two engines and a functional pilot went at full throttle, but the halt, the one-engined, the burning and the otherwise combat-impaired struggled to stay aloft. Some of the crews were lured to their death by the thought that if they could just keep flying for five more minutes, they could bail out over British-held ground. Those with a burning engine or wing had to decide when to help their wounded out. When to jump. Or when to die.

Shortreed, Sanford and Sellers stopped to watch a C47 with burning engine and wing come to their moment of decision overhead. They were flying slowly at 800 feet when a figure hurtled from the cargo door. The three troopers held their breath waiting for the guy to open his chute. None came and he hit the ground not far from where they were standing. Right after that, another figure appeared in the door and leapt out. To everyone's surprise, this chute was on a static line and opened quickly.

"A paratrooper!"

"What the fuck is going on here?"

"He's probably some wounded trooper who got up off the floor and jumped," Shortreed said. He had the wild thought "Maybe it's Skidmore." Then he realized it couldn't be. Skidmore was dead on the floor of Plane Number 3, and when it hit the ground it killed him again. Skidmore was double dead.

"Let's get him before the Krauts do!" Sanford demanded.

They watched the parachute descending and saw the man try to maneuver the chute.

"He's going to land close to where we are. Down on the road."

They heard the sound of a motorcycle approaching and stopping. By this time the parachute was down below 300 feet and drifting toward the road. The troopers figured out where the chute would land and took off running.

Before they could reach the spot, the parachute landed on the far side of some tall trees about half way to the road. They redoubled their efforts, but they heard a short burst from a machine pistol and knew they were too late.

"That fucking motorcyclist shot him!"

In silent fury they descended on the spot from which the shot had come. Crouching low and running, they came to where the parachute had caught in a tree. The now dead paratrooper hung a few feet from the ground, and a German soldier was going through him, looking for a souvenir. They all shot at once, and the German fell to the ground dead.

Down at the road, the remaining German soldier heard the sound of American weapons firing and made a run for it. The motorcycle with its sidecar screeched back up onto the road and took off, with the rider hunched down over the gas tank and the engine roaring.

Wordlessly the three troopers threw their weapons to their shoulders and fired a hail of bullets at the fleeing German rider. He slumped onto the gas tank and the motorcycle careened off the road and tumbled into the bushes.

Abruptly on the other side of this patch of woods, there came the noise of a furious firefight. From the sounds of the weapons, it was obvious that the Germans had superiority by about two to one.

"Now what?" Sanford looked questioningly to Shortreed.

"Come with me, but stay scattered out."

He took off on the double for the road below, and the others followed.

At the road, Sanford stopped to examine the body of the dead German who had tried to get away on the motorcycle.

"He's *kaput,*" Sanford said, as he rejoined the others.

The sounds from the firefight changed as the outnumbered troopers began withdrawing under covering fire. They listened for a moment.

"That's probably Lieutenant Best and the front end of the stick," Sanford said.

"What are we going to do?" Sellers asked.

"First I'm going to see what's happening over there," Shortreed told them. "You guys watch the road."

"Should we shoot if we see Krauts?"

"Only if you can whip them."

Shortreed sprinted across the road and disappeared, still running, in the direction of the gunfire. The other two lay down and took cover in the bushes with their guns before them. This was for concealment. For fighting they would have to move to a more advantageous position.

Overhead the sky was clear with no planes or flak, and except for the gunfire on the other side of the woods, things were quiet locally. From much further away, near the DZ, there came the sounds of combat. The ragged gunfire gave way to a more organized sound as the regiment formed up and started clearing out a landing area for the soon-to-arrive gliders. Over toward Brussels, on the allied side of the Rhine, the glider serials waited at attack altitudes. They would be the second stage of the airborne assault.

Alert about their surroundings but otherwise relaxed, Sellers and Sanford waited. Sellers lit up a cigarette. "This is our last jump. It's the end of the war for us."

Sanford ignored him. Sellers dragged on the cigarette and daydreamed out loud, "When I get home, I'm going into politics."

"Who'd vote for you?" Sanford asked. "You ain't nobody!"

"Wait till Johnny comes marching home." Sellers framed an imaginary poster with his hands. "William R. Sellers fought for you. Now, you vote for him. A vote for Honest Bill Sellers is a vote for good government."

"Honest Bill huh," Sanford said derisively. "That's a wet dream if I ever heard one."

"Four years in the paratroopers, an unblemished war record, solid citizen, family man." Sellers enumerated, self-satisfied. "I'll be in the state senate before I'm thirty," he predicted.

Both reacted as a small sound behind them brought Sellers abruptly out of his daydream. But it was only Shortreed.

"Why did you sneak up behind us like that?" Sellers sounded pissed off.

"I wanted to see if you had your head up your ass."

"What did you find out?" Sanford asked.

"You were right. It looked like the Lieutenant and the front end of the stick."

"Let's go join them!" Sanford was ready.

"They're already past the main body of Krauts and on their way to the regiment." Shortreed said. "We'll have to find our own way back."

He started to say more, but fell silent at the sound of an engine approaching rapidly on the road. They listened intently as it came nearer.

"Sounds like a tank," Sellers said.

Shortreed shook his head. "It's coming too fast for a tank,"

"Whatever it is, what're we going to do about it?"

"Blow it up, " Shortreed said.

'With what?"

"Grenades. You guys go across the road and take up positions," he instructed.

"Shoot when we see them?" Sanford wanted to know.

"First I hit them with a grenade," Shortreed said." Then, if there's any of them still kicking, start shooting."

Sanford nodded and hurried across with his BAR to take up a position with a good field of fire. Sellers ambled after and stretched out near him, as Shortreed disappeared into the bushes.

'What's Shortreed bucking for?" Sellers asked peevishly.

"Quit bitching will you!" Sanford told him.

"We don't have to be fighting these bastards."

"That's what we're here for."

They fell silent as it became apparent that the vehicle would come into sight in a matter of seconds. When it rounded the corner, they saw that it was an armored truck. It was going fast, headed for the ambush at full speed.

On the other side of the road, Shortreed cocked his arm and threw the grenade. It hit the truck squarely, demolishing the engine and wrecking the front end. Just in case, Sanford raked the cab with a few short bursts from his BAR. Then everything was quiet.

They watched for a moment, then approached the truck cautiously, guns in hand. Smoke still hung in the air from the explosion. Sanford and Sellers stood ready as Shortreed yanked the truck door open. The driver, an SS lieutenant, tumbled out onto the road, dead. On the passenger side another SS officer slumped dead, mangled by the explosion.

"Keep your eyes open," Shortreed told the other two. "I'll check the back end."

Sanford watched as Sellers rifled systematically through the pockets of the German lying on the road, finding and examining pictures from the dead man's wallet.

"His wife was ugly," he said critically.

"Put it back," Sanford said with disgust.

"What's the matter with you?"

"They're family pictures!"

Suddenly they heard the shrill, hysterical "BRE-E-ET!" of a Schmausser machine pistol. Cutting across this was the deeper sound of a burst from Shortreed's tommy gun. Instantly they hit the ditch. After a moment, Sellers called, "Shortreed."

"It's okay," Shortreed assured them. "It's all over."

They rose from the ditch and joined him. A third dead SS officer sprawled on his back before the opened door of the armored truck. His machine pistol lay nearby.

"What happened?"

"He almost got me," Shortreed said. Stepping over the dead man, he went to the rear door of the truck and climbed inside. Sellers, meanwhile, stooped and picked up the dead man's machine pistol and examined it.

"Hey, come over here!" Shortreed yelled from inside the truck.

They went to join him. Sellers peered inside, but Sanford, ever wary, held back, alert and vigilant, his eyes always moving.

"Come in here! Both of you!" Shortreed yelled again.

Sellers vaulted into the truck and, after a last glance around, Sanford followed. They discovered that Shortreed was kneeling before a large chest that he had already opened.

"What is it?"

"Money!" said Shortreed. "A lot of money!"

They crowded closer around the chest. Shortreed took a sheaf of bills and examined them.

"French thousand franc notes."

"They're probably no good."

"Is that why they were carrying it in an armored truck?' Shortreed challenged . "With three officers for guards?"

He took up a ledger that was lying in the chest with the money. While the others stared bug-eyed at the pile of bills, he tried to read it.. Unable to make heads or tails of it, he held the ledger out to Sellers who didn't take it.

"Hey, you know German," Shortreed said.

"Only enough to ask for pussy and booze."

The ledger was of no interest for Sellers, whose complete attention was on the stacks of money in the chest.

"Read it!" Shortreed shoved the ledger into Sellers' hands.

"I told you I only learned enough German to ask for-"

"Pretend it's pussy," Shortreed cut in. "And tell us what it says."

His voice had the ring of an ultimatum. Sellers looked to Sanford for support, but he was clearly with Shortreed.

"Yeah, tell us what it says." There was more than a hint of menace in Sanford's voice.

With no other choice, Sellers shrugged and began to turn the pages of the ledger. After puzzling over it for several moments, he handed it back to Shortreed. "Best I can tell it's the record of some kind of bank account."

"Where?"

"It's just numbers."

"How much is in the account?"

"Don't know." Sellers shook his head. "But there's a shit pot full of money right here."

"They must have been stealing it," Sanford decided.

"Who cares. It's ours now."

"And it's real!"

They were momentarily stunned. Then, almost simultaneously they began grabbing money out of the chest.

"We're rich!" Sellers capered about with a fistful of money! "We're fucking rich!"

Back on the British side of the Rhine, the gliders were already formed up in attack formation. The first C47's and their gliders were already in the approach corridor and roaring down the slot toward the landing zones captured for them by the paratroopers. The second stage of the airborne assault had begun.

<u>End of Chapter 3</u>

Chapter 4

While the others were still grabbing sheaves of money, Shortreed unslung his musette bag and dumped out the shaving kit, socks, and other personal items that it contained. The other two were quick to follow suit.

"Load up," Shortreed told them, "and let's get out of here."

"We can't carry all of this," Sellers complained.

Sanford suggested, "We could bury the rest,"

"Fill your bag with thousand franc notes," Shortreed said..

"But what about the rest?" Sellers persisted.

"We'll burn it."

"You're out of your fucking mind, Shortreed!"

"Yeah," Sanford seconded.

"If someone finds a looted truck with a bunch of French money lying around, there's going to be questions!"

Hastily and in silence, they finished stuffing the musette bags with thousand franc notes. Shortreed looked around and found the spare gas can.

"Now get out!"

"Hey, there's still a lot of money here-"

"Get out!"

Reluctantly Sellers and Sanford jumped down from the truck. Shortreed loosened the lid, tipped over the gas can and tossed it down, then leapt from the truck.

Hugging their musette bags, Sellers and Sanford made a dash into the woods. Shortreed lingered long enough to pull the pin on a white phosphorus grenade. He tossed it into the truck then dashed after the others. He had almost reached the woods when the grenade exploded and, with a big "Poof!" the gasoline ignited.

They watched the truck burn for a moment. Then Shortreed spoke.

"This way all they'll find is three German stiffs and a burned-out truck."

By now the sky over the approach corridor had become crowded with C47's towing gliders. Sporadic small arms fire was directed at the formation but, with one exception, there was no ack-ack. The exception, a lone, clip-fed ack-ack, opened up briefly, then fell silent in a hail of grenades and small arms fire from a sizeable group of attackers.

"Hey! That sounded like our guys!"

Although the sounds had come from a half mile away, they took off toward it at a run. They were close enough to their regiment that it was likely a patrol from the 705th that had knocked out the ack-ack gun. If they linked up with all that firepower, they would be home free.

Over the approach corridor the glider assault still streamed overhead in a modern version of the old full-blooded cavalry charge. Win or die, there would be no turning back.

For the Germans, number two of the one-two punch was already gliding down onto German soil. It was going to be a long day for them.

As the three reached the far side of the woods, a burst of machine gun fire in the distance started a firefight with a squad of troopers who returned their fire. Near at hand the enemy had set up a mortar in a clearing. When the small arms fire began, the mortar joined in, and together the mortar and the machine gun had the troopers pinned down.

When the mortar started firing, Shortreed saw at once what was happening and understood that if they didn't take out the mortar, the pinned-down troopers would die. Quickly they assessed the situation and approached as close as possible. The area had been the site of a battery of 88's. Now it was cratered and desolate, with the guns destroyed and the gun crews dead or missing. The softening up process of bombing and strafing had been accurate and severe. The machine gun was firing from somewhere on the far side of this desolation, but the mortar was another thing.

They fell on it from all sides like a pack of wolves. A grenade, a couple of bursts of full automatic fire from the BAR and the tommy gun, and the German mortar had been put permanently out of action. Such ease of success was only possible during the confusion of the early stages of the airborne invasion when paratroopers were everywhere and militarily there was no front.

Quickly, Shortreed, Sellers and Sanford crossed the bombed-out area and began the deadly business of stalking the machine gun. The gun was well-placed and commanded a broad field of fire. By listening to the sounds of the machine gun fire and being able to see where the bullets were striking, they located the gun position.

It had been put where it could harass traffic on the road below. The machine gun and the mortar together had been able to control a large stretch of the road. But now the three men discovered that the closer they got to the gun, the more difficult it became to find it.

It took them several minutes to locate the lone sniper who controlled the approach to the machine gun. But when they did, Sellers had no trouble getting the sniper whose attention was focused on the pinned-down troopers. Even so, his mind was on the thousand franc notes.

"What good will that money be if I get killed?" he asked himself. It was a question Sellers would ask himself many times in the days to come.

When the sniper fell to the ground, they approached cautiously, but they could not locate the well-concealed and camouflaged machine gun.

"Sanford, have you still got a white phosphorus grenade?" Shortreed asked.

"Yeah, why?"

"Give it to Sellers."

With a shrug Sanford removed the grenade and handed it to Sellers.

"See those two trees?" Shortreed pointed. "Put the grenade right between them."

"It's just going to make a lot of smoke," Sellers protested.

"The burning particles will fall down in their holes and land on them. When they start jumping around, me and Sanford will take care of them by shooting into the smoke."

Sellers fitted the grenade onto the launcher, calculated the trajectory and fired. The grenade landed in one of the trees and exploded as it fell toward the ground showering the area with particles of white phosphorus. They would burn until they were consumed or given no more air.

There were cries, and the machine gunner and his crew leapt out of their hiding place in a frenzied effort to free themselves from the burning phosphorus particles. Immediately Shortreed and Sanford fired several bursts, each burning off a clip as they thoroughly swept the smoke-clouded area.

There was silence and then a shout from down below. The troopers who had been pinned down were signaling for the newcomers to come join them. But with the wariness born of long experience, they did not approach across the open field. Instead they followed the curve of the woods and finally came upon Lieutenant Best and the remains of the front end of the stick.

"Shortreed, Sanford, and Sellers," Shortreed reported to Best. "That's all of us, sir."

"What about the others?" Best asked.

"They didn't get out of the plane, sir."

"What happened?"

"The wing came off just as I got out."

"You're sure they're dead?"

"Yes sir."

"Corporal Martinez has a big hole in his right thigh and even with morphine, he can only walk by leaning on someone. Turk is dead. So is Kelly. Danford has a shrapnel wound in his shoulder and is still losing blood. But if they can get the bleeding stopped, Danford can walk out on his own."

Shortreed asked, "Sir, what happened to Sergeant Burns?"

"I saw him hit the ground," the lieutenant said. "But he disappeared and I never saw him again."

They had no medic, but Jones and Bergetti had given Danford his quarter grain of morphine and had sprinkled on wound powder. Now they sought to staunch the blood by stuffing a gauze bandage into the wound. It was rough and ready, but with a little luck Danford could make it to the regiment and eventual evacuation.

They were only about six hundred yards from where most of the regiment had landed and from the glider troops who were now almost all down and fighting. The moment the glider riders started to form up, the paratroopers attacked along predetermined lines for the purpose of clearing the roads and surrounding area of all enemy combatants and setting the stage for tomorrow's crossing of the Rhine by the British. By this time the approach corridor had been cleared by the paratroopers, and the tail end of the glider assault went over without being fired on from the ground.

Lieutenant Best moved his wounded and his able-bodied men to a point near the end of the woods where troopers from the Second Battalion were manning an observation post and standing by to call mortar fire when targets were observed on the road.

"Where's Regimental Headquarters?" Best asked the corporal in charge of the detail.

"That way, sir, about a thousand yards."

They were interrupted by an over flight of B24 bombers flying low and much faster than had the earlier formations of C47's. It was resupply coming for the paratroopers. The B24's had been picked for several reasons, the foremost of which were speed and payload. With para-bundles in the bomb bay, they could fly relatively low to make their drop.

The cargo chutes were much larger than those used by the paratroopers. At altitudes estimated at 250 to 300 feet, the bundles would drop free of the plane. The parachute would open, chute and cargo bundle would oscillate once or twice, then hit the ground. A human could not survive such force unscathed, but ammunition was another matter.

Once the supplies were dropped, aircrews waved and the four engines raced at full throttle. The big bombers, with those ear-challenging four engines blasting, pulled up and away so fast that the enemy gunners firing from German-held territory had no chance at them. They did in 30 seconds what would have taken a C47 an often lethal minute and a half.

The bombers were gone and the dropped supplies were being retrieved, when Lieutenant Best and his men reached Headquarters Company. After leaving Corporal Martinez and Private Danford with the medics, they fell out near the switchboard and rested. They found other demolition guys there from another plane and there was a brief exchange of questions and answers regarding those who were killed, missing in action, wounded or present. None of them had seen Sergeant Burns or knew anything about him.

Shortreed tried to pretend that it was just a matter of time until Burns would show up but in his heart he knew better. Burns was dead and he knew it. But until someone actually reported seeing him dead, Shortreed would continue to hope that his hunch was wrong and that Burns was okay.

Shortreed went to where Perine was running the regimental switchboard.

"Have you heard anything about Burns?"

"He's listed as missing in action. That's all I know."

Shortreed turned to leave, but turned back when Perine spoke.

"Tippett was in your plane, wasn't he?"

"The wing came off as I was getting out. Tippett was still in the plane."

"Oh."

"Sorry, Perine, but everyone from number thirteen on back went in with the plane."

"Murray too?"

"I'm afraid so."

Perine was much affected by this news and turned away abruptly to hide the depth of his grief.

"Oh-h-h fuck! They're both gone."

Murray and Tippett had been Perine's drinking buddies;

Shortreed touched Perine lightly on the shoulder. "I'm sorry, Perine."

He turned away and left, and went to where the others awaited the return of Lieutenant Best. Absently he opened a K ration and ate his first bite since breakfast. As he munched on canned bacon and egg, Shortreed glumly considered the number of his friends who had died on the jump. Turk, Skidmore, Tippett, Murray, Hiner and probably Burns.

"They were all good men," Shortreed thought. "That makes me and Sanford and Sellers the last of the original Demolition Platoon."

It was then that the news started coming in from the battalions. The new modus operandi for the troopers was simple. About half of the German troops opposing them were composed of old men and sixteen-year-old boys, none of whom wanted to fight, but were held in the line by SS officers who ruthlessly shot those who failed to make a hundred per cent effort.

The paratroopers' solution was to press hard for a brief moment, slack off, wait, then press them again and back off again. Usually, after a little of this, the Germans would shoot their SS officers and immediately surrender.

Then bit by bit, resistance began to collapse and prisoners began flooding into POW compounds. So many were the POW's that there were no enclosures that were not full. The overflow soon outnumbered those that were behind barbed wire.

In actuality the Germans had tried to buy time by putting what they considered trash troops in the way of the advancing airborne soldiers. Unfortunately for the German plans, the paratroopers shot their way through the trash troops and engaged the hardcore *Waffen SS* troops before they could dig in properly.

Interrogation of prisoners indicated that for ten days the Germans had given the highest priority to the ack-ack guns they were moving into the area. It was little wonder, since Montgomery had been in position for fully two weeks, but would neither shit nor get off the pot. The Germans realized that if Montgomery crossed the Rhine here, he would have airborne troops spearheading the attack. There were only a few places suitable for drop zones and the Germans deployed their ack-ack along the few approaches to these few DZs. There was little wonder at the carnage in lives and burning planes.

Lieutenant Best returned to them and said, "Give me your attention, men."

They fell silent and listened closely as he continued, "We have no demolition duties at the present time. Sanford, Sellers and Shortreed will be attached to H Company. Tomorrow when the British get their tanks across the Rhine, H Company will climb aboard and spearhead the attack. When the attack has a demolitions problem, you men will take care of it."

This was an important job and these were the best men for it. The Lieutenant unfolded an area map and laid it on the ground. "Okay you three, let me orient you."

The three troopers joined him. Lieutenant Best continued to speak, indicating points on the map. In the distance there were sounds of small arms fire.

"We're right here. Over there is the main road. A mile east on that road is the town of Hochberg. H Company is along this ridge. That's about a thousand yards from the outskirts of the town. The first farm building along the ridge is Company Headquarters. Any questions?"

"What about the British, sir? What's their timetable?'

"Before sunrise their infantry will attack across the Rhine in rubber boats. By 0900 hours they will have a pontoon bridge across and will bring three hundred plus tanks by 1000 hours. When they link up with us, we'll climb aboard and attack down the main road to Muenster."

"How far is that, sir?"

"Fifty-five kilometers."

Hearing that, Sellers whistled softly.

"It's not as bad as it sounds. We'll make it in two days."

Sellers grinned. "The war might be over by then."

"I've heard that rumor too. Who knows." Lieutenant Best laughed, then said, "Okay then. Report to H Company as soon as you can get there. The rest of us will be going on night patrol, so we'll see you tomorrow."

"Yes sir." As they turned and left at a fast walk, a cluster of 88's straddled the road. The distant crunches of the explosions and the sound of shrapnel reminded them that the war was still there, still going on, and still deadly.

Lieutenant Best had turned to the others. "All right, men, we're headed to Third Battalion Headquarters. Stay spread out and follow me."

They moved out and a minute later a salvo of counter battery fire from the glider-borne 75 mm pack howitzers roared over toward the 88's. The uproar of battle changed in scope and intensity as the newly landed glider troops joined the fray..

It was about an hour before sundown when Shortreed and the other two men arrived at H Company Headquarters. When they got there, H Company riflemen were in a firefight with a German force some five hundred yards to the east. The Germans were withdrawing with the help of mortar fire and covering fire from two machine guns.

The area where the main body of H Company's riflemen were dug in was receiving more or less steady harassing fire from the self-propelled 88's that were firing on them from somewhere near the outskirts of Hochberg. Abruptly the Germen riflemen broke contact and were gone. The combined firepower of the mortar and self-propelled artillery had extracted them successfully. This done, the firing tapered off to nothing.

Shortreed led them to the building that housed H Company's Headquarters. It was a German farmhouse. Beyond it, a stone barn had been demolished by a C47 that had crashed into it earlier with both engines burning. The wreckage still smoldered and the smell of burnt flesh was strong.

The dirt road that led to the farm had been the scene of a sizeable battle when H Company had driven the Germans out. The dead of both sides lay where they had fallen amid the rubble of combat. In the farmyard a knocked out German tank sat with its turret blown askew by a gammon grenade. The German crew lay dead in and around the tank.

The three passed by an H Company machine gun dug in to cover the approaches to the farmhouse. A voice called out.

"Hey Shortreed!"

They stopped. It was Cardone.

"What happened to Tippett?"

"The plane crashed before he got out."

"Shit!"

"Have you heard anything about Sergeant Burns?"

"He's missing?"

"Yeah," Shortreed said glumly. "Keep your head down."

"You too."

They continued on and passed several dead troopers on their way to the farmhouse. When they went inside, a corporal directed them to the basement where they found Captain Lindenberger, the CO of H Company, The captain was alone except for Staff Sergeant Mathieson.

The ground level windows of the basement had been blacked out. In the middle of the room the captain was seated at a woodworker's bench that served as a table. He was in the process of sending out a patrol under Sergeant Mathieson. The purpose would be to find out if there was any activity on H Company's left flank.

"Sergeant, this is not a combat patrol. Don't fire unless you're fired upon."

"Yes sir."

"And along the eastern edge of these woods," the captain indicated a spot on the map, "one of our gliders has disintegrated against a stone wall. They've seen movement at the wreckage. There could be survivors. Check it out."

"Should we take a stretcher, sir?"

"Take a medic. If there are any wounded to be carried out, we'll come back for them."

"Yes sir."

Mathieson started for the door, then had a thought.

"We'll need fragmentation grenades, sir."

"The ammunitions dump is upstairs in the kitchen. And stay out of the booze."

"I beg your pardon, sir."

"All the alcohol in the area is up there also," the captain said. "Tell them you have my orders."

At the word "grenade", Shortreed remembered.

"Sir, we need grenades too. Can Sanford go with Sergeant Mathieson and get some more?"

"Go ahead, Sanford."

"Yes sir."

Sanford hurried after the sergeant, and the captain asked, "Where's Lieutenant Best?"

"They're patrolling for battalion tonight, sir," Shortreed told him. "But they'll be here in time for the attack tomorrow."

Captain Lindenberger pointed to the map. "There's a bridge here about half way to Hochberg. It's not worth a damn because their tanks can go down into the streambed and cross. But it's a good spot for an ambush."

"Do you expect them to counterattack, sir?"

"No, but they will be probing our positions. We have three riflemen and a bazooka at the bridge. Dig in with them"

"What then, sir?"

"Lieutenant Franks already has his mortars registered along the road." Lindenberger handed Shortreed a map and a walkie-talkie. "If the Germans try anything, you'll be calling mortar fire."

"Yes sir."

"When the tanks get here tomorrow, you guys will climb aboard and ride to Muenster with the rest of us."

"Sounds like the Krauts are starting to fold, sir."

"They're still fighting, so keep your heads down," the captain said.

Three mortar rounds landed one after another. They were uncomfortably close and each of them flinched.

Stanford returned as Lindenberger shook his head in irritation and said, "I wanted to move the command post. But battalion wants us here."

The field phone rang and the captain answered. "Lindenberger here. Oh, Colonel Breit. Yes sir."

He signaled for the demolitions men to leave and they went away up the stairs.

"My situation, sir?" Lindenberger continued on the phone, "We have only light contact with the enemy. My CP is taking harassing mortar fire from the enemy at the rate of twelve an hour. Company strength is one hundred seventy eight. I have only one officer on duty. Lieutenant Carson was KIA, Lieutenant Egan is severely wounded and Lieutenant Youngblood is MIA, I have two walking wounded and three litter cases."

More mortar rounds landed outside. They were so close that the building rattled.

The daylight was beginning to fade when Shortreed, Sanford and Sellers arrived at the bridge. The three riflemen were sitting near their holes, holding an animated discussion on a favorite subject: How soon would the war be over ?

The bazooka man was across the road and the only one watching for Germans. Shortreed spoke briefly to the bazooka man and decided they would dig in near the bazooka. Quickly he appraised the situation and realized that their position was vulnerable to attack from along the road or from those approaching from the cover of the dry streambed. He and Sanford selected a spot where the BAR could cover both approaches. All three of them dug in near each other.

Shortreed dug his hole quickly and then began to reconnoiter the area. He was curious about how much money he had, but knew that Sellers would count his over and over. They all had about the same amount, which was as many thousand franc notes as you could stuff into a mussette bag. Sellers' numbers would be close to his.

Later, he thought, he'd count it himself, but for now he was busy watching out for his ass. He made himself fully aware of the strengths and weaknesses of their position and had a good idea of how the chief terrain features could be exploited by the attackers or defenders. Satisfied that he had done all he could, Shortreed returned to where Sanford and Sellers waited. It was

Seller's first real chance to look at his money and, as Shortreed had expected, he sat in his hole counting it.

Shortreed watched and laughed.

"What's so funny?" Sellers asked.

"I knew you'd be doing that."

"You mean you're not going to count yours?" Shortreed noticed that Sellers' voice was faintly slurred.

'When I have the time."

"I've already counted mine once. This'll be the second time."

"How about you, Sanford?" Shortreed wanted to know.. "Have you counted it yet?"

"No. But I've been thinking about what I'm going to buy," Sanford told him..

"You'll put it in houses and lots." Sellers mocked. "Whore houses and lots of whiskey."

It was clear to Shortreed that both of the other two men had been drinking.

"Okay, Sanford, where is it?" he demanded.

"Where is what?"

"The bottle you stole when you went for the grenades."

Sanford held up a half-empty bottle." Want a drink?"

Shortreed took the bottle and smelled it. "That's Calvados."

He turned the bottle upside down and spilled it out on the ground.

"Hey! What're you doing?" Sellers demanded belligerently.

"You guys can't get shitfaced tonight."

"Who says?"

"Remember the day Lieutenant Best got hit and I pulled him out of the snow bank?"

"What does that have to do with getting drunk?"

"Right after Best got hit, we came to the farmhouse where me and you and Sanford and Sergeant Burns wiped out eight or nine Krauts in nothing flat without getting a scratch."

"I don't want a lecture!"

"You know why we could do that so easy?" Shortreed persisted. "Because the Krauts were all shit-faced drunk!"

"You've already poured out the booze, so what're we talking about." Seller shrugged in sullen disgust and returned to counting his money back into his mussette bag.

By now there were a few artillery rounds going in both directions and the countryside was dusking. Sanford sat on the edge of his foxhole with his sack of money cradled in his arms. He was half-drunk, and was feeling faintly sorry for himself.

Shortreed had taken a cursory glance at the money stuffed in his own mussette bag and had concluded that the packets of thousand franc notes must be worth about three-hundred fifty to four hundred thousand dollars. Whooeee, that was a lot of money!

He lay back in his foxhole and relaxed as he watched the moon rising. "What would he do with all that money?" It was an intriguing thought, and there seemed to be many attractive answers to the question.

Sellers came over and joined Shortreed. He carried his mussette bag and his rifle. Clearly the Calvados was taking effect and both he and Sanford were drunk. Sanford began talking to no one in particular,

"When I was fighting in the Garden the sports writers would come around." He thought for a moment, then shook his head sadly. "But it wasn't like they were my friends."

"I got almost four hundred thousand dollars worth of francs," Sellers bragged.

"So do we," Shortreed countered, then turned his attention to Sanford. "What about your seconds? They must've been friends."

"Nah, it was just a job to them."

Deliberately provocative, Sellers asked, "Feeling sorry for yourself, Sanford?"

The moon had cleared the horizon and the countryside was bathed in the glow of moonlight.

"You don't know nothing about being an orphan! So shut up!"

Sanford stared at the moon for a moment. Then five hundred yards or so off to their left front, there was an outbreak of small arms fire which petered out after a couple of minutes. Sellers and Sanford ignored the outbreak of shooting, but Shortreed listened and concluded that it had been short and sweet because it was a probing action. They could expect more of the same before the night was over.

"One time I was going against a Cuban light heavy, name of Bustamente. It was ten to one against me and no takers. They asked me how I was going to fight him. Just like a sparrow, I told them." He fell silent, waiting for a response None came.

"They didn't even know what I meant," Sanford said.

"You're drunk," Sellers told him.

"You know what it means, Shortreed?" Sanford was insistent.

"I'm afraid not."

During this, an artillery duel had been developing. The shells were going both ways but not landing close. A German artillery round passed overhead with a loose rotor ring. The click-clank of the loose ring could be plainly heard.

Sanford began singing softly, "A bluejay pulled a four-horse plow. Sparrow why can't you?" He stopped and grinned expectantly.

 Sellers who had his hand inside his mussette bag, was fondling his money and daydreaming about what he was going to buy. Shortreed just looked blank.

Sanford tried once more to explain. " A bluejay is four or five times bigger than a sparrow. If a bluejay can do it, that ain't no sign a sparrow can."

"I don't get it."

"It means when you ain't got a chance, you go ahead and fight anyway. Because all you got left to lose is your pride."

"Like paratroops," Shortreed said.

Sanford accepted this in silence, then began singing again. "Redbird sitting on a sycamore tree, pouring out his soul. Along came a big black snake and ate that poor boy whole..."

"How long were you in the ring?" Shortreed asked him.

"Too long. Sometimes the next day I was so sore I couldn't move. But while the fight was going, I was somebody. Everyone was watching me."

"Now you got all that dough, you'll have a lot of friends," Sellers told him and laughed nastily.

"I'm going to buy me a gym." Sanford grinned at the thought. "Where the fight crowd can hang out."

"We'll never make it through the war," Sellers said glumly. "We'll never spend a fucking penny of this money."

"When Graves Registration rolls me over and finds all that money, the first thing they're going to do is check my dog tags. Augustine Sanford. They'll tell their grandkids about the trooper they buried that had all that money."

"Here we are, practically millionaires, and we got a life expectancy of zero, " Sellers complained..

"You've got the same odds you had before we took the money," Shortreed told him.

"All that money and no place to spend it," Sellers said.

"The time will come for that."

"We ought to desert."

"Shut up, Sellers!" Shortreed exploded.

"Fuck you!"

"Any more talk about deserting and you're in some shit with me!" As an afterthought he added, "And with Sanford."

"He doesn't always agree with you."

"We agree on one thing! We're both paratroopers!"

"What does that make me?"

"Chickenshit!"

Shortreed turned away and lay down in his foxhole to sleep. It was clear to him that Sellers and Sanford would be out of action until they slept off the effects of the hundred proof calvados. The last thing Shortreed heard before he fell asleep was Sanford singing softly to himself.

"Wild geese flying through the air, Through a sky of blue, They're going where the chilly wind don't blow, Why can't me and you?"

Around three in the morning, the bazooka man awakened Shortreed. It was his turn to act as sentry. The moon had moved over toward the west, and the new angle gave the moonlight a mysterious quality. For a moment Shortreed listened to the sounds of the night. From somewhere way off there came the sound of small arms fire as two patrols tangled briefly.

After that it was quiet until just as the moon was starting to set and the light was getting dim. Then from the dry streambed there came the faint sound of stone moving slightly under the weight of a foot.

Shortreed was instantly alert and readied his tommygun for instant use. Almost as quickly Sellers appeared at his shoulder with his M-1 ready for action. He still smelled like calvados, but some sixth sense had prodded him from his drunken sleep and now he was ready to fight. He and Shortreed conferred in whispers.

"What is it?"

"Krauts."

"Where?"

"In the stream bed to our right front."

"What are they up to?"

"Can't tell."

Then from the streambed there came a moan, as if someone was in pain, and a voice cried out in English, "Help." This was followed by more moans, and again the cry for help.

"That's one of our guys!" Sellers started to rise, but Shortreed yanked him back. "Idiot! That's a trick!"

"Help! Help!" The voice came again.

"Listen," Shortreed said. "That voice is too strong for it to belong to a wounded person. They just want to know if we're here."

The bazooka man joined them.

"They're just probing," Shortreed told him. "Go across the road and tell those guys to hold their fire and to keep quiet."

The bazooka man went across the road and carried the message to the three riflemen.

"Suppose they came to blow up the bridge?" Sellers asked.

"They wouldn't be making all that noise yelling for help, if that's what they were up to."

They listened for more sounds, but for a few minutes none came. They were just starting to breathe easier, when the voice began again.

"Help! O-h-h-h my God," the voice moaned. "Someone help me!"

There was a long moment of silence and the light from the setting moon continued to diminish. Giving up on the success of this approach, the Germans switched tactics.

"Fuck America!" they yelled. "Americans eat shit.!"

Trigger fingers were tightening on both sides of the road, but after a long moment it became clear that the insults had been a parting jibe and the Germans were gone. One of the riflemen took over sentry duty from Shortreed. The moon dropped below the horizon and the countryside was plunged into almost total darkness.

Before he fell asleep, Shortreed listened to the sounds of a flight of bombers flying over way up high. Briefly he speculated on what it would be like to be a crewmember in a bomber. To be present in a world of cockpits. Pilots, bombardiers, gunners, all flying through the sky in a large four-engined target. He drifted off to sleep, thankful that he was a paratrooper.

The rest of the dark hours were uneventful for Shortreed and the group of troopers at the bridge. When sunrise came, Shortreed awakened and watched and listened. He listened carefully for sounds of battle coming from the Rhine crossing. The plan called for a Highland Light Infantry unit to attack across the river in rubber boats before sunrise. The local scene started up with a short artillery exchange that passed over going in both directions. As for the river crossing, it was too far away and Shortreed could hear nothing.

Beyond the bridge the town of Hochberg had been bombed and badly shot up. Close at hand the bazooka man sat on the edge of his foxhole, eating a K-ration. Someone had raised

Shortreed on the walkie-talkie, while Sellers peered into his sack of money, his uneaten K-ration open beside him, and Sanford still slept.

This was the beginning of another day of combat. For Shortreed, it was another day closer to the end of the war. For Sellers, it was another step closer to the bank. For all of them today might be a door that opened onto eternity.

Shortreed hurried over to tell Sellers admiringly. "Hey! The Brits fought their way across the Rhine with bagpipes blowing."

"No shit!"

"Their tanks are already coming across the pontoon bridge!"

"We'll be riding tanks before you know it."

"It looks like it." Shortreed handed him the walkie-talkie. "Lieutenant Best is going to be on the radio in a minute. Talk to him while I wake up Sanford."

Sellers took the radio. "When will the tanks get here ?"

"Pretty soon I guess." Shortreed left him and went over to where Sanford snored on his pillow of money.

Lieutenant Best's voice began on the radio. "Calling Little Dog Four. Calling Little Dog Four."

"This is Little Dog Four."

"Is that you, Sellers?"

"Yes sir."

"There will be a patrol passing your position soon. I want you to go with them."

"Excuse me, sir, but why me?"

'The grenade launcher."

"Sir, that must've come off the last time I fired a grenade. I don't have it any more." As Sellers spoke, he was busy removing the launcher.

"Let me talk to Shortreed," Best said.

"I'll have to get him, sir. It'll only take me a minute."

Sellers laid the radio down and quickly finished removing the grenade launcher. He tossed it into the weeds, then brought the radio to Shortreed.

"The Lieutenant wants to talk to you."

Shortreed took the walkie-talkie from him.

"This is Shortreed, sir."

"We're sending a recon patrol into the village. There will be a British tank and seven troopers."

"I can hear the tank now, sir."

"Send Sanford with them. They'll need the BAR."

Shortreed glanced over at Sanford, who sat on the edge of his foxhole, nursing his hangover. "Yes sir. Is that all?"

"For now. But the main body of the tanks has already started across the pontoon bridge. Be ready to move out and stay close to that radio."

"Yes sir.."

"Over and out."

The sound of the tank was coming nearer, as Shortreed snapped off the radio and told Sanford, "Get your stuff. The Lieutenant wants you to go with the patrol."

In a moment the British tank stopped before their position. Riding on the tank were seven paratroopers. The tank revved its engine impatiently while Sanford slipped into his ammo gear of loaded BAR clips and pulled on the harness of his mussette bag. This done, he hurried to the tank and climbed aboard and the tank moved out toward Hochberg. Sanford waved once to Shortreed and then was gone.

Shortreed watched the tank until it disappeared into the village, then sat on the edge of his foxhole. From there he could still see down the road to Hochberg. Closer at hand, he could see Sellers continuing to touch the bulge of his mussette bag for reassurance.

Shortreed lay back in his foxhole and heard the riflemen across the road arguing about how soon the end of the war would come. Listening to them, he began to daydream about it himself. Unlike Sellers and Sanford, for Shortreed the money was secondary. He was glad he had it. Among other things, it would pay for a party, of course. A big one. Beyond that, he had no plans. First he had to get through the war in one piece.

Right at dark the night before, a patrol from H Company had knocked out the mortar that had been harassing their command post. After that brief outburst, the night had been fairly quiet. No artillery, no mortars, no firefights. The airborne assault had been so overwhelmingly complete that all resistance seemed to have collapsed. Yet German patrols had been probing the American positions most of the night. Shortreed concluded that even if the Krauts had been overwhelmed yesterday, there were still German soldiers out there who could and would fight.

As if to confirm this, there was a brief flurry of small arms fire from the village. The German guns, being of a different caliber, were clearly distinguishable from the American ones. The exchange went on for about five minutes in one position, then became more fluid as the outnumbered patrol began trying to withdraw under covering fire from the British tank.

The radio sprang to life and Lieutenant Best's voice called urgently, "Big Dog to Little Dog! Big Dog to Little Dog!"

Shortreed hit the talk switch. "Little Dog to Big Dog, over."

"We've lost contact with the patrol in the village," Best said. "Can you tell anything about what's happening?"

"Sir, there's a firefight going on, and it sounds like we're really outnumbered."

"We've been trying to call them back."

"Why is that, sir ?"

"S2 has changed their mind. Hochberg is crawling with Krauts. The Third Battalion is moving to clear them out of there. But we've lost contact with that patrol and can't call them back."

While they were talking, the sounds of combat increased in the village. Tanks were firing at such short range that the propelling explosion was overlapped by the sound of the projectile exploding against the target. After a few minutes of this, there came an ominous silence and a pillar of black oily smoke could be seen rising from somewhere inside the village.

"Sir, I see a cloud of smoke coming up and the German tanks have quit firing."

"They got our tank?"

"It looks like it, sir."

"Anything else?"

"It's quiet, sir. No small arms fire. Nothing."

"I guess the Krauts won."

From somewhere in the outskirts of the village, there came the sound of Sanford's BAR and the answering small arms fire from the enemy.

'Sir, I can hear Sanford still firing! Send a squad and we'll go get him!"

"The tank support is already here. We'll be there in fifteen minutes."

"I'm going by myself then."

"No you're not! That's an order!" Lieutenant Best told him. You'll do him more good calling in mortar fire."

In the distance, Sanford could be seen running from ruined building to ruined building, firing the BAR on the run as he tried to fight his way back to the outpost.

Sellers brought his gear and stood at Shortreed's shoulder, listening and watching. Shortreed took the area map from his jacket and was checking the coordinates as he spoke into the radio.

"Lieutenant Franks. Lieutenant Franks, This is Little Dog Four. Come in please!"

Sellers tugged at Shortreed's jacket and pointed at the outskirts of Hochberg. Sanford had just made it out to the main road. He was still almost four hundred yards away, but he could been seen running quickly from cover to cover, pausing now and then to rake the pursuing Germans with bursts of fire from his BAR.

"Lieutenant Franks! Lieutenant Franks!." Shortreed called urgently into the radio. "I've got targets for your mortars! Lieutenant Franks, please come in!"

Now at the edge of the village, Sanford's chances of survival were quickly diminishing as more Germans joined in the pursuit.

Shortreed was frantic. "Come on, Lieutenant Franks! Get your head out of your ass!"

Lieutenant Franks voice on the radio was calm. "What's all the excitement?"

"Shortreed gave him the coordinates and added, "Two squads of infantry. Give them all you've got!"

"I'll have to check that with Captain Parker," Franks said. "My orders are not to fire until the attack starts."

"God damn it! Start shooting, sir!" Shortreed snarled into the radio.

Lieutenant Best's voice cut in. "Calm down, Shortreed! Lieutenant Franks, this is a legitimate fire mission," he explained. "We've got a man out there."

"Repeat the coordinates."

Shortreed gave him the coordinates and immediately could hear the mortars as they coughed a salvo of H.E. rounds in a high-arching trajectory. As they waited for the mortar rounds to impact, he continued on the radio. "Sir, can we get machine gun fire on that road?"

"I'll call Sergeant Adams."

"Sir, please tell him to start shooting as soon as he thinks he can hit them."

On the outskirts of Hochberg, Sanford had gained a little and now had almost a hundred yards on his pursuers. Then the first mortar rounds began landing in the midst of the Germans. They faltered and, from the high ground behind Shortreed, burst after burst of machinegun fire punished the area and the Germans took cover. The machine guns pinned the enemy down, while the mortars pounded them.

This gave Sanford the break he needed and he no longer ran from cover to cover. Instead he made a straight line for the outskirts of Hochberg and the regiment. For a brief moment, it looked like he had it made. But then a German tank roared onto the main street behind him and, with machine guns blazing, charged in pursuit.

The American machine gunners on the ridge switched their fire to the front of the tank, in the hope of forcing the tankers to shutter their observation ports to mere slits. This would restrict their vision and hamper their effort to get Sanford. But in spite of this, while Shortreed continued his frantic efforts to extricate Sanford, the tank continued to close in on him.

For Sanford, the whole event was like a condensed version of his life. He was an underdog and alone in the arena with his enemies. Forced again to run from cover to cover, exhausted, hampered by the weight of the bag of money, he stumbled and fell. Quickly he rolled behind a piece of masonry from one of the bombed out buildings.

Some of the most repulsive and sickening battlefield atrocities of World War II were committed by German tank crews high on their daily ration of methedrine and burning with patriotic zeal. The crew inside the tank pursuing Sanford were a more or less typical German tank crew. They had been flying on methedrine for three days and, from this jangled perspective, their harrying of the American soldier took on mythic proportions. Unsure of where Sanford had gone to ground, the tankers sprayed the area where he had taken cover with burst after burst of machine gun fire.

Reluctantly Sanford removed the cumbersome bag of money and then waited until the next salvo of mortar rounds burst close to the tank. Even a direct hit from a mortar would not damage the tank, but the head rattling bang of a hit or a close miss would give the tankers a bad moment. Taking advantage of this, at this moment Sanford sprinted across the open space and into the next cover, leaving the bag of money behind. He stood behind the corner of a stone house, panting convulsively, his body gaunted by great racking sobs as he struggled to breathe.

The tank started toward him, just as two smoke rounds from the mortar landed, billowing clouds of white smoke. Sanford hesitated for a moment then, under cover of the obscuring smoke, ran back to where he had left his mussette bag. Just as he grabbed the money, the tank emerged from the smoke.

For a split second everything stood still. There was no escape for Sanford and the tank was in no hurry. He began firing his BAR and the bullets from it splashed all around the left hand machinegun port of the tank. It was a futile defiant gesture on Sanford's part that was cut short by answering bursts from both of the tank's machinegun ports. Sanford flopped over, face downward, on top of the money. He was dead before he hit the ground.

Watching at the bridge Shortreed was stunned by Sanford's death. The distant tank squatted over Sanford's body like some great carnivorous insect devouring its prey, raking it with burst after burst of needless machinegun fire. This done, the tank spun around and rumbled toward the bridge, bent on obliterating all those who dared to invade their homeland.

"You motherless, motherfuckers! " Shortreed bellowed and shoving the radio into Seller's hand, he grabbed a half of a camouflage parachute that one of the riflemen had been using for bedding. He began stringing it like a tennis net across their end of the bridge, instructing the others, "Peel the outside cover off your K-rations and toss them to me! Hurry!"

"They won't come here," one of the riflemen protested. "Why would they?"

"Start snapping shit! " Shortreed said. "Gimme those K-rations!"

The others began tossing their K-rations to Shortreed, who placed them on the road in the pattern of a minefield. Approaching from the direction of Hochberg, the tank would first be confronted by the visual barrier of the parachute and, beyond that, what appeared to be blocks of explosives. It wouldn't stop the tank, but they would slow down and shoot the K-ration "minefield" to bits before continuing. Just in case. Shortreed wanted them off the bridge and moving slow. The fake minefield ought to do the trick.

"Don't fire on them until they're off the bridge!" Shortreed shouted to the bazooka man. "Take cover! I'll get them from behind when they come off the bridge."

Shortreed slipped beneath the bridge and the others crouched in their foxholes. The tank roared up onto the bridge but stopped a few feet before the parachute barrier. There was a long moment when nothing happened and time stood still for the waiting paratroopers. Then suddenly the tank's machine guns opened up, shooting the parachute to shreds and scattering the harmless ration boxes about the road. The tank crew were satisfied that the whole thing was a hoax and the tank moved off the bridge, sweeping the area with its machine guns.

When the tank had cleared the bridge, the riflemen began shooting at the tank's observation ports. The bazooka man fired a round at the tank that blew a tread off and the tank started to spin crazily on its one remaining tread. When the riflemen began firing, Shortreed came from under the bridge and flung a gammon grenade just as the tank started to spin. The grenade exploded right where the turret joined the tank and the explosion blew the turret awry.

Another bazooka round slammed into the tank and soon it was burning furiously. From within the tank came the screams and moans of the wounded and dying crew. One wounded German managed to get the lid open and tried to escape from the burning tank, calling out frantically, "*Kamarad*! *Kamarad*!"

Shortreed threw his tommygun to his shoulder. This was one of the bastards that had killed Sanford! But he was too late. The tank's ammo began exploding and the German tanker fell back into the burning interior. A few more of the tank's 88 rounds cooked off as the tank burned in a cloud of oily smoke. Shortreed could tell at a glance that Sellers and the bazooka man were okay. He crossed the road to check on the others.

One of the riflemen was dead, another had a sucking wound in his chest. The third was unscratched and was caring for his wounded comrade. He asked Shortreed, "When does the attack start?"

"Any minute now." He told the wounded man, "They'll have a medic."

Shortreed was still struggling with what happened to Sanford. It wasn't denial so much as it was delay. Some inner awareness made him realize that Sanford's death was a wound to his psyche that would never heal and there would be plenty of time for sackcloth and ashes later. For now his best bet was to keep on being a paratrooper and every time he shot a Kraut, he'd dedicate it to Sanford's memory.

His moment of introspection was cut short by a thundering cannonade from the airborne artillery. As every battery fired time on target, the town of Hochberg was rocked by a hail of artillery rounds that landed more or less simultaneously. Fifteen seconds later the guns fired another time on target salvo, and so the attack began.

Shortreed returned to his foxhole and grabbed up his gear. Sellers was still clutching his mussette bag of money to his chest, seemingly uninvolved in all that was going on around him.

"Hey Sellers, get your gear on! They'll be here in a minute," Shortreed told him.

Sellers rose reluctantly from his foxhole and slipped into the harness of his bag of money. Then, with his M1 on his shoulder, he joined Shortreed, saying "We need more grenades."

"Yeah."

More artillery shells screamed over to impact on Hochberg. A moment later there came a tremendous explosion. Apparently the Krauts were pulling out and had blown up their ammo dump rather than leave it behind, and it was then that they began taking fire from several of the self-propelled 88's that were in and around Hochberg. The Germans were retreating in good order and this was no doubt part of their rearguard action.

H Company began passing on the road. Shortreed and Sellers fell in behind a tank and moved out with the column. German mortars had the road zeroed in and immediately began harassing the column. It was a long way to the outskirts of the town but continual heavy artillery support began to wear away the defenses. The lead tank in the column knocked out two of the self-propelled German guns and from there on it started to get a lot easier.

Shortreed and Sellers came at last to where Sanford's riddled body lay face down and stepped out of the column. Shortreed knelt by the body for a moment and took a long painful look at Sanford. If he was ever going to weep, this would have been the time. He closed his eyes and prayed silently. While Shortreed prayed, Sellers started pulling the bag of money from under Sanford's body. Just as he got it clear, Shortreed opened his eyes and saw what was happening. Furiously, he snatched the bag from Sellers.

"Hey!" Sellers protested. "He don't have no use for it."

"Shut up!" Shortreed told him flatly. He returned to the body and gently lifted it by the cartridge belt. He shoved the bag beneath Sanford, then rose and for a long minute stood looking down at the body. "So long, Sparrow."

He turned away and fell in behind a passing tank. Sellers joined him. More artillery rounds screamed over to land on enemy positions. The attack was gaining momentum.

End of Chapter 4

Chapter 5

All that remained of the defenders of Hochberg were the remnants of a company of *Waffen SS*. These highly skilled and battle-seasoned soldiers were fighting a desperate delaying action. Their numbers were too few to confront the combination of tanks and troopers that bore down on them. Their only recourse was to stay fluid and harass the column with cleverly hidden ambushes. So compelling was the attack on Hochberg that H Company shot their way through the town quickly at the cost of one KIA and three litter cases. German casualties were unknown. As for the German tanks, one was knocked out and two got away.

On the far side of Hochberg, H Company and their supporting tanks paused while more tanks arrived. The troopers of H Company climbed aboard and, with the rest of the tank-mounted regiment strung out behind them, they took off down the road to Munster. The Germans had several self-propelled guns in the area and these took turns harassing the column.

The favorite tactic for the self-propelled guns was to stay ahead of the column and position themselves where they had an observed field of fire that gave them the option of firing on any of several killing zones. When a tank or a concentration of men entered one of these zones, the self-propelled gunners would slam a few rounds into the target then disappear.

As the column moved along through areas of zero resistance, the few houses they passed had white sheets hung in their windows as a token of surrender. An occasional artillery piece had its muzzle depressed in sign of surrender. The almost complete absence of local resistance and the display of accepted signs of surrender made the troopers and tankers euphoric. The Krauts were folding! They were all giving up!

There was no need for the column to lose momentum just so they could blow breechblocks off surrendered ordinance. What the fuck! The war was almost over and everyone would be going home soon. The end-of-the-war fever was catching but, to Shortreed's way of thinking, unless those "surrendered" 88's were disabled, it was only a matter of time until some Kraut cranked the muzzle up and started firing on an unsuspecting column of men.

At the front of the column an 88 screamed in and narrowly missed the lead tank. It came from a self-propelled gun firing from cover some fifteen hundred yards to the south. The lead tank took off at top speed down the highway with its load of paratroopers hanging on grimly. The SP gun fired twice more as the tank raced along looking like a duck in a high-speed shooting gallery. But the British tanker was experienced and brave and he raced to close the escape route for the self-propelled gun.

The column stopped, while the lead tank and the SP gun played out a deadly game of cat-and-mouse in the distance. The SP gun, being only lightly armored, was lighter and faster than the tank, but had so far to go that it soon became apparent that the tactic of shoot and run would not work this time. The British tank had shut the door on the SP gun's escape route. If the SP gun was to escape, it would have to shoot its way past the British tank.

While both the tank and the SP gun maneuvered for a shot, Shortreed and his buddies aboard tank number two were startled to hear the tank gunner's warning yell, "Fire in the hole!" They were getting ready to fire on the SP gun! The troopers had no time to bail before, with an unbelievable roar, the second tank's gun fired. It missed, and the SP gun maneuvered, and then fired a close miss at the first British tank.

"Fire in the hole!" the gunner on number two shouted again, and the tank's gun roared for a second time. This round was a direct hit and was followed by another direct hit from tank number one. The SP gun went up in smoke and flame, to the cheers of Shortreed and his fellow passengers on the second tank,

"Hey Shortreed!" a voice called from the ground. It was Beale. He was at the wheel of a jeep. At his side was Lieutenant Youngblood, formerly missing-in-action. Even though Beale was visibly glad to see him, Shortreed recoiled slightly. Beale was a full time twenty-four hour a day Jonah of biblical proportions. Because of this, Beale was shunned by his messmates.

"The Lieutenant wants you and Sellers to come with us," Beale called out, above the sound of idling tank engines.

Shortreed leapt down from the tank, followed closely by Sellers. "I'm glad to see you made it, sir," Shortreed said, as he and Sellers got into the back of the jeep.

Lieutenant Youngblood grinned. "Thanks."

Then turning serious, he briefed the newcomers. "Colonel Breit doesn't want to stop the column to disable surrendered or disabled field pieces."

"The column's going to stop anyway, sir, when they get one of our tanks or kill a bunch of people," Shortreed said.

"That's where we come in," Youngblood told them. "We're now a mobile deactivation unit."

There was something faintly derisive in Youngblood's voice. He was only twenty-five years old. He had married just before the regiment left the states two years ago. Now, with the Germans retreating on both fronts, the war was almost over. Yet here he was on a dangerous mission like this. What a bunch of shit!

With a lurch and a roar, the tank column got underway again. Beale tucked the jeep in between a couple of tanks and became the second vehicle in the column. The tank that had shut the door on the SP gun waiting for them down the road.

Sellers was still cocooned in a fantasy of his money and where it would take him. Most of the time this allowed him to avoid confronting the realities that lay just beyond. It also made him dependant on Shortreed for his moves. He could be uninvolved until the shit hit the fan and still come out okay by cuing off Shortreed. It was a dumb idea, but such was the growing love affair between Sellers and the money that he thought it to be clever.

The column buzzed along without incident until around noon when a German fighter plane flew over at about eight hundred feet. It was flying a path directly over the road and was headed toward the Rhine with the engine snarling at full throttle. The plane was going very fast and it was clearly on a recon mission. Every trooper in the column took a shot at it, but the window of opportunity was short and the plane came and went so quickly that no one even came close to hitting it.

Right after that they came to their first field piece with its muzzle depressed in surrender. They dropped out of the column and Beale parked the jeep near the abandoned gun. "Keep the motor running," Lieutenant Youngblood told Beale. He dismounted, with Sellers and Shortreed who took the demolitions bag. "This could be a trap, so let's spread out," Youngblood told them.

They approached the gun with caution. While Shortreed finished setting the charge, the Lieutenant and Sellers served as an alert backup for him. Shortreed inserted a blasting cap with a short fuse into the booster charge, pulled the fuse lighter and hastily joined the others as they took cover from the impending blast. Seconds later the explosive charge went off. A quick visual inspection showed the field piece to have been totally disabled.

Shortreed carried the demo bag back to the jeep and they loaded on and rejoined the still passing column of tanks and troopers. Lieutenant Youngblood ordered Beale to move over into the passing lane and they took off for the front of the column.

As he drove, Beale was thinking of many things. The war was almost over and he'd be going home soon. And any minute some holdout Kraut could pop up and kill him. Shit! Beale had been pissed off and depressed ever since he had become such an outsider that he'd asked to be transferred to H Company. There was at least a man there from his home county in Tennessee. Unfortunately that man went out on a stretcher the day Beale arrived.

"Tuck in behind the lead tank, " the Lieutenant ordered as they reached the head of the column.

As Beale obeyed the command, he concluded that the one bright spot in his life just now was Shortreed. It was he who had taken Beale's side when Choquette, who was a bully, announced to one and all that Beale was the official outcast of Headquarters Company. He did this in front of Beale and for this Shortreed had jumped Choquette and beat the shit out of him so badly that he had to have stitches and was on limited duty for a week.

Shortreed had been put on company punishment. Beale could tell that Shortreed liked him. That was good, because no one else did. As for Choquette, he was pushing up daisies in Normandy and good riddance!

From the direction of the Rhine there came the roar of an aircraft engine and the crackle of small arms fire as the German plane returned from its recon mission. The return flight was a replay of when the plane had sallied forth. Everyone in the column fired at him but missed. Grudgingly Shortreed could not help but admire the courage and determination required of the pilot. It took a lot of balls to make that flight.

"There's another gun!" Lieutenant Youngblood pointed and Beale pulled out of the column and parked at the side of the road. The gun was located on a low rise that gave it a good visual field of fire. The muzzle was depressed in surrender and the camouflage netting hung awry. There was another gun with depressed barrel and a white flag some three hundred yards southeast of the first gun. Apparently this was the remnants of a battery that had been hastily dug in, and then abandoned when the attack overwhelmed them.

Shortreed and Sellers dismounted from the jeep. The lieutenant asked Shortreed, "How many breechblocks can you blow with what you've got now?"

Shortreed peered into the demo bag. "I've got enough C2 for eight more and plenty of blasting caps and about a mile of primacord. But we've only got five booster charges left," he warned Youngblood.

"What about fuse lighters?" the lieutenant wanted to know.

"We could use some," Shortreed said. "'But they might as well bring more of everything else except primacord."

"I have to report to Captain Lindenberger anyway. I'll see if they can send it up, Youngblood told him and added, "Beale, you go with Shortreed."

"Yes sir."

The lieutenant began talking into the radio. Reluctantly Beale took his .30 caliber carbine and followed Shortreed and Sellers toward the 88. Three hundred yards to the southeast, the depressed muzzle of the gun with the white flag was being slowly cranked into firing position. Such small deliberate movements attracted no attention in the high-speed world of combat.

Unaware of this, Shortreed went about the business of disabling the field piece before him. The C-2 and the gun cotton booster charges were so stable that they could be pushed together and molded into position without danger. But with the addition of a fused blasting cap, the charge became more demanding of respect. All of which was automatic with Shortreed. He finished setting the charge and pulled the fuse lighter.

Shortreed shouldered the demo bag, and the three of them started back for the jeep where Youngblood had dismounted and was taking a leak. All at once the 88 to the southeast fired at a tank that had entered a kill zone. Lieutenant Youngblood was standing directly in the line of fire and the artillery round took off most of his head before impacting against a tank on the road behind them. It penetrated the tank, killing or wounding all the tankers inside. With one exception, the troopers who had been riding the tank escaped serious injury.

The response was immediate. Three tanks in the column fired almost as one. All three rounds impacted on or close around the German 88. The column slowed just enough to give a wide berth to the burning tank. The troopers who had been aboard the stricken tank pulled the survivors from the flames. Almost simultaneously Shortreed's explosive charge wrecked the 88 behind them. The cry "Medic! Medic" went up near the burning tank.

Beale took one look at Lieutenant Youngblood's mangled head and threw up. He'd seen a lot of shit, but nothing like this. Sellers fought off revulsion by convincing himself, in spite of a twinge, that this was just another stiff on the battlefield. He retreated even deeper into his cocoon of denial

A medical jeep raced up and stopped. The four medics dismounted and began working with the wounded.

"Need a medic down there?" a voice called from the road.

"No." Shortreed called back. Turning to Beale and Sellers, he told them, "Get in the jeep."

He stowed the demolitions bag and got behind the wheel. Once the others had mounted up, Shortreed took off for the now silent 88 that had fired the fatal round. While he drove he was thinking that, even if no one looked back at the lieutenant's body as they left, what had happened to Youngblood would leave a wound on their memories, an unhealing scar that would throb painfully at unexpected moments for the rest of their lives.

Lieutenant Youngblood's death was spectacular and tragic because he was a good man and a good soldier. But just because he got his head blown off didn't make him any deader than someone whose chute didn't open or someone who caught a bullet between the eyes. Shortreed had armored himself with this hard-nosed logic of acceptance. Dead was dead. If there were other considerations, he'd deal with them later.

The main issues for Shortreed were the war and survival. The war had been thrust upon him by the times, but survival was his own private war against oblivion. So far he was winning, but what happened to Lieutenant Youngblood had reminded him that the war was not over yet.

They fell out of the moving column and parked near the 88. After getting out of the jeep, they started for the gun with a high level of alertness and caution. The chance of the gunner having survived the three tank rounds was slim. But who knows? He might have had a deep hole. This set of circumstances even pulled Sellers from his money-driven fantasy of luxury in a better world. In the background the roar and rattle of the tank column continued as the three men approached the 88.

Beale might well have been the regimental pariah but, when it came to this kind of business, he was deadly. In spite of the fact that he was armed only with a .30 caliber carbine, he was a tiger among tigers, clearly sharper set than either Sellers or Shortreed. Shortreed had assumed that it was just Beale trying to earn acceptance, but it was that and more.

The gun emplacement had taken one direct hit. The other two rounds had been close misses. On the floor of the gun pit, a German soldier lay with a serious wound in the leg. He was only a lad of fifteen years or so and he was weeping softly.

"A kid! What the hell is this?"

A check of the place showed a well-constructed hidey-hole that enabled the kid to survive although wounded. Shortreed knelt beside the boy.

"Do you speak English?"

There was no answer.

"We're going to take you to the road where there are medics. Doctors."

The kid's eyes followed Shortreed's every move, but he remained silent. Shortreed removed his own first aid kit from the camouflage netting on his helmet and took out the morphine syrette.

"This will make you feel better."

He prepared the syrette and, as he bent over to inject the painkiller, the German boy spat full in Shortreed's face. At the same time he reached under the uniform jacket that lay at his side and came out with a hand grenade. As he pulled the pin, he started to shout "*Heil Hitler!*"

But "*Heil*" was as far as he got before Beale sealed his lips with a fast shot to the head. Shortreed was for once in his twenty-two years totally at a loss what to do.

"Goddamn little bastard!" Beale cursed, as the three troopers scrambled for the grenade. Then, just as the grenade was about to explode, Sellers got a hand on it and flung it outside the gun pit where it immediately exploded harmlessly.

Shortreed pulled out his shirttail and wiped the spit from his face.

"How do they get these kids so hyped up?" he asked himself and turned to the work at hand. As he prepared the charge, Shortreed could not help but consider the fate of the poor boy who lay dead at the bottom of the gun pit. He had lived and died at the whim of his government, his mind stunted by the acceptance of political bullshit from on high. The kid had no choice, but maybe his parents did. What a bunch of assholes!

The fused blasting cap was next and Shortreed automatically cleared his mind of all distractions. The important thing now was to be safe and do it by the book. Respectfully he inserted the fused blasting cap into the booster charge. A couple of more moves and Shortreed had the charge set. He pulled the fuse lighter and the three of them took cover outside the gun pit. The charge went off with a bang and Shortreed peered into the pit to check his work. The gun was demolished.

He tried not to look at the dead boy on the floor of the pit, but his eyes could not stay away. Shortreed had found two C clamps attached to the gun, one on the transversing mechanism and the other on the elevating mechanism. Some adult had zeroed the 88 on the road and limited its actions with the clamps, so that the kid had only to crank the elevating wheel until it hit the clamp and he would be on target. What a lousy thing to do, Shortreed thought.

"Hey Shortreed! Hadn't we ought to get going?"

It was Sellers, who was worrying about getting back to the front of one of the tank columns.

Shortreed turned from the gun pit and together they returned to the jeep. After stowing their gear, they started up took off for their place at the head of the column. Sellers returned to his fantasies, and Beale sunk back into his mire of low self-esteem. Shortreed could not keep his mind off the kid. He would like to get his hands on the prick who set up the artillery and left the kid to die. What a bastard!

In the next 8 kilometers they blew the breechblock from three more abandoned guns. During that time not a shot was fired and, amazingly, the column of trooper-laden tanks reflected that state of affairs. Where before there had been menace and power in the column, now the menace was muted by the high spirits of the soldiers on and in the tanks. No one was sharp-set. The tanks were no longer attacking; they were transporting paratroopers to Munster. Finally even the superstitious and the skeptics like Shortreed had to acknowledge that resistance was crumbling and that the war in Europe was rapidly coming to an end.

For Sellers this thought fueled his already ravening appetite for luxury and power. These were things you could buy and he had a big bag of money. He would use it to parlay his wartime record into a political career.

He could see himself at a big political rally, a war hero with a pretty wife who would look up at him adoringly. He'd be a state senator by the time he was thirty! He was almost delirious in anticipation. Once he got his foot in that door, he'd just get richer and more powerful. People would bow and scrape to him! He loved it.

Beale combated his self-loathing with his hatred of the army and their refusal to let him belong and for the smugness of those who were no better than him but did belong. Fuck them!

As for Shortreed, he had no real plans for after the war. Of course he'd go home to see his folks, but aside from that he had no plan. For now he was going to stay on the alert as if these were the first days of the war when the German resistance was strong. The Germans would be fighting differently now that they were losing. There was going to be a bunch of sneaky shit going on, anti-personnel mines, trip wires, booby traps, hit-and-run sniping. Demo was going to be busy disconnecting a lot of high-risk junk.

And on top of all this, he had Beale around his neck. He knew that as long as Beale was with him, the odds of his survival were grim. He shook his head in disgust. Sellers had his head up his ass and Beale was a Jonah with a proven track record. The initiative, if there was to be one, clearly lay with Shortreed himself.

The roadside was changing. There were more houses along the road. They all had white bed sheets hanging from the windows. They were entering the outskirts of Munster.

Here the paratroopers and the tanks parted company. The troopers dismounted and went further into the suburbs of Munster on foot. Before they actually entered the city proper they halted the regiment and, after sending out patrols, went about the business of billeting the troops. They still maintained a perimeter and aggressively patrolled the surrounding area.

Within the perimeter, the men were billeted in the houses of an upper middle class neighborhood where owners had hastily vacated at the first sign of the column of troopers. For the men these houses furnished an unaccustomed touch of luxury. Some of the men even managed to bathe, but to Shortreed it seemed strange to wash your body clean then dry on dirty towels and put on the same dirty clothing you had gotten out of.

The troops were deliriously happy at the prospect of soon being homeward bound. Their elation was further reinforced by the fact that there had been no artillery or small arms fire for hours and here they were, quartered in an elegantly furnished house. Nonetheless, all the old guys found it difficult to let their guard all the way down. Somewhere in the back of their mind they all had one eye on the door.

They had no way of knowing then that this would be true for the rest of their lives. There is something about serious combat that burns such patterns into the most primal levels of the human mind. There it exists as a scar that serves as a sentry for the inner being.

While the rest of demolitions was reveling in the thought that peace was at hand, Shortreed went foraging. As far as he could tell the war was just catching its breath. Then there would be more. Peace rumors were airy and insubstantial. In the real world a bottle or a good wiggle was more comforting than rumors of peace. If he was lucky enough, he might get both.

Colonel Breit and his staff were ensconced in a mansion in the middle of the regimental perimeter. The first order Breit gave his men on this day of victory was typical of this prick among pricks: "All ranks will take this opportunity to shave." This order was greeted with boos and catcalls from the entire regiment. Nobody shaved.

Gill, one of the new men, was worried. "Suppose Colonel Breit throws an inspection?"he asked.

"As long as we have live ammunition, you won't see old Piss-and-Tears," Parker told him.

"He knows if we get the chance, we'll get him," Watkins added with feeling.

"Piss and Tears?" Gill questioned.

"He calls us his Roughnecks and we call him Old Piss and Tears," Parker said.

Watkins laughed. "Or sometimes we just call him Shithead."

"I can see Shithead," Gill said. "But why Piss and Tears?"

"You know how they call Patton 'Blood and Guts' because he's so game he'd fight a buzz saw?" Parker asked.

Gill nodded,

"Well Breit is so chickenshit he runs for his rear, rear command post when the shooting starts."

"Pissing and moaning all the way," Watkins added vehemently.

"He jumped into combat didn't he?" Gill challenged hotly. Not that he gave a damn about Breit. But he hated Parker and wanted to provoke him into swinging on him.

"Breit's not even a soldier," Parker said contemptuously. He was as big and as mean as Gill and had a short fuse, and he was also getting hot.

Gill demanded, "If he's not a soldier how did he get to be a colonel?"

"He was a fucking P.E.instructor who married a general's daughter!" Parker bellowed.

By now their loud, angry voices had begun to penetrate the fog of euphoria and dreams of peace that enveloped the other men in the room and they began to gather around. Parker and Gill were equal in size and temper. Either one of them could pound you into the ground.

But Watkins, the banty rooster, would kill you. When he was pissed off, the look in his eyes would bore a hole through the strongest man's confidence. He moved right up into Gill's face and said, "Just before we pulled out of Normandy, a bunch of 88's landed in the Headquarters Headquarters Company area while General Hobart was there to see Breit."

Parker interrupted the little man loudly. "And you know what Breit did when the shells started landing? That cocksucker jumped into his jeep and hauled ass for his rear CP!"

Covertly Watkins undid the snap fastener that held his trench knife in its scabbard and started loud-talking Gill. "And General Hobart who was a man stayed in the regimental area and took charge of moving the wounded out!"

"You know what that makes Breit?" Parker demanded angrily. "A piece of crawling shit!"

The room fell silent and for a moment this tableau of anger and confrontation hung suspended in time. Then just as things were about to get bloody, the side door opened and Shortreed swaggered into the room with a bottle in each hand.

"Hey. Look what I got!"

Almost no one took any notice of Shortreed. The main event was the three troopers who teetered on the brink of mayhem. Sizing up the situation, Shortreed walked over quickly and stopped between Gill and the other two. He pulled the cork from one of the bottles with his teeth and held it out to Gill.

"Have a drink!"

Gill pushed it aside, snarling, "Can't you see I'm busy?"

"If you're too busy for a drink, you're too fucking busy," Shortreed told him.

Others in the room joined in.

"Yeah Gill, have a drink."

"Don't be an asshole, have a drink!"

Gill grabbed the bottle, took a big drink and handed it back to Shortreed. Clearly this was what was needed, for he began to relax visibly. But when Shortreed held out the bottle to Parker, the big man shook his head and said, "I'm not thirsty."

"Come on," Shortreed urged.

"I told you, I'm not thirsty!" Parker growled.

"You'd rather suck your thumb, is that it?" Shortreed taunted him.

Parker drew back his fist to hit Shortreed, but before he could deliver the blow, he found himself looking at a very sharp trench knife in the hands of Watkins. Not a word was spoken, but Parker found himself suddenly reminded of why people gave the little man a lot of room.. The little bastard was sharpset to kill him!

Slowly, Parker reached out for the bottle and drank from it deeply He finished and held the bottle out to Watkins. Plainly it was meant as an olive branch and, after replacing his knife in its sheath, Watkins took it.

Until this moment, the others in the room had been holding their breath. Now that the tension was rapidly dissipating, there was an audible sigh of relief.

Shortreed placed the other bottle on a table in the middle of the room and announced, "These two bottles are for everyone."

Plainly this was a cause for jubilation. While the men of the demo squad wasted no time in starting the bottles around, Shortreed's eyes searched the room, looking for Sellers. He found him off in a corner, apart from the others and living in his private world in which there was nothing but Sellers and his schemes for the money.

"Come with me."

"What do you want, Shortreed?"

"I want to show you something."

Reluctantly Sellers got to his feet and, taking his musette bag of money, followed Shortreed from the room and out onto the porch. They closed the door behind them.

"What do you want, Shortreed?" Sellers asked.

Shortreed pointed to the house next door. " You see the second window from the back on the ground floor?"

"What about it?"

"I'll be there. If we move out, come get me."

"Okay."Sellers nodded consent and added, "Just to be safe, why don't you leave your money with me?"

"Thanks, I'll keep it with me."

Shortreed turned away and went swiftly across the yard and, as Sellers watched him, knocked at the window. It was opened from the inside and there was a glimpse of a bunch of blonde hair and a bare arm as Shortreed climbed in and the window closed behind him. After a moment Sellers turned away and went back inside.

<u>End of Chapter 5</u>

Chapter 6

Shortreed awakened with the sun and while Ilse slept on at his side, he spent almost half an hour contemplating his situation. The war was winding down and the Germans were beginning to surrender here and there in large numbers.

To Shortreed these were the most dangerous days of the war. Some Germans fought, others surrendered, and the war was almost over. It was a time when soldiers let their guard down and made mistakes. War was not forgiving of such mistakes. He realized that constant vigilance of a high order would increase the odds in his favor

But in the back of his mind Shortreed knew that training and a high level of motivation were not enough. Luck ruled the battlefield and was distressingly too often the determining factor in who lived or died. So far his luck had been good in the matter of booze, women and survival. Was there anything else? Not for now, he concluded philosophically.

Pleased with this thought, he drank deeply from the bottle of wine that stood on the nightstand and leaned back on his pillow. Soon duty would call. Until then there was Ilse and this moment in time and space. Nothing else existed.

Next door the remnants of the demolition squad were stirring. The lack of artillery or small arms fire together with the two bottles of wine had ensured a good night's sleep for all hands. Sellers had been the lone exception. He had slept fitfully with his head pillowed on his bag of money.

The other troopers awakened in an ebullient mood. Was the war not almost over? There was something faintly ludicrous about the way the day started. So accustomed were they to morning calisthenics while in garrison that even now some of the troopers began this day with impromptu push-ups and side-straddle hops, which if nothing else, demonstrated the army's success in replacing thought with habit patterns and conditioned responses. No one thought of it that way. It was just how the day usually started.

Sergeant Lisenby was the only sergeant left in demolitions. All the others were dead, wounded or missing in action. In garrison Lisenby was a spit-and-polish no-nonsense sergeant because, as he put it, "It keeps the army off our ass." But in combat his loyalties were one hundred percent with the troops and fuck the establishment. He and Lieutenant Best were distant and formal toward each other in military matters, yet they respected each other for their bravery and accomplishment as soldiers.

The first thing Lisenby did when he rejoined demo early that morning was to send Beale back to H Company.

"What about the jeep?" Beale wanted to know.

"Tell them it hit a mine," Lisenby told him.

"But--" Beale started to protest.

"Demo needs it worse than they do!" Lisenby told him

Beale picked up his carbine and slouched away glumly in the direction of H Company just as Shortreed showed up. He watched Beale as he left, then saw Lisenby.

"Hey Lisenby! I heard you got hit."

"I had a couple of close calls, but I'm still here."

Both men laughed. They liked each other. Lisenby would still have been a corporal had it not been for the fact that every time Shortreed made sergeant he would get busted within six weeks time.

It went like this. In combat Shortreed showed natural leadership and looked good. In the absence of other non-coms he would take charge and the men would follow him. He would be promoted to sergeant and everything would be great until they returned to base. Then Shortreed would again start doing as he pleased, blithely ignoring all the petty rules and regulations with which the army hassled the troops.

It became obvious that Shortreed was not ever going to play the garrison game. So once again he was busted to private and this time he stayed there. Which suited him fine.

Lieutenant Best entered the room and Lisenby called out, "Tenshut!" The troopers popped to attention. Best was carrying his rifle and wore his pack

"At ease, men," Best ordered. "Here's the latest from Division. The 705th is to proceed to the town of Essen on foot. There is a big Krupwerke there and a large group of holdouts. Our job will be to get them out of there."

This was greeted by a stunned silence. The men had assumed that their mission had been accomplished and that the war was over for them.

Best went on. "First we'll try to starve them out. If that doesn't work, we'll go in and get them. Any questions?"

No one spoke.

Best glanced at his watch. "All right then, men. Get into your gear and assemble in the street. Turn your squad out, sergeant," he ordered and left the room.

The troopers scrambled for their gear. There was a lot of bitching and grumbling.

"Quit sniveling and get moving," Lisenby told them.

Within the 705th perimeter, men were leaving their billets reluctantly. The luxury of sleeping inside on beds, couches and rug-covered floors was hard for them to leave behind. In the street they assembled in loose groups while the sergeants counted noses.

Captain Farlow stood in the middle of the street, conferring with Best, Newberger and Wilson, his three remaining lieutenants. First Sergeant Widdison went around getting the nose count from the sergeants of each of Headquarters Headquarters four sections. Beside Demolitions, there were Message Center, Communications and S2. This completed, Widdison went to report to Captain Farlow.

"Sir, we have one hundred and twenty three men reporting for duty."

"Is that all?"

"Yes sir."

Captain Farlow shook his head grimly. He started to speak but stopped, as everyone's attention was diverted by the accented voice of a young woman calling, "Shortreed! Shortreed!"

All eyes turned to watch Ilse hurrying from the house next door to where Demolitions had been billeted. She was a really good-looking German girl with long blonde hair and a great figure. Spotting Shortreed, she hurried to him with his dog tags held high. The troopers watched silently as this mini-drama unfolded.

Here was Shortreed in front of the whole company, with Ilse making it obvious that they had spent the night together. While he was still in a state of shock Ilse stood on tiptoe and put Shortreed's dog tags around his neck, then embraced him and kissed him warmly. For one agonized moment Shortreed was totally nonplussed, but he quickly regained his composure. Never one for halfway measures, he gave as good as he got and kissed Ilse back with equal warmth. After a brief moment they broke the embrace and Ilse stepped away.

Spontaneously all of the enlisted men broke into cheers and applause. The three lieutenants were grinning, but Captain Farlow was furious.

"Tell Shortreed to report to me immediately!" he snapped.

Sergeant Widdison strode to the demolitions squad and called out in a stentorian voice, "Private Shortreed, report to Captain Farlow immediately!"

Shortreed left his squad and went directly to where Captain Farlow stood bristling with indignation. He stopped before the captain and stood at attention.

"Private Shortreed reporting to the company commander as directed, sir."

"Don't you salute anymore, soldier?" Farlow demanded angrily.

"Sir, your orders were that you were not to be saluted in combat so it wouldn't identify you as a target for snipers." Whereupon Shortreed clicked his heels and saluted smartly.

If Farlow caught the implication of this, he ignored it, but Lieutenant Best winced. Shortreed was crazy to push his luck with Farlow who was a prick and a stickler for military courtesy and discipline. It was Farlow who had as good as murdered Dignon by sentencing him to permanent first scout for S2. All because in a moment of drunken exuberance Dignon had fired his rifle in the air a couple of times.

"Well, what have you got to say for yourself?" Farlow demanded.

"With regard to what, sir?"

"The girl!"

"We spent the night fucking, sir."

It was a moment before Captain Farlow could trust himself to speak. "Did you read your non-fraternization card which expressly forbids such behavior?"

"No sir, I did not."

"Your orders were to read it," Farlow sputtered.

"Sir, I had no such orders. I found the card on my bunk when I returned from a work detail."

"You know what it said," Farlow said accusingly.

"Sir, at the top it said Headquarters 12th Army Group and at the bottom it was signed Lieutenant General Bradley. Since we're in the First Allied Airborne Army which is part of the 21st Army Group under the command of Field Marshal Montgomery, it didn't seem like it applied to me."

Captain Farlow shook his head in disgust. A career officer, he did not want his record of achievement with Headquarters Headquarters Company to be besmirched by a disciplinary court martial of one of his men. But he would be damned if he'd let Shortreed get by with this kind of crap.

"From now on anytime S2 is on patrol, you will be their first scout," Farlow ordered. "Dismissed."

"Thank you, Sir." Shortreed saluted smartly, did an about face and returned to his squad.

Captain Farlow turned to Lieutenant Best. "He's your soldier. Was he being insubordinate?"

"How's that, sir?

"Thanking me for making him first scout."

"No sir, I think he'd rather be dodging bullets than pulling mines and de-activating booby traps."

Farlow let this go by without response; He had the reputation of being ruthless and was considered to be a tight-assed GI bastard by his men. His favorite method of punishment was to put an offending soldier on permanent dangerous duty until he was killed. It was a tactic he had borrowed from Colonel Breit who had raised it to an art form. Farlow's nickname among his men was "Foxhole Farlow", because in common with Colonel Breit he was a coward and bully who took refuge in his foxhole any time the shit hit the fan.

Soon the 705th was strung out along the road in the beginning phase of what was to be almost three days of marching with only an occasional sniper impeding their advance. Along the way they moved through war-ravaged villages, past the tottering walls of bombed out buildings, across pastures strewn with whole herds of bloated dead cattle. At the site of pitched battles the dead of both sides lay where they fell, ripening in the sun. The stench of death was all-pervasive.

The troopers' end-of-the-war euphoria was dampened by these stark reminders of the cost of war in terms of human and animal life. Gone were the ebullience and sense of victory that had prevailed the day before. The troopers were silent and introspective. The remnant of humanity that remained active in their collective psyche recoiled at this tableau of inhumanity and secretly more than one of them felt dirtied by the part they had played in the war.

The next day of the march the regiment was sullen and moody. The joking and horseplay were missing. Gone were the ribald parodies of popular songs. At one point Headquarters Headquarters Company was forced to wait at a road intersection while a convoy of trucks passed on the main road.

The trucks looked like cattle trucks with slotted sideboards. Each was fully loaded with bodies stacked like cordwood. Many were identifiable as paratroopers by their jump boots. The stench was overwhelming as was the whole goddamned thing. There was not a trooper among them who did not suffer a momentary pang of survivor's guilt. A few men wept openly and unashamedly.

It was only with the greatest difficulty that Shortreed held himself together. For a moment his defenses were demolished and his inner being lay naked and undefended in the midst of this sense of monumental loss. Sanford, Turk, Tippet, Stoyle, Murray, Shepherd, Burns. All good men, all gone forever. Was there no end to it? It was a grim company of troopers who bivouacked at the end of the day's march toward Essen.

For Shortreed the day was not over. He had just got his foxhole dug when Sergeant Kramer and a patrol from S2 stopped on the road before where demo was dug in.

"Hey Shortreed," Kramer called out. "Captain Farlow wants you to come with us."

Shortreed slipped into his vest of clips for his tommy gun, then into the harness for his mussette bag of money. As he joined the patrol, Kramer told him, "You know you're first scout," and added, "You won't need that mussette bag."

"I've got some bread and cheese in it," Shortreed said.

Kramer shrugged noncommittally and spread out a map on the ground. "Let me orient you."

The two of them squatted before the map. As Kramer spoke he indicated points on the map.

"We're here. Two kilometers south on this road we will intersect with the main road to Dorsten. F Company is deployed at the intersection and on the high ground just west of the intersection. Got that?"

"Yeah, I got it."

"After we pass through F Company's roadblock we will continue south to Dorsten,"

"How far, sergeant?"

"Five kilometers,"

"We can do that before dark."

"It will be dark before we get back."

"Any enemy activity reported along the road?" Shortreed asked.

"F Company's been sniped at all day and we can expect the same thing. We're supposed to find out where their main body is located."

"If they still have a main body." Shortreed laughed.

Sergeant Kramer folded the map and both men rose to their feet.

"This is not a combat patrol. Don't shoot unless we're shot at."

"Okay, Sarge. When do we start?"

"Right now."

"How much of a spread between me and the patrol?"

"Just walk at a good pace. I'll adjust the gap."

Shortreed slung his tommy gun over his shoulder and struck out.

"All right, men," Kramer ordered. "Move out in extended order. And keep your head out of your ass. There's still plenty of Krauts out there somewhere."

Silently the patrol started to move out with a gap of ten feet or more between them. By now even the replacements were tough and battle wise. The 705th was a regiment where you either learned quick or died quick. These guys had learned.

The patrol moved at a good pace until they came to F Company's roadblock at the intersection. The first familiar face Shortreed saw was that of Corporal David Waters, an old pal from jump school. He was on a machine gun dug in to cover the approaches to the intersection.

"Hey Shortreed! What's demo up to?"

"This isn't demo. It's S2."

"Then how come they got you on point?"

"That old dry-balled son of a bitch Farlow found out I got laid."

Waters laughed. " If you'd got drunk he'd have chewed you out and left it at that."

"Fuck the bastard."

"Hey Shortreed, get moving!" Kramer yelled as the patrol started closing up on the roadblock.

Reluctantly Shortreed broke off with Waters. "Keep your head out, Davie."

"You too."

Shortreed struck out on point. Waters waited until he knew Kramer would be sure to hear him, then called after Shortreed, "If you have to come back by here after dark, the password will be kiss my ass!"

Several of the privates in the patrol grinned and gave thumbs up as they passed Waters and the machine gun. But Kramer ignored the bullshit and kept the patrol moving.

They went along without incident for the better part of the five kilometers to Dorsten. Then they moved into the outskirts of the town which had been strafed and bombed often because of the rail yards located there.

As Shortreed moved along the main road through the devastated town, he began to understand the seriousness of the sentence given him by Captain Farlow. His main function as first scout was to get the enemy to expose themselves by drawing their fire.

Essentially he was little more than a duck in a shooting gallery. First scout was such a dangerous job that in most patrols the men drew lots to see who was to be first scout or the job was rotated. Here he was, doomed to be first scout until he was dead or the war was over. Behind that, he had to wait until he was shot at before he could shoot at the enemy. What a bunch of shit!

With this realization Shortreed sloughed off all of his flippant jauntiness and reduced himself psychologically to the barest essentials. Every fiber of his being, both the physical, the touch-it, feel-it reality, and the felt but unseen dimension of spirit were tuned to the highest levels of alertness and awareness. Somewhere in his inner being he knew there lay a sixth sense that had warned him unasked many times in the past. Given his present circumstances he did not scruple to call upon this inner resource.

Always before that sixth sense had seemed an airy and insubstantial mean of explaining the vagaries of chance. Now he called upon it as if it was a reality and asked that it stand sentry for his survival. There was no explaining it. Perhaps it was a gift from beyond the grave, ancestors, dead relatives. Who gave a fuck! It was there and he didn't have to understand it to call on it for help.

His moment of introspection was sundered by the almost electric shock of awareness that peril in the highest was lying in wait close at hand. His adrenal levels surged and suddenly he was walking on the balls of his feet with his tommy gun ready. He was sharp set for whatever was in the wind.

Behind him the men in the patrol read his body language. The lack of enemy resistance had allowed the members of the patrol to lapse into a state of low vigilance. But when Shortreed's body language called out to them, Alert! Alert! a metamorphosis took place and, without a word, the gap between the men increased, safeties were clicked off, and Sergeant Kramer abandoned his position in the middle of the road and fell in behind the left hand file of men. In less than an instant the patrol had gone from being relaxed but vigilant to being alert and deadly.

Ahead of the main body Shortreed was passing the bombed-out shell of a three-story building of masonry. As he passed the far end of the building it was clear to the others in the patrol that shit was getting ready to hit the fan. Anxious eyes searched the area near Shortreed for signs of an ambush.

Suddenly Shortreed dashed off the road at the end of the building and disappeared from view. This was followed by two short bursts from his tommy gun. The patrol hit the ditch. Sergeant Kramer shouted, "Cover me!" as he raced toward where Shortreed had disappeared.

When Kramer rounded the corner of the building he found Shortreed some thirty yards away in the shrubbery flanking the next building. He was looking down at a German soldier convulsing in his death throes.

"You okay, Shortreed?"

"Yeah. Where's the patrol, sergeant?"

'Why?"

"I want to know if there's anyone before the building there." Shortreed jerked his head toward the derelict structure.

"They're in the ditch at the other side of the building."

"Would you please check and make sure?"

Kramer moved so he could see down the road and reported, "It's all clear."

Returning to where Shortreed stood, he asked, "What's this all about, Shortreed?"

"Watch this, " Shortreed said as he took an electric spark generator from near the body of the now dead German. A wire ran from the generator to the derelict building and entered it through what had once been a window.

"What is it? A communications wire?" Kramer asked.

"Nope." Shortreed told him. "Watch."

Shortreed shoved the plunger down, and within the building there were a series of small explosions that blew the tottering front masonry wall down. It fell across the road in such a way that, had the patrol been there, it would have been destroyed.

The Sergeant looked dumbfounded and it took a moment before he spoke. "Man, than was close. Good work, Shortreed."

Kramer signaled to the patrol and they rose from the ditch and started moving out as before. He told Shortreed, "We have to go as far as the railroad yards. We ought to try to make it before dark. So let's move out."

Once more Shortreed took up his position as first scout. The patrol started out again, with a newly sharpened awareness of the complexities of the deadly end game that the Germans were playing. They were on edge and sharp set but they made it to the rail yards without incident. Just as they reached their destination a string of bullets from a machinegun struck the road right beside Shortreed and, as they whined away to the rear, he hit the dirt behind a pile of masonry from a bombed-out building.

A second burst of fire raked the pile of masonry savagely, then the gunner switched and began spraying the road with bullets. The second burst of fire cost the gunner his life, for it enabled Sergeant Kramer to spot the gun and he fired a tracer round into the gun's position. The patrol knocked the gun out in a fusillade of rifle fire. This was followed by an eerie silence as the paratroopers waited in the gathering gloom. There was a sniper out there somewhere who had been protecting the machine gun. Where was the son of a bitch?

Shortreed knew that if he showed himself now, the sniper would get him Darkness was only minutes away and, with a little luck, he could slip away after dark. Shortreed and the other members of the patrol waited tensely as darkness slowly fell. The silence was sinister and oppressive. After a few minutes it was darker and Shortreed was about to leave his place of concealment when a voice called from nearby on his right front.

"*Herr Falschirmjaeger*! I want to surrender."

Shortreed reacted immediately and pointed his tommy gun at the sound of the voice. The voice spoke again in a mixture of German and English.

"I want to surrender. *Danke schoen*."

"*Vuffer niederlagen?*" Shortreed responded in bastard German.

"*Jah, jah! Wiederstandt es sindlos.*"

"*Komen sie mitt hande hoch!*"

"*Kamarad! Kamarad!*"

Shortreed heard the unmistakable sound of a grenade being activated. It was too late to run and he squeezed off a short burst from his tommygun then plastered himself prone against a piece of shattered building. There was a dirty red flash overlapped by a deafening explosion. In the midst of this he heard his own voice scream once and felt a searing pain in his left leg. Then came oblivion.

End of Chapter 6

Chapter 7

The grenade had been a concussion grenade. Shortreed lay in the darkness, stunned, deaf and so confused that he had no idea that a fierce firefight raged around him. Sergeant Kramer had brought the patrol forward in an effort to extricate Shortreed if he was still alive. The Germans had another machine gun firing down the road and what sounded like a squad of riflemen who were concentrating their fire on the area near where Shortreed lay dazed in the rubble.

Kramer's patrol was scattered out and firing from cover in the area near Shortreed. There were two grenade launchers in the patrol and they were lobbing fragmentation grenades into the area where the enemy fire was originating. As a matter of pure luck, one of the grenades landed right on the machine gun nest knocking out the gun and its crew. After that, the Germans began withdrawing. They left behind them a wounded German who began calling for help but fell silent when a fragmentation grenade landed close by and healed his pain.

Shortreed was still deaf and still dazed. Were it not for the pain in his leg, he would have thought himself dead. Then friendly hands were checking him over for wounds.

"Are you hit, Shortreed?" one of the men asked, but Shortreed could not hear and did not answer.

"That concussion grenade must have blowed his ears out."

Two of the men pulled Shortreed into a sitting position and began feeling around on his torso for wounds. This gave Shortreed a point of reference and apprised him of his situation. He grabbed one of the hands in the darkness and pushed it to where his leg was throbbing with pain.

"There. I'm hit there." Shortreed realized that his hearing was gone, but that he could move his leg without increasing the pain. He concluded that all of his leg was there and that it was in working order. Aside from his ears everything was still functioning. Thank God!

Then someone was cutting his first aid kit open and moments later he felt the sting of the morphine syrette. Then they stood him up to see if he could walk.

"I can't hear."

Sergeant Kramer came over to where they were working with Shortreed.

"How is he?"

"He's got a flesh wound in the calf of his leg and he's deaf."

"Is he bleeding bad?"

"He's bleeding a little but we got wound powder and a bandage on him and gave him a shot. He can walk."

"It's time to head back. Peringian, you stay with Shortreed," Kramer ordered. "If we have to hit the dirt, make sure he knows it."

"Is everyone else okay, Sergeant?"

"We lost Evans."

"Dead?"

"Yeah."

"The poor bastard."

"Let's move out," Kramer said.

The patrol gathered on the road and after making sure that everyone was accounted for, Sergeant Kramer started the patrol back to base with Private Townsend as first scout. Peringian walked at Shortreed's side and carried his tommy gun and pack for him as they walked.

Shortreed's confusion started to dissipate and he began taking stock of his injuries. He couldn't hear, but that should clear up in a day or two. At least that's the way it was when Osborne had a concussion grenade go off near him in Normandy. His leg worked and no longer hurt. It was likely that the functionality and lack of pain was due to the morphine. He'd have to wait and see, but at least his head was starting to clear a little and he didn't seem to be limping. He concluded that anyone who can't hear in combat is up shit creek. Fuck!

With his ears gone and his wounded leg leaking blood, Shortreed found the five kilometers back to the roadblock to be the longest 5K he had ever done. He was beginning to stumble frequently and his mind reeled under the effects of concussion and worry about the extent of his wound. One part of his mind tried to rally the jangled portion of his consciousness, but the only solid assurance he could find was Peringian's presence at his side. At least he was still with his buddies and they were looking out for him.

After identifying themselves, the patrol passed through the roadblock and continued on to where Headquarters Headquarters Company was bivouacked for the night. The aid station was in the basement of a house. Peringian took Shortreed directly there and stayed with him while the medical team on duty prepared another wounded G.I. for evacuation.

The morphine was beginning to wear off and Shortreed was starting to hurt. He was also aware that his left boot was wet with blood from his wound. The medic was working in the light from two Coleman lanterns, and Shortreed decided to have a look at his leg. With Peringian's help he pulled the blood-soaked bandage to one side and was shocked to find a piece of curled metal from the grenade deeply embedded in the calf of his leg. It had cut a gash in the muscle as it went in, but a tentative tug showed it to be lodged firmly in the tissue at the bottom of the wound. "Shit!" Behind that it was starting to hurt a lot.

Just as the medic finished stabilizing the wounded man on the table, another stretcher case came in. It was a sergeant who had had his foot blown off and his leg from the knee down hamburgered when he stepped on an anti-personnel mine. The sergeant went directly to the table, where the medics hooked him up to plasma and began stabilizing him for the trip to a field hospital.

This left Shortreed still waiting, but in spite of his own pain, he felt sorry for the sergeant. The poor guy was going to lose his leg from the knee down. What a bunch of shit this war was!

After what seemed an interminable wait, the medics finished with the sergeant and it was Shortreed's turn. Peringian explained that Shortreed's hearing was gone and that the only wound they had been able to find was in the back of his leg.

"How long since he had morphine?" the medical officer asked Peringian.

"Six and a half or seven hours, sir."

The medical officer took an otoscope and examined Shortreed's ears while an assistant gave him another shot of morphine.

"Well, his ear drums are not ruptured," the officer, said. "How did it happen?"

"It was a concussion grenade that got him, sir."

"He won't be able to hear for a few days, but after that his hearing should come back okay."

"What about his leg, sir?"

"We'll check that as soon as the morphine takes effect."

The surgeon stepped back and lit a cigarette. "This is only the third casualty today. Where did this happen?"

"We were on patrol near Dorsten, sir."

"Were there a lot of Germans there?"

"I can't say, sir," Peringian told him. "It was just two patrols in a firefight."

The surgeon went on smoking while his assistant removed the bandage from Shortreed's leg and sterilized the area around the wound. This done, the surgeon flipped the cigarette to the floor and stepped on it. Then he went to work on the wound. He removed the curl of metal with a pair of forceps, cleaned the wound and put in a few stitches and applied a new bandage,

"That does it," he said. He'll have to be on limited duty until he can hear again. The leg won't bother him unless it gets infected."

"Here's sulfa pills." He held out an envelope to Peringian. "The instructions are on the envelope and he <u>must</u>

drink plenty of water. Tell him to come back if the leg starts hurting."

"Thank you, sir."

They helped Shortreed down from the table. Peringian and Shortreed started for the door but stopped when the assistant called out.

"Wait a minute, soldier."

Peringian made a gesture to Shortreed and they turned to face the medic, who came over to them and handed Shortreed the piece of metal taken from his leg.

"You can show that to your grandkids."

Everyone but Shortreed chuckled at this, He solemnly stuck the piece of metal in his pocket and he and Peringian left the aid station. They went to where Demolitions was dug in and reported to Lieutenant Best. The Lieutenant had heard that Shortreed had been hit, but had no idea whether it was serious or not. He arranged for Watkins to stay with Shortreed and see that he hit the ditch when shells came in or when there was shooting, and dismissed Peringian, who gave Shortreed back his pack and tommy gun and left for where S2 was dug in.

Shortreed sat in the dark and waited while Watkins dug him a foxhole. Shortreed was well liked in the platoon and several well-wishers came by, but could only pat him reassuringly on the shoulder. Someone, he never knew who, shoved a bottle of schnapps into his hand then left. It felt good to know that his buddies were there and that someone gave a damn whether he lived or died.

When the hole was finished, he and Watkins finished off the bottle of schnapps, which was only about half-full. Thus reinforced, they crawled into their foxholes and called it a day. As the schnapps mingled with the morphine given to him at the aid station, Shortreed's anxieties and conflicting emotions dissolved in a rosy glow and he fell asleep.

The night was quiet in the Headquarters area. Toward three o'clock, two patrols got into a brief firefight somewhere faraway to the east. Only the sentries heard, and Demo slept peacefully, except for someone who cried out from the depths of a nightmare. Just before sunrise Shortreed could hear a phone ringing somewhere and struggled mightily against the bonds of sleep. It seemed to him that he must answer that phone. It was close by, but in the transition zone between sleeping and waking, his body at first would not respond. After a few moments of frustration, his mind prevailed and he awoke only to find that the ringing sound was in his head. It was not at all like a phone ringing, but his mind had sought to deny this by identifying the sound as that of a phone.

Shortreed sat up abruptly and the tinnitus subsided to the point where it no longer dominated his awareness. Warily he looked about and oriented himself. In the hole next to him, Watkins was snoring peacefully Right by his foxhole, his tommy gun was propped up against his musette bag. Quickly he checked and he still wore his tommy gunner's vest of clips. Like any combat soldier, his first thoughts were of the basics, a gun and ammunition. Thus reassured, he checked to see if the musette bag was really his. They all looked the same and you never knew. Pushing the piece of a parachute he had placed on top of the money to one side, he was reassured by the feel of many packets of thousand-franc notes.

He lit a cigarette and sat on the side of his foxhole. It could have been a lot worse, he thought, as he remembered the poor guy in the aid station who had his leg blown off. What the hell, Shortreed told himself, he might get all the way through the war with no more harm than the minor wound in his leg and the buzzing in his head. The wound would heal quickly and if his ears were like Osborne's, they would be okay in a day or two. There was no way that the war in Europe could last much longer. Of course there was still Japan, and the rumors were that nobody was being discharged until the Japs were whipped.

The dawn was at hand and the early risers were beginning to stir. Shortreed was surprised to see Sellers going from hole to hole and peering in, apparently searching for him. He stood up and attracted Sellers' attention by waving his arms. Sellers hurried over to him.

"I heard you got hit."

"I can't hear you," Shortreed told him. "I got my ears blown out by a concussion grenade."

"I heard you got hit in the leg."

"I can't hear you," Shortreed repeated.

Sellers looked blank, then caught on. Shortreed could talk all right, but he couldn't hear. He felt about do for a pencil, but couldn't find pencil or paper.

"I'll be right back."

Sellers turned and left in the direction of the message center. Shortreed shrugged and sat back down on the edge of his foxhole. He opened the last of his K-rations and started munching his breakfast. He was getting tired of potted meat and energy bars. The crackers and the four cigarettes were okay, but everything else was dogmeat. As he ate, he could see Sellers hurrying toward him again and wondered what was on that crazy bastard's mind. It was something mean-spirited and trivial, no doubt.

Sellers arrived and wrote with self-importance on the message center pad he had brought back with him. When he finished, he held out the pad to Shortreed. It read: "Are you going to stay with the regiment?"

"Why?" Shortreed asked.

"If you go to a field hospital, they'll find your money," Sellers said.

"I told you I can't hear!" Shortreed said in exasperation.

Quickly Sellers wrote on the pad and held it out to Shortreed who read it.

"So what are you proposing?" he asked.

Sellers started to say something, but one look at Shortreed's face and he scribbled his answer on the pad and once more gave it to Shortreed. It read: "If they find your money, they'll start sniffing around to see who else has money."

"I'm not going to a field hospital," Shortreed told him.

Quickly Sellers wrote again on the pad. "Suppose your leg gets infected or your ears never come back?"

"Let me guess," Shortreed said sarcastically. "If I go to a field hospital, you want me to leave my money with you?"

Sellers wrote on the pad eagerly: "You can trust me."

"Nice try, Sellers, but I'm not going to a field hospital. " Shortreed took the pad and pencil from Sellers and tore the written page from the pad. He put pad and pencil in the pocket of his gunner's vest, then struck a match to the torn off page.

"I'll keep the pad and pencil. They'll be my ears for a while."

Sellers turned to leave, but as an afterthought, turned back to tell Shortreed. "You ought to think about what I said."

Shortreed pointed to his ears and grimaced.

Unhappily Sellers turned and stalked off. Shortreed watched him for a moment, then made a jerk-off gesture and returned to his K-rations, Finishing, he lit a cigarette and pondered his situation. Not being able to hear was going to change things for a while. How?

That was the question troubling his mind when Watkins roused up from his hole and lit a cigarette. He offered the pack to Shortreed who held up his own lit cigarette. Watkins yawned lavishly, then grinned at Shortreed.

"I've got a pad and pencil if you need to tell me anything," Shortreed said.

Watkins held out his hand for the writing gear, scribbled and handed it back. It read: "You okay?"

"I still can't hear," Shortreed told him. "But everything else is okay."

Watkins gave him thumbs up and devoted himself to opening a K ration. As the wrapper came away, the look on his face changed to chagrin.

"Motherfucker! Potted meat again!" he complained. He was hungry so he ate it anyway, but he would have preferred something else. Sometimes the K's had bacon and eggs which were identifiable only by the label. Actually the K's weren't that bad, but they were monotonous.

Finally even the late risers of Demolition were up and ready to move. First Sergeant Widdison got the head count from the platoon leaders and reported to Captain Farlow. They had lost no one from Headquarters Headquarters Company the previous day, but Shortreed was listed as being on limited duty.

"What's this about Shortreed?" Farlow demanded.

"A concussion grenade went off near him, sir," Widdison reported

"And?" Farlow asked testily.

"It blew his ears out and he got a piece of shrapnel in his leg, sir."

"Have him report to me immediately!" Farlow snapped.

"Yes sir."

Widdison turned and went to tell Watkins that Shortreed was to report at once to Captain Farlow. Watkins wrote on the pad and showed it to Shortreed. They followed Widdison back to the command post and went in and over to the table where the captain sat waiting.

Shortreed saluted. "Private Shortreed reporting as ordered, sir."

Farlow ignored this and said, "I didn't send for you, Watkins."

"Sir, Lieutenant Best assigned me to go with Shortreed wherever he went to let him know when to hit the dirt."

"Wait outside for him." Farlow ordered.

"Yes sir." Watkins took the pad and pencil from his pocket and set them on the table before the captain. "Here you are, sir."

"What's that for?" Farlow asked, eying them suspiciously.

"So you can write to him, sir. It takes the place of his ears. He can't hear."

"Stay here, Watkins."

'Yes sir."

"I'll talk, You write." Captain Farlow ordered.

"Yes sir."

Watkins retrieved the writing gear from the table and took up a stance at Shortreed's side, pencil poised above the pad, ready and waiting. There was something faintly ludicrous and derisive about it, but Farlow's attention was focused on Shortreed.

"Listen, Shortreed, if you think you're going to goldbrick your way out of being first scout, you're-"

"Not so fast, sir, I'm getting behind," Watkins interrupted.

Farlow fumed while Watkins wrote with exaggerated haste.

"Where are you?"

Watkins read with feigned difficulty, "Listen, Shortreed, if you think you're going to goldbrick your way out of being first scout—" He paused and looked to Captain Farlow expectantly

"You're crazy!" Farlow finished the sentence. As Watkins wrote this down, he continued, "If I catch you malingering, I'll have you shot!"

Watkins paused in his writing and looked puzzled for a moment. "Sir, how do you spell malingering?"

"What the hell difference does it make if you can read it!" Farlow exploded...

"Sir?" Watkins seemed confused.

"Watkins, get out of here now!" the captain shouted.

"Yes sir." Watkins saluted exaggeratedly and left, taking the pad and pencil with him. Outside he was grabbed by First Sergeant Widdison.

"What the hell's going on in there?"

"The captain's flipped his lid," Watkins told him angrily.

"Sounds like combat fatigue to me," Widdison said.

"How the fuck would he get combat fatigue?" Watkins demanded to know. "He hasn't been out of his foxhole since the war started!"

From within the command post Captain Farlow could be heard ranting and raving. Concurrently Shortreed's insistent voice could be heard protesting, "I can't hear you, sir! I can't hear!"

Finally there came a silence, after which Shortreed came outside. Captain Farlow strode after him and shoved a piece of paper into Watkins' hand.

"Make sure that Shortreed reads this."

"Yes sir."

"No one can say I didn't warn him!" the captain declared vehemently and went back into the command post, slamming the door behind him.

Watkins read the note and looking surprised, handed it Shortreed.

"What does it say?" Widdison asked.

"Farlow claims that if he catches Shortreed malingering he will shoot him and he won't even have to give him a court martial!"

Widdison shook his head.

"Is that true?" Watkins asked. "Can he shoot Shortreed without a court martial?"

"We're in combat," Widdison said. "I'm afraid so."

Watkins scowled. "I guess the bastard doesn't know we can do as much for him."

"Don't talk that way, Watkins," Widdison said. "And that's an order."

"Why?"

"Because you're just stirring shit!"

Watkins shrugged noncommittally.

"I'm getting ready to turn the company out," Widdison told them. "You two ought to be getting into your gear."

As they turned to leave, Widdison patted Watkins on the arm. "I know it's a bunch of shit, Watkins. But be patient. The war's almost over."

Watkins grinned. "You're okay, Sarge," he said, and left with Shortreed to get their gear.

The 705th was like a dragon uncoiling from a copse of woods. Each of the three battalions formed up in the road before their positions and at exactly six o'clock they moved out along separate lines in the general direction of Essen. Headquarters Headquarters Company marched with the Third Battalion, which was the reserve battalion. Headquarters Headquarters had two demolition men with each battalion as well as a radioman with each company commander. Headquarters Headquarters marched out in two files, one on each side of the road. Both were strung out in combat spacing and stayed close to the ditch on their side of the road.

At noon they stopped long enough for everyone to eat a K Ration, smoke a cigarette and take a piss. After that they were back on the road. The only news was that Captain Farlow had commandeered the jeep that Demo had taken from Beale.

Just at dusk they came to a sunken part of the road. Here the road went through a cut where the banks on both sides of the road were as high as ten feet in places. At some time during the last ten days or so, a German horse-drawn supply column had been caught in the cut by elements of the Allied air forces. The column had been bombed and strafed into oblivion and for the entire length of the sunken road there was a nightmarish tangle of death and destruction.

Giant dray horses lay dismembered, disemboweled and scattered throughout the wreckage of the supply wagons. Lying amidst all of this carnage were sodden loaves of bread and moldy wheels of cheese. Equally disintegrated and mangled were the bodies of the German wagoneers. 20mm rounds and anti-personnel bombs produce horrific destruction to the yielding flesh of men and animals. After rotting in the sun for more than a week, their stench was so overwhelming that the human mind lacked resources to describe it.

The advance party had passed this way an hour earlier and had seen no reason to report this to the main body. But when the troopers of Headquarters Headquarters Company came upon this grisly sight just at dusk, the company morale plummeted. They had seen plenty of mutilated soldiers before, but the dismembered dray horses were another thing. Presumably the German soldiers were willing accomplices in Hitler's scheme of world dominance and tough shit for them. The horses however were innocent victims..

Private Eccles, who was driving for the captain, had been steering a path through the dead horses and men when the jeep engine coughed a few times then quit. It was out of gas. Sourly

Captain Farlow dismounted and shouldered his musette bag. Eccles helped Forgetti, the captain's radio operator into the harness of his radio, and the three of them joined the moving column. By this time the dead horses were indistinct mounds in the gathering dusk. Only the smell remained to remind them of what lay around them.

It was dark when they reached where they were to spend the night. Lieutenant Best, who had been in charge of the advance party, had chosen a little settlement that was only a few kilometers from the outskirts of Essen. The advance party had selected billets that dispersed the company in a loose perimeter, thus giving them the ability to quickly form a firebase of formidable proportions.

Meanwhile elements of S2 were aggressively patrolling the surrounding area. The Third Battalion, still in reserve, was dug in on a hill a thousand yards to the east; Headquarters Headquarters had not fired a shot all day, and it was decided that it was not necessary to dig in for the night. But ominously, in the distance, the dark sky flashed intermittently and the rumble of artillery could be heard from far away. There was still a war out there somewhere.

Lieutenant Best reported to Captain Farlow, but while he was briefing him, it became clear that the captain was only half-listening.

"Are you all right, sir?" Best asked.

"I don't have a jeep anymore," Farlow told him testily

"Sir, I wasn't aware that you had one."

"I commandeered it from Demolitions."

"Oh – that jeep. What happened to it?"

"It ran out of gas. Have you any idea where to get some?"

Best considered for a moment then said, "The Second Battalion moved down the same road we're on as far as the canal."

"Well?" Farlow prompted eagerly,

"Their jeep hit a mine about a mile back up the road."

"Did it burn?"

"No sir. But it killed the corporal riding shotgun."

"But it didn't burn. Good." The captain was pleased. "And it still had some gas in it."

"Probably," Best concurred.

"Send a patrol," Farlow ordered. "If there's any gas, get it!"

"Yes sir."

"And report to me immediately when they come back."

"Yes sir."

The lieutenant left and went to where Demolition was billeted. He sent Peters and Wilson to check the ruined jeep for gasoline, picking these two men because they had been with the Second Battalion when the jeep had hit the mine. They'd have no trouble finding it.

The moon was just starting to rise as the two set out and being combat wise, they hugged the shadows where possible. When there was no shadow, they moved smoothly, without abrupt movements that invited attention. Although there had been no enemy reported along the road, the Germans were skilled at night patrols. It didn't pay to take chances. In about twenty minutes they arrived in the area of the ruined jeep, but lingered in the shadows when their noses were assailed by a sour smell like that of stale onions. Krauts! It was common knowledge among combat veterans of both sides that the other side smelled.

Peters was a replacement after The Bulge and a little green. Wilson had come to the regiment as a replacement after Normandy and was combat wise. The Germans, he knew, liked to load their night patrols with machine pistols. If fired upon, they retaliated by spraying the immediate area with automatic fire and tossing hand grenades at random. That complicated the situation for the two paratroopers. It would be easy to surprise the Germans and get a few of them, but it would also be suicidal unless they could gain a real advantage.

The two troopers silently searched the night for signs of the German patrol. But in spite of the fact that their scent was strong, they could find no movement in moonlight or shadows.

Then from behind them came the sounds of movement! The two men shrank back even further into the shadows. They automatically separated and flopped down in the ditch. Wilson laid his two grenades before him and partially removed the safety tape. If they were going to die, they wanted to take as many Krauts with them as they could.

But something was funny here. The sounds that were approaching them were uncharacteristically loud for a German patrol. Tensely they waited, with weapons poised. Then, unexpectedly, a cow with a calf at her side ambled into view, walking down the middle of the road. What a relief!

But before they could really relax there was a flurry of gunfire and the sound of grenades coming from several hundred yards further down the road. For almost five minutes they could hear a small but furious firefight. Then the sounds of gunfire and grenades tapered off into silence. The Krauts had blundered into the Second Battalion reserve company!

"Come on, Peters!" Wilson whispered loudly and the two of them sprinted to the demolished jeep. The dead corporal lay sprawled on his back beside the jeep with his face glowing white in the moonlight, They ignored him and grabbed the two jerry cans they found on the jeep and retreated with them to the shadows. All this movement spooked the cow and her calf and they left the road and trotted noisily away cross-country.

The two troopers took off down their back trail, headed for Headquarters Headquarters. They were relieved that the Kraut problem had fallen to the Second Battalion and pleased that they had salvaged two ca ns of gasoline. It was only after they had lugged the two jerry cans the long mile back to Headquarters Company that they discovered that one of the cans held water. The other, at least, was full of gasoline. They delivered it to Lieutenant Best, who took it at once to the company commander.

Captain Farlow was delighted. "Good work, lieutenant."

"It was Wilson and Peters who retrieved the gas, sir." Best reported.

Farlow ignored this. "Have a couple of men take the gas and go get my jeep."

'Yes sir."

Best picked up the can of gas again and started for the door.

"One moment, lieutenant!" Farlow growled.

Best turned back to face the captain. "What is it, sir?"

"Send Shortreed and Watkins," Farlow ordered.

'Shortreed can't hear, sir"

"What's to hear? There are no Germans back there."

"But, sir, he's —" Best tried to protest.

"The captain overrode him. "That's an order, lieutenant."

Best turned angrily and left the room without the usual Yes, sir. Leaving Farlow glaring after him, he went to where Demo was billeted and gave the jerry can of gasoline to Watkins, informing him of the captain's orders.

Immediately Wilson and Peters both volunteered to take Shortreed's place.

"All you got to do, sir, is keep Shortreed out of sight," Wilson urged, "and we'll take care of it."

But when Watkins wrote this on Shortreed's pad, Shortreed vetoed the plan.

'I'll go. Otherwise we'll get Lieutenant Best in a bunch of shit."

Sellers, who had been listening to the conversation, grabbed the pad and wrote. "Use your head, man and stay here . Otherwise you could lose everything." He underlined the word "everything" heavily.

"Fuck it! I'm going," Shortreed said. "So let's cut the bullshit and get on the road!"

After that there was really nothing more to be said. Watkins hefted the jerry an while Shortreed put a match to the incriminating page and struck out with Watkins for Captain Farlow's jeep.

As they left their billet the moon was shining brightly and their eyes adjusted quickly. The two men walked fast and took turns lugging the can of gasoline. As they walked they could see flashes in the distant sky and Watkins could hear the sounds of artillery far away. Somewhere someone was catching hell. Thank God that things were quiet where they were. After half an hour of walking, their noses told them they were approaching the sunken road.

As they moved along in the moonlight they found it a simple matter to avoid the larger mounds of the fragmented dray horses and German wagoneers, but the smaller stuff was different. Once Shortreed stepped on something slick and almost fell down. The combination of what they smelled and what they could see in the moonlight filled both of them with an overpowering sense of dread. They had seen a lot of stiffs before, but they had always been freshly made.

As they approached the jeep they were startled to see large low figures scurrying away from them. Hogs! Stray hogs!

"My God," Shortreed thought. "That's what it all comes down to. You fight and fight until you're killed and then the hogs eat you."

Quickly they poured the gasoline into the jeep and after they fiddled with it for a few minutes, the engine sprang to life. The jeep had lights but turning them on in a combat zone would have been foolhardy. So Watkins began driving by the light of the moon. They had a couple of hundred yards to go before they would be out of the shot-up supply train. The going was slow, and as Watkins threaded his way past the obstacles, Shortreed was thinking of the incongruity of all this.

Some guy in a fighter plane flying at four or five hundred miles per hour had hammered on the slow-moving wagon train and produced all this annihilation. Then he flew back to base, had a shower and went to town and had a couple of beers and got laid. He didn't have to hear the screams and the terrified neighing. Nor could the pilot see the scattered body parts and the sight of a three-legged horse, wide-eyed in terror and pain, dragging its entrails as it tried with its dying breath to climb the wall of the killing ground.

There was something wrong with that, Shortreed concluded. The pilot ought to have to come and look at the obscenity he created. Otherwise his detachment from it was dishonest and dirty.

Finally Shortreed realized that he couldn't go on thinking this way. He was in danger of driving himself crazy. The problem was that not being able to hear had isolated him within himself. Deprived of his interaction with others, he was becoming a loner like Beale. His mind, cut off from the ameliorating influence of his comrades, was free to dwell on unwholesome things. Without the usual input from others his mind could go from dwelling on the unrelieved horror of war to obsessing on it.

It was time to quit thinking about weird things and pull himself together. The war was almost over, but if he didn't start practicing mental hygiene he'd never live through it. Once again he set his mind to fashioning a psychological lifeboat, one that would carry him past the perils that stood between him and the end of the war.

First among the dangers that confronted him was Captain Farlow. That bastard hated him and was trying to get him killed. Maybe he ought to try to placate Farlow. He could tell the captain he was sorry about Ilse….Nah, that would just infuriate the bastard. Farlow was not mad about the broken regulation forbidding fraternization. It was because Shortreed had gotten laid. Farlow was a sick twisted bastard who couldn't get laid in a whorehouse with a hundred dollar bill dangling at the end of his prick. His anger at Shortreed had been sexual jealousy, plain and simple.

There was another problem relating to Captain Farlow. He was so generally hated by his men that someone was bound to kill him if they thought they could get by with it. And if that happened, Shortreed would be a prime suspect. Shortreed resolved that he would work on giving everyone the impression that he was contrite and that the punishment meted out by Farlow was just and proper. He knew that he wasn't supposed to get laid, so it was his own fault. The soldiering part of survival he could handle. Captain Farlow was another matter. One way or another Farlow was the major obstacle between Shortreed and the end of the war.

The moon was getting low on the horizon when they got back to the company. After turning Captain Farlow's jeep over to Private Eccles they went to their billet and turned in. It was late and they needed all the sleep they could get. Tomorrow the regiment would take up positions for the assault on the German soldiers that were holed up in Essen.

When morning came, a corporal from supply went to each of Headquarters Headquarters sections with the news that two supply trucks were waiting near the colonel's billet, One held rations and spare equipment. The other held ammo, grenades, and demolition supplies. Each trooper was to draw two days K-rations and bring their equipment up to regulations. They were also to bring their ammo up to the basic load of two bandoleers of rifle ammo and two fragmentation grenades per soldier. Beside all of this, demo was to carry one 2-pound block of C2 plastic explosive per soldier. Demolition was also to draw a loaded demo bag for each of its two squads.

This news changed the mood of Headquarters Headquarters Company. Men looked to their equipment or scribbled V-mail letters to loved ones. A few went to see the chaplain, but the change in most of the troopers was more subtle. They walked different. There was something cocky and aggressive about them that showed even in simple things, like the way they flipped a cigarette butt away. At this level soldiering was a profession and it was a group of professionals who drew their ammo and rations, then fell out on the road. Just as soon as they kicked these Krauts' ass they'd be going home. At least the survivors would be.

As the 705th began their approach march, they moved out in combat spacing. A few kilometers away 88's could be heard impacting on the outskirts of Essen. Shortreed rejoiced that he could hear these sounds. To him they were vague and apparently somewhere far off. But his hearing was starting to come back! Now if he could just avoid Farlow's vindictiveness, he was confident that he could fight his way past anything else that lay between him and the end of the war.

A couple of 88's screamed in and landed at the head of the column. As the shells came in, Headquarters Headquarters hit the ditch, then the cry of "Medic! Medic!" went up. As they rose from the ditch more shells landed in the column, and Lieutenant Best, Sergeant Lisenby, Shortreed and others began exhorting the column, "Don't bog down! Keep moving! Keep moving1 They've got the road zeroed in!"

Those who could, kept moving. The medics would take care of those who couldn't.

<u>End of Chapter 7</u>

Chapter 8

The regiment moved into position by battalions under harassing fire from the German artillery. The troops called it "dodging shrapnel". In spite of the fact that it produced few casualties, it jangled everyone's nerves. Aside from occasional skirmishes, there was no other enemy action. They used up most of a week tightening the noose around the German positions.

So far the going had been easy compared to what had happened right after the jump. This only fueled the storm of end-of-the-war rumors. At the noon break Sellers held forth on the end of the war in the ETO and how, after furloughs, the 705th would then spearhead the attack on the home islands of Japan with high casualties. The more gullible were gap-mouthed in believing every word of this, but Gill spoke for the majority when he spat contemptuously, "The wind blew and the shit flew and you couldn't see Sellers for a day or two!"

There was a chorus of agreement.

"He's right, Sellers."

"You're full of shit, Sellers."

"As soon as we whip the Krauts," Gill told him, "we're going home."

"Bullshit!" Sellers answered. "Nobody's getting out after Essen. You'll see, if it ain't the Japs it'll be the Russkies. Either way we'll be fighting someone."

Right after that, a convoy of transport arrived for the 705th. The trucks, jeeps and trailers would simplify life for the troopers. Instead of carrying enough supplies for two or three days, the men could limit themselves to carrying enough rations and ammo for the business at hand. With the transport came the news or rumor that they would have artillery support for the coming attack which was to begin at dark that evening.

While this was going on, everyone was eating their rations and Watkins was helping Shortreed take the stitches out of his leg. The wound had healed, but Shortreed couldn't reach all of the stitches by himself. He had taken the last of the sulfa pills and, in spite of a slight ringing in his ears, he could hear again and was now off of limited duty.

S2 had taken a prisoner who had given them a lot of intelligence, including the fact that the Krauts had a huge commissary depot inside their perimeter. It had formerly served the SS officers' messes through the Ruhr valley and the northern reaches of the Rhine and was stocked with the finest wines, chocolate from Holland and Belgium, hams, canned delicacies and more. It was the edible portion of the plunder of Europe. So much for starving them out.

They also had ample stores of ammo and artillery shells, and the German commanding officer was a fanatic who expected his men to fight to the last man. The bright side of all this was that most of the German enlisted men wanted to surrender, but were held in line by a bunch of SS bastards who summarily shot those who showed weakness. The defenders consisted of a few small regular units, together with stragglers who had been trapped in Essen by the rapid advance of the American paratroopers.

The present situation was more or less past the stage where regimental patrols were useful. The attack would begin tonight right after dark. Shortreed and Watkins were assigned to H Company, who were to spearhead the Third Battalion's attack.

Still the rumor mill ground on, with a rumor to fit every hope and every fear. Ordinarily the troops didn't get worked up over rumors, but with the end of the war so close, it was easy to get caught up in the game. The rumors were about equally divided between optimism and pessimism.

Shortreed and Watkins reported to Captain Lindenberger at H Company. He sent them on to Staff Sergeant Mathieson who briefed them on their mission.

They were at the edge of the rail yards. The problem was that the Germans had littered the planned attack route with derelict autos, burned out tanks and trashed out railcars. In addition, the few trees in the area had been felled across roads and tracks. All of these obstacles were hiding places for a tangle of trip wires, booby traps, and anti-personnel mines. Their job would be to deactivate this tricky stuff and lay a trail of luminescent tape through the cleared area to guide the riflemen of H Company in the after-dark assault. Sellers and Gill would not be with them. They had been assigned to F Company.

Captain Lindenberger ignored the rumors that were flying and went about the business of getting ready to attack. He was battle wise and too practical to succumb to wishful thinking. The mines and trip wires in his line of attack had to be cleared. He sent a detail of riflemen as protection for the demolition men and went about readying his company for the attack.

The riflemen were led by Corporal Rivera, a tough little Mexican guy from the barrio in Los Angeles. He had been with the regiment since day one and should have been the poster boy for the Combat Infantry Badge. He totally understood the role of the rifleman in combat and had the balls to put that understanding to work.

Shortreed and Watkins had both worked with H Company many times before and had a great deal of respect for H Company riflemen. They knew Rivera both by reputation and at first hand by having been through a lot of shit with him. If the Germans thought they could run them off, Rivera and his bunch would make them think again.

It was about an hour before dark when they began clearing a pathway through the minefield. Shortreed removed his bag of money and put it against the shell of a building, but kept his tommy gun close at hand.

He and Watkins worked well as a team. Watkins went first, taking care of trip wires and probing for mines. When he found a buried mine he marked the spot and Shortreed would then remove it. The only tricky part was unscrewing the detonator. They worked swiftly and carefully. They were about half finished when artillery fire began landing all around the mined area. When the 88's started landing, Shortreed was in a double bind. The artillery fire was so accurate that the shrapnel was whining by, dangerously close. When it began, he was in the middle of removing a doubled mine.

The mine on top was pretty much a standard anti-personnel mine. When stepped on, there was a five second fuse time at the end of which a small charge exploded. This hurled a canister filled with many small projectiles some ten feet into the air, where a second more powerful charge exploded. This blew the projectiles all over the area producing many casualties. During this sequence, the second bottom mine would explode. The troopers called them "Bouncing Betsies".

Aside from the noise, the bottom mine contributed little. It was placed there as a trap for unwary demolitions men clearing the area. The weight of the top mine held down a spring-loaded striker on the bottom mine. If the top one was lifted off, the striker would be released and flip over to detonate the bottom mine, killing the demo man.

When the shelling started, Shortreed had already removed the detonator from the top mine and had worked his hand underneath to hold the striker down on the second mine. As the shrapnel started ricocheting around him, he panicked momentarily. But with great will power he pulled himself back together. He realized that if he was going to get out of this, he had to use his head.

Back when they started clearing the minefield, he had asked himself, where will I go if they start shelling this place? He had already picked a place. In a quick flash of insight he shoved the already deactivated mine back on top of the striker. Then, between shells, he grabbed up his tommy gun and sprinted to the only building still standing in the area.

It was two-storied and built of stone. Except for the fact that all of the windows had been blown out, it was intact. A salvo of 88's screamed in just as he dashed inside the stone building. When Shortreed burst into the front room, he came very close to being shot by the riflemen of Rivera's detail. Fortunately recognition overcame reflex, and the riflemen lowered their weapons, only to succumb once more to reflex when Watkins dashed in a moment later. The riflemen grinned.

"What the fuck are you guys doing here?" Shortreed demanded.

"Someone is calling in these 88's and this is the only place where they can see where you guys were working," Rivera told him. "We're going to get the bastards."

Together the troopers made a sweep of the first floor and found it empty. But when they began on the second floor, they ran into a hornet's nest. There were two machine pistols and a rifleman firing from a barricade of sandbags near the window.

Ritchie and Ortega went down in the first exchange of gunfire. Ritchie was clearly dead from a bullet between the eyes and Ortega had taken a bullet through the shoulder. The troopers fell back to the bottom floor.

"They're sandbagged by the windows," Ortega muttered between clinched teeth as he was helped back to the first floor. While his comrades worked over his wound and gave him morphine, Shortreed and Rivera conferred.

"We can't frag them," Rivera said. "They're sandbagged."

"I've got a white phosphorus grenade," Shortreed told him.

"That'll do it," Rivera said.

After leaving a man with Ortega, they once again moved to attack the enemy position on the second floor. Rivera and his riflemen waited near the top of the stairs. Shortreed went a little further up, where he pulled the pin on the white phosphorus grenade. He used up two seconds of fuse time, then hurled it into the room where the Germans were barricaded. Before they could throw it back the grenade exploded, releasing a dense cloud of white smoke and particles of white phosphorus that rained down on the men behind the sandbags.

The Germans began screaming in pain and yelling, "*Kamrad! Kamrad!*" as they came running from their sandbagged position, slapping desperately at the particles of white phosphorus that stuck to their flesh and clothing. As long as the particles were exposed to air, they would continue to burn. One diehard came out with his machine pistol held behind him, but when he raised it up to fire Rivera killed him with a single shot from his M1.

They left the German forward observer and the two others under guard and went into the now-burning room. Behind the sandbags they found the forward observer's radio. Rivera picked it up and pressed the talk switch.

"*Achtung! Achtung*!"

The voice that answered said something in German.

"Fuck you, you Kraut bastard!" Rivera yelled back. He threw the radio to the floor and smashed it with the butt of his rifle.

Outside, another cluster of 88's crashed near the building, and they all flinched. Seconds later, an answering salvo passed over, going in the opposite direction. The 705th now had artillery support! The attack was getting under way!

It was almost dark and the two demo men returned to the minefield where they tied a rope to the doubled mine and after taking shelter, exploded it by pulling the top mine off. With the double mine neutralized, they began removing the remaining mines and trip wires.

While they were busy with this, an artillery duel was building. Salvos of German shells screamed over as the Germans switched their artillery targets from the rail yards to the American batteries. American guns seemed to ring the German positions. In a very short time this artillery battle grew to gigantic proportions in the gathering dusk.

Corporal Rivera came to where Shortreed and Watkins were just finishing the laying of the luminescent tape that marked the trail they had cleared through the minefield. Rivera carried a walkie-talkie.

"You guys finished?"

"It's going to take another few minutes," Shortreed told him.

They all hit the dirt as a salvo of American artillery screamed over and a short round landed too close for comfort. The artillery was increasing in intensity and the now dark sky was alive with flashes from the guns of both sides.

"The second battalion is already on the attack and the rest of H Company will be here any minute."

"We'll be ready." Shortreed said.

"You guys stay here and direct traffic."

"What about you?"

"We're the point," Rivera told him. "When the captain gets here, be sure to tell him that we left Ortega in the building. He'll need a stretcher."

"What about the Krauts?"

"I left a man guarding them."

"Okay, we'll tell the captain."

Rivera stuck his fingers in his mouth and gave a low whistle, and his detail of riflemen came from the building and joined him.

"Stay between the two tapes and you'll be okay," Watkins told them.

Rivera and his men started moving away.

"Keep your head out," Shortreed called after them.

Someone called back "You too!" and they disappeared into the night.

Far away to the east there came the sounds of a lot of small arms fire. The Second Battalion had already made contact! Simultaneously, the Third Battalion's H Company began arriving in battle array, while overhead one thunderous artillery salvo after another screamed over from both sides.

At about this time, somewhere near the *Krupwerke*, a large holding pen of slave laborers, mostly Russians and Poles, were either turned loose or broke out of confinement. Unlike the Hollywood version of such events, these people didn't start singing their national anthems and dancing in the streets. Instead they picked up guns and clubs and lit into the civilian population. Soon portions of the city were burning as these escapees burned and raped and killed their way through.

The American and German troops were too busy with each other to stop this rapine and slaughter, and for the time being it swept unchecked across the city. At the minefield most of H Company was safely past the mined area. While Watkins stood directing the tail end of H Company through the cleared trail, Shortreed reported Corporal Rivera's message to Captain Lindenberger. The captive Germans were marched to the rear to a POW enclosure and Ortega went to the rear on a stretcher.

At the same time the monumental artillery battle clicked up a few more notches on the intensity scale and a continuous cannonade passed overhead in both directions. About three hundred yards down the road the leading elements of H Company made contact with the Germans, and there began a blazing firefight that escalated rapidly until most of H Company was involved.

Sergeant Francini stood at the captain's side staying in constant touch with those at the firefight by means of a walkie-talkie. The building where the white phosphorus had routed the German forward observer was now illuminating the area as it burned brightly. In the distance the sounds of battle were joined by the sounds of 88's firing at point blank range. Either tanks or self-propelled guns had come in on the German side.

After a few minutes of this, Francini spoke. "Sir, the Krauts have two tanks in close support and they've got us stopped. We're taking a lot of casualties."

The captain turned to Beale, his radioman. "Get Battalion for me."

Beale did not respond. Instead he stared straight ahead at nothing.

"Hey Beale! Get Battalion for me!"

Beale mumbled unintelligibly.

"Snap shit, Beale! Get Battalion!" Captain Lindenberger repeated the order impatiently.

Beale roused out of his daze and began calling Battalion on the radio while Shortreed and the others listened to the sounds of battle. The tanks were firing as rapidly as possible and the tide of battle was fast shifting to favor the Germans. Mutely Beale handed the hand set to the captain then sank sullenly to a sitting position. Shortreed removed the earphones from Beale's head and slipped them over Lindenberger's ears.

"Hello. Lindenberger here. We're on a very narrow front and the Krauts have two tanks in close support. They're pounding us with pointblank fire. It's turning into a meatgrinder."

Lindenberger listened patiently to the Battalion Commander on the other end. Meanwhile Shortreed was keeping a close eye on Beale who was hunched over, staring glumly at the ground.

Lindenberger spoke into the handset once more. "Okay, we can hold out that long, but every minute counts."

He listened a minute then spoke. "Yes. But hurry, we're getting hit hard. Over." After a short pause he signed off with "Out".

"They're sending a recoilless 57," he told the two men at his side, while he handed the earphones and the handset back to Beale.

"It's going to take forever for them to get here," Shortreed said.

"They're coming in a jeep," Lindenberger told him with relief. "Five minutes at the most."

Silently Shortreed called the captain's attention to Beale who sat with the handset and the earphones in his lap. He was still hunched over and seemed to be working himself up with an animated and inaudible conversation. A cluster of artillery rounds screamed over high up and Beale flinched as if they were landing on top of him.

"Keep an eye on him," Lindenberger said.

Shortreed began removing the backpack radio from Beale who made no response, seeming unaware of what was going on.

"Sir, it's Lieutenant Barnes." Francini held out the walkie-talkie to Lindenberger." He has seventeen men dead or wounded. He wants permission to withdraw to a less exposed position."

Lindenberger took the walkie-talkie. "Barnes? You have to hold out there. Colonel's orders!"

He listened for a moment. "I know, but there's a recoilless 57 on the way." There was another pause while

Lindenberger listened. "Okay, okay. After we get the tanks you can pull back a little and we'll pound them with the mortars."

Overhead the artillery rounds still screamed over in both directions, only now the German response had begun to diminish. Intermittently, through this varied wall of sound they could hear a jeep engine as it drew closer to the little group at the minefield. At last the jeep roared into the area, lighted by the burning building, and skidded to a stop before Captain Lindenberger and his group.

"Where do you want the recoilless gun?"

"Down the road at the fire fight," the captain told them. "The area here is mined and there's only a foot path cleared."

"We can't take the jeep?"

'You have to go on foot from here."

Overhead the artillery duel had degenerated into a one-sided pounding of the German position with only an occasional response from the Germans. But at the firefight it was the German tanks hammering on the Americans with very little return fire.

Quickly the three men with the recoilless gun dismounted from the jeep. After being guided through the minefield, they took off running in the direction of the firefight. One man carried the gun and the other two carried ammunition.

Overlapping the arrival and departure of the gun crew a wire party from regiment arrived on foot. They had laid a wire to battalion where they learned that the battalion wiremen were all either dead or wounded. When they found this out, they had volunteered to bring the wire here to Lindenberger and H Company. The wire party had started from Regiment as a seven-man detail, but now was down to three able-bodied men and two walking wounded. Somewhere behind them they had left one KIA and one litter case. The casualties were all victims of artillery fire.

The sergeant in charge of the wire party handed Captain Lindenberger a field phone with a wire attached. "Sir, Regiment and Battalion are at the other end."

"Good work, sergeant."

"Is there a medic here, sir?" the sergeant asked.

"They're at the fire fight," Lindenberger told him.

"I have two walking wounded with me."

"Can they walk to the battalion aid station?" the captain asked.

"One of them is about to collapse right now."

"Take the jeep," Lindenberger ordered.

"Thank you, sir. I'm leaving two men with you. They have two spools of wire. If you move, they'll extend your wire."

At the fire fight there came the sound of the recoilless 57 firing several times and then there was no more firing from the German tank. During this, the wire sergeant loaded his wounded onto the jeep and took off for the battalion aid station.

While the little group around the company commander listened to the sounds of combat, Watkins came from the minefield and joined them. With the tanks knocked out the Americans were once more dominating the firefight.

Suddenly, Beale sprang to his feet with a cry of despair, a cry that could only come from one grievously wounded in spirit. The group watched dumbfounded as Beale yanked a captured Luger from his belt and pointed it in the general direction of the others.

"Knock it off, Beale!" the captain ordered sharply. "We don't have time for this kind of bullshit!"

Overhead, a German artillery round screamed over with a loose rotor ring that clanged a discordant counterpoint to Beale's rapidly disintegrating emotional state.

"You want bullshit?" Beale shouted. "I'll show you bullshit!"

He shoved the safety off the Luger and raised it to firing position. This was met with the sound of safeties clicking off as Shortreed, Watkins, Francini and the two wiremen covered Beale with their weapons.

For a moment everything stopped and the only sounds came from the distant firefight.

"Put the gun down, Beale!" the captain ordered.

"Fuck all of you bastards!" Beale said.

Shortreed handed his tommy gun to the captain and holding his hand palm up, he started advancing slowly on Beale.

"Watch your step," Lindenberger cautioned.

"Hand it over, Beale."

"You're just tired, Beale," the captain told him. "All you need is a little R and R."

"All I need is a friend!"

"We're your friends."

"Fuck you! I tried to be friends. Nobody wanted me!"

"The captain says he wants you to go on furlough," Shortreed told him. "Wouldn't you like to go to Paris? Get a bottle of French wine and a French woman?"

"I'm not interested," Beale snarled.

"Wouldn't you like to get fucked?"

"I was born fucked!" Tears were beginning to run down Beale's cheeks.

"I'm your friend," Shortreed told him. "Didn't I kick Choquette's ass when he fucked with you?"

There was a rising note of hysteria in Beale's voice and his face was distorted into a mask of inner torment as he continued, "Every night over and over I have the same dream. Me and you go back to where Lieutenant Youngblood lay with his head scattered and you say let's put him back together. I bring you the pieces and you stick his head back together. When it's finished, you say, 'Hey come look.' When I look it's not Youngblood's head, it's mine! It's me that's dead."

There was a guilty silence as Beale struggled to continue. "And --- every night I run to the company and yell, "Beale's dead! He got his head blowed off!"

From the innermost recesses of his tortured being there came a strangled cry of naked anguish. He placed the Luger against his temple.

"And you know what? None of you bastards give a fuck!" You're all too goddamned busy being buddy-buddy with each other!"

Just as it became clear that Beale was going to kill himself, a shot rang out. Beale screamed out in pain and the

Luger flew away into the shadows. At the same time Shortreed lunged forward and grabbed Beale. It was Watkins, the cold and deliberate, who had fired the shot.

Like a puppet with broken strings Beale collapsed in an ungainly heap at Shortreed's feet. There he lay moaning in pain and sobbing in misery. Everyone was riveted in place by the intensity of Beale's anguish.

Shortreed knelt beside Beale and started cutting into his aid kit. While he was preparing the morphine syrette, the two wiremen pulled Beale to a sitting position and checked him over to see if he had other wounds from bullet fragments.

While this was going on, the firefight tapered off to a few scattered rifle shots. Forgetti, at the walkie-talkie, called out to the captain, "Sir, the Krauts are pulling back."

The American artillery fire continued to pass over, headed for the German positions.

"Tell Lieutenant Barnes to keep pressing them until he has all of his men across the canal," Lindenberger ordered.

"Lieutenant Barnes is dead, sir."

"Who are you talking to, sergeant?" the captain asked.

"Sergeant Malloy, sir."

Lindenberger took the walkie-talkie. "Hello, Malloy. What's your situation?"

He listened, then said, "I know about Barnes. What about Lieutenant Neuberger?"

"Neuberger too?" He shook his head, then continued, "You are in command until we get there. Get a squad of men across the canal and have them dig in deep."

Again, he listened for a moment, then signed off, "Over and out."

Calling Shortreed to him, he handed back his tommy gun and spoke quietly, "I want you to personally walk Beale to the aid station."

"Yes sir."

"And make sure they know he's suicidal before you leave."

The field phone rang and one of the wiremen answered it.

"Sir, it's the colonel." He handed the phone to the captain, who paused long enough to tell Shortreed to get moving.

The men finished bandaging Beale's hand, and Shortreed started to the Battalion aid station with him. In spite of the morphine Beale was still agitated and continued raving on about his angers at the army and the injustices of a system that refused to cull the bad apples from the chain of command. His anger, which had focused on Colonel Breit and Captain Farlow, was so impassioned that Shortreed concluded that Beale had totally flipped.

These were common angers among the troops and were more or less accepted as something that came with the territory. Then Shortreed remembered how quickly he had lost his own perspective when he was isolated from his comrades when his ears were not working. This awareness gave him insight into Beale's madness and he marveled at how Beale had lasted as long as he had.

The poor bastard was the regimental pariah and this had deprived him of meaningful interaction with the others. Thus, each instance of petty vindictiveness from Colonel Breit or Captain Farlow had festered alongside his hunger for acceptance. Dignon, his only friend, had been essentially murdered by Captain Farlow when he had sentenced him to company punishment as a permanent first scout for S2.

"Goddam that cowardly glory-robbing son-of-a-bitching Colonel Breit!" Beale screamed loudly, then lapsed into a meaningless babble of thoughts and fragmentary sentences until his voice trailed off to nothing and his eye locked in a fixed stare.

Patiently Shortreed took Beale by the arm and steered him to the Battalion aid tent. The casualties from the attack were beginning to arrive and the place was bustling. The triage officer directed Beale to a waiting area. Shortreed explained to him that Beale was suicidal and had received morphine twenty or thirty minutes earlier. Meanwhile Beale still held conversation with himself, babbling in a rising-falling inflection.

Two enlisted medics led Beale to a cot and, after getting him onto it, quickly strapped him down. An officer came over with a hypodermic needle.

"This will sedate him."

"Let me try to talk to him first, sir." Shortreed spoke with such urgency that the doctor paused.

"Hurry."

Shortreed took Beale's uninjured hand into his own and spoke from the heart.

"Beale---this is Shortreed. Come out of it. I want to say something to you."

He repeated this several times while Beale rattled on. Then slowly Beale's eyes no longer rolled about in his head and his mind pulled back from the brink of the abyss that yawned before him. For a moment Beale's mind returned to the here and now.

"I'm your friend," Shortreed said in a voice that was burdened with emotion.

Beale remained silent, but for a brief moment Shortreed could see past the veil of madness into the very center of Beale's tortured soul and know that Beale had heard him and was glad. Then Beale's overburdened mind slid back into its refuge of madness.

Shortreed stepped back and Beale's story ended as the doctor administered the sedative. There would be no new chapters for Beale. This chapter would play over and over until at last it was all over.

Shortreed stepped out of the triage tent and lit a cigarette. The first thing he noticed was the eerie silence. There was no small arms fire, no artillery. Except for low moans and cries of pain from the triage tent, all was quiet.

End of Chapter 8

Chapter 9

As Shortreed started back to the minefield and the burning building, his mind was on the silenced guns. Had the Germans surrendered? Was the battle for Essen over? Or were both sides only waiting for sunrise?

For a brief moment his mind toyed with the thought that the war was over. Just before the attack started the Russians had announced that they had already begun what was their final push to take Berlin and were attacking along a forty-five mile front.

Then Shortreed's survival instinct took over and pushed these thoughts from his mind. Even if the shooting had stopped, danger still lurked in the thousands of trip wires, mines, booby traps, unexploded aerial bombs and tottering walls that were part of the rubble of what had once been the city of Essen. It would be up to Demolitions to neutralize all these dangerous leftovers from the war. If he was going to come through all this in one piece, he'd have to keep his mind clear and aware of all the dangers that threatened him.

When Shortreed got to the minefield, Watkins was still probing for mines by the diminishing light from the burning building. Where before there had only been a trail, he had already begun on the business of removing the entire minefield.

"Why don't we finish this after the sun comes up?" Shortreed asked.

"The First Battalion is coming through at sunrise," Watkins told him. "The colonel wants the whole thing cleared by then."

Resigned, Shortreed unslung his tommy gun and began carefully removing the flagged mines. As he worked, he was mindful of the doubled mine he had found earlier. They worked silently until the sky in the east began to show signs of the coming sunrise. Shortreed removed the detonator from the last mine. Together he and Watkins stacked the neutralized mines to one side and draped them with bright orange warning tape.

Something had been eating on Shortreed's mind ever since he had rejoined Watkins but, in keeping with his resolve to stay focused while doing dangerous things, he had pushed it from his thoughts. Now with the mines out of the way, his thoughts returned to what was gnawing at him. Consequently it was with only half a mind that he helped Watkins make preparations to dispose of the dangerously sensitive detonators he had removed from the mines.

First they located a likely crater and placed a primed charge of a quarter pound block of TNT in the bottom of the hole. While they were gathering the detonators, the answer to what had been bothering him came to Shortreed: Where was his bag of money? Whoa!

It was while he and Watkins were carefully placing the detonators in with the TNT when Shortreed remembered that he had lost track of his money during the excitement surrounding Beale's collapse. Watkins pulled the fuse lighter.

"Okay, let's go!" Watkins told him.

They ran to cover behind a wall, but Shortreed was still hung up trying to remember where he had left the money. His thoughts were interrupted by the loud explosion when the TNT and the detonators went off. Simultaneously the shock wave brought down the wall behind which they were sheltering. Only their razor-sharp reflexes enabled them to leap out of the way at the last possible second. Like idiots they had taken shelter behind the tottering wall of a bombed-out shell of a building.

"What a couple of fuck-wits we are!" Watkins said with feeling.

Shortreed didn't answer. He moved out of the cloud of brick dust that was rising from the tumbled wall. "Fuck the goddam money!" he told himself silently. If he hadn't been thinking of the money he would have had enough sense to stay away from that wall. It could have cost him his life. Hadn't Sanford died because he couldn't turn loose of his money? Would he be next? Right then and there he made up his mind to leave the bag of money where it lay. He would rather be alive then to have all of that money.

The dust from the collapsed wall still hung in the air when the lead elements of the reserve First Battalion began moving past them in combat array. Someone called out, "Hey Shortreed! How's your hammer hanging?"

Still dazed and rattled by the near miss from the falling wall, Shortreed managed a dispirited, "It's hanging."

Near the end of the column, C Company's radioman Corporal Collins stepped from the line.

"Hey Shortreed! Captain Farlow wants you and Watkins to report to him immediately."

"Where is he?"

"On this side of the first canal."

"There hasn't been any shooting since last night," Watkins said. "Did the Krauts surrender?"

"Nobody knows yet," Collins told him and turned to rejoin the passing column.

The two demo men watched the column of men as they moved through the rubble.

"I guess we ought to get going," Shortreed said.

"Yeah," Watkins agreed. "Don't forget your musette bag. It's right over there."

"Fuck the bag!" Shortreed said. "Let's go!"

Watkins shrugged and together they turned and started walking. But after a few steps, Shortreed stopped and hurried back to get his bag of money. The war was almost over, he reasoned, and if he kept his head out he would live to spend it. He overtook Watkins and together they struck out for Regimental Headquarters.

The guns were still silent and both men were lost in thought. It was well past sunrise, yet no attack had started. Maybe the war really was over and they'd be going home soon. Wouldn't that be great? But what about the Japs? They were still fighting. These thoughts occupied the minds of both men as they walked in silence.

After half an hour they were approaching the regimental area when they came upon a machine gun dug in by the side of the road. The gun was there, but strangely there was no crew present. There were several foxholes nearby and they too were empty.

"What's going on here?" Watkins asked.

Shortreed shrugged and, as they looked about for an explanation, they could hear loud voices coming from a nearby copse of wood. Together they went to investigate, and shortly they arrived at a clearing in the woods. Standing in the middle of the clearing was a corporal, waving a half-full bottle as if it were a conductor's baton. Seated before him were the rest of the gun crew and its complement of riflemen.

The corporal and all of the others were gloriously drunk. Several bottles were being passed around.

"Okay, let's try it again," the corporal said. "One, two three." With that, he began conducting the chorus with his bottle. They responded enthusiastically and off key.

"Fuck 'em all. Fuck 'em all, the long and the short and the tall. We'll never be mastered by some G.I. bastard, So cheer up my lads, fuck 'em all!"

"Hey!" Shortreed yelled.

The singing stopped and all eyes turned to Shortreed and Watkins.

One of the troopers shoved a bottle into Shortreed's hand. "Have a drink!"

As Shortreed started to pour it on the ground, a man snatched the bottle back.

'You guys are really fucking up!" Shortreed told them.

"The Krauts surrendered!" one of the troopers yelled. "The war is over!"

"What?"

"I don't believe it!" Watkins said.

"They surrendered. It's all over! Have a drink!" the troopers variously responded in a show of drunken camaraderie.

"Sorry," Shortreed said. "We have to report to Farlow."

"You can't," one of the drunks told them. "Farlow's dead."

"Dead?" Shortreed and Watkins both reacted to the news.

"He got blowed up."

"How did it happen?" Watkins asked.

"Dunno," said one of the troopers. "All we know is that him and Gill got blowed up."

"Who's company commander now?

"Who cares?"

The corporal again raised his bottle like a baton.

"All right, start over from the first. One, two, three…"

All of the drunken troopers joined in. "Fuck 'em all. Fuck 'em all, As back to the barracks we crawl, There's Sally and Susie, You can't be too choosy, So cheer up my lads, Fuck 'em all!"

Shortreed and Watkins watched this in disbelief. After a moment Watkins spoke.

"You think the war is really over?"

Shortreed shrugged. "How would these guys know?"

"They couldn't find their ass with both hands," Watkins said in agreement.

"We won't know until we get back to Headquarters."

They returned to the road littered with the debris of war and walked on toward Headquarters. Here and there the dead bore mute testimony to the deadly effects of last night's 88's. One dead trooper in particular summed up this scene of desolation.

He had apparently been a wireman. At his side a one-man spool of field communication wire had a huge piece of shrapnel embedded in it. His combat jacket had been pulled open, revealing grievous wounds to his upper body. Nearby, an empty plasma bag hung from a tattered bush, and the tube ran from there to the needle that was still stuck in the dead man's arm. The first flies were beginning to gather.

Shortreed had a momentary twinge, knowing that it could have been he himself, lying there with his life's blood spilled out on the ground. That poor bastard almost made it through the war, only to die in what was probably the last artillery barrage fired at the 705th What a bunch of shit, Shortreed thought to himself. To get that close to the end of the war and get killed.

Both men were preoccupied with their own thoughts and walked on in silence. They were almost to Headquarters Headquarters Company when they met with a wire party from Regiment. During last night's attack the communication wires had simply been laid in the ditches or to the side of the road. Now the wiremen were moving the wire up off the ground onto trees and such to keep it above vehicular traffic.

The wiremen were jubilant. The Germans in Essen had surrendered! Besides that, the Russians and the Yanks were within thirty-three kilometers of a link-up and Berlin was already in range of the Russian artillery! Yippee! The war was over for the 705th and would soon be over for everyone in the ETO!

The wire party moved on and for a moment Watkins and Shortreed were stunned by this news.

"We made it!" Watkins exploded in a yipping, yelling dance. "The fucking war is over!"

As Watkins capered about jubilantly, Shortreed joined in the shouting. But after a moment he fell silent. As they hurried the last half mile to Headquarters, Watkins continued to cut loose. But Shortreed wasn't listening. His mind raced all the way back to Normandy. He recalled the names and faces of his dead and mangled friends who lay scattered along the Regiment's back trail. The hedgerows, the snow banks, and the ditches were littered with the bodies of men who had not made it through to this day.

Spiritually some part of Shortreed lay in the hedgerows, the snow banks, and the ditches alongside those dead faces, those mangled bodies, those brave men. His was a sadness and grief beyond tears and lamentations. It was a spiritual darkness that lay beyond human comprehension and was the first twinge of survivor guilt.

In Shortreed's mind he sought to dismiss this feeling by distilling it to its essence and concluding that it was a reminder that, for all of us, Eternity is always only a step away. He had no way of knowing that the part of him that lay beside his dead comrades was a partial payment on the debt that we all owe to the scheme of things. Nor was he aware that only time and the final payment would make him whole again. With the remarkable resilience of spirit that had enabled him to steer his way through the horror and insanity of combat, Shortreed willed himself to break off this moment of introspection as they entered the Regimental area. Was it not time to celebrate? Was not the war over? It was time to rejoice!

Headquarters Headquarters Company was clearly in an end-of-the-war mood. Men were standing around, laughing and talking. Some had left their rifles with their gear, while others, from long habit, still had their rifles slung over their shoulder. This air of celebration was heightened by the presence of many bottles of wine that had been "liberated" from the SS Commissary before Colonel Breit had posted guards. Men drank openly and no one called them down for it. Those few men with assigned tasks went about their duties lightheartedly.

After a few celebratory and ritual drinks of wine, Shortreed and Watkins found their way to Company Headquarters where they reported to Lieutenant Best, who was now the acting company commander.

"Sir, we had orders to report to Captain Farlow."

"He's dead," Best told them.

"We heard, sir." Shortreed said.

"What about Gill, sir?" Watkins asked

"He died at the aid station."

Neither Shortreed nor Watkins gave a damn about Farlow, but Gill, whether they liked him or not, was a comrade-at-arms. One who had come within hours of surviving the war. This gave them a momentary pause of sympathy for the poor bastard.

"Captain Farlow had you both on a shit detail," Best told them.

Both men acknowledged this with a grimace.

Best continued, "You're both old timers in the regiment. And good soldiers. So, I've got you on regular duty, unless you fuck up."

"Thank you, sir," Watkins said. Both he and Shortreed grinned.

"Do you think the war is really over for the 705th?" Shortreed asked.

"It is for the ETO," Best told them, "but there's no telling about the Japs."

"Those motherfuckers," Watkins muttered.

"However," Best continued, "there's an estimated three hundred escaped slave laborers running loose around the area. They've picked up guns and booze and are raising hell. They have to be rounded up. Besides that, Demolitions has to start blowing down tottering walls and unsafe buildings."

"Sir, I don't really want to do any more demolitions unless I have to," Watkins objected.

Best said, "There's a detail of riflemen going after the escapees. They'll be here any minute."

"Can I do that, sir?"

"There's a tommy gun and a vest in the corner. Leave your M-1 and take the tommy gun."

"Thank you, sir."

"Wait outside for the truck."

'Yes sir."

As Watkins left, Lieutenant Best turned to Shortreed. "Besides the shaky walls, S2 is going to be searching for mass graves."

"Mass graves?" Shortreed was puzzled. "I didn't know that they had any."

"They worked slave laborers on half rations until they couldn't work anymore," Best told him. "Then they shot them."

"What a bunch of coldhearted sons-of-bitches!"

"What do you want to do, Shortreed?"

"Get drunk, get laid, and sleep for two days."

Best laughed. "Yeah, but what do you want to do for the army?"

"Blow the walls, I guess."

"Okay. Take the demo jeep and a full demo bag."

"Yes sir."

"And take Abbot and Sellers with you." Lieutenant Best opened a map and spread it out before him.

"Sir, are you going to be the new company commander?"

"Captain Breckenridge outranks me," Best said.

"Suppose he gets promoted to major?"

The lieutenant shrugged.

"And you get promoted to captain?"

They both grinned at this. Pointing on the map to the area where he was to work, Best instructed Shortreed to use Abbot and Sellers to warn others away when there was fire in the hole.

"If you find unexploded aerial bombs, mark them well and we'll get them later."

"Why is that, sir?"

"If you shoot the big stuff first, all those shaky walls might come down at once."

"Yeah, I got it," Shortreed said. "We might injure someone."

"I'm sure you can deal with it."

"Thank you, sir."

As he started for the door, Best called after Shortreed, "Keep your head out."

Just outside the building, he found Sellers waiting for him.

"What are you doing here, Sellers?"

"Watkins told me you were in there."

"You're supposed to come with me."

"Why?"

"We're going to blow some shaky walls."

"You and me gotta talk," Sellers demanded.

"You got some kind of a crazy idea. I can tell."

"Let's get out of here."

"What do you mean?"

"We can be in Switzerland before anyone even knows we're gone."

"You're as big a loser as Beale!" Shortreed turned and walked to the demo jeep. He looked back at Sellers. "You coming?"

"I guess." Sellers made no effort to join him.

"Get Abbot and meet me back here. He's supposed to go with us."

"Why?"

"Just get him."

Sellers started to leave, but instead turned back to Shortreed.

"Don't you care about the money?"

"The war's over, Sellers. We'll have plenty of time for the money."

"If it's over, why aren't you celebrating?"

"After we shoot those walls, I'll celebrate," Shortreed told him.

"Everyone else is already celebrating." Sellers wouldn't let go of it.

"Go get Abbot!"

Again Sellers started to say something, but Shortreed cut him off. "Now!"

After Sellers left, Shortreed felt a strong urge to join the others in what was now a boisterous celebration of the war's end. His hard-nosed practicality overcame the urge. For him the war would not be over until there were no more high explosives that he had to shoot. That time was not far off, he concluded. If he kept his head out.

Before going to draw the explosives for his assignment, Shortreed followed the communications wire to where they entered a window in the mansion where Colonel Breit had his command post. Peering inside, he found Perine at the switchboard.

"Hey, Perine," Shortreed called quietly.

Perine looked up and held his finger to his lips. It was clear that he was listening in on a call. This continued briefly, then Perine stopped listening and spoke excitedly.

"Boy, have I got some news for you!"

At that moment, the colonel's Chief of Staff Major Bolen came into the room. Perine quickly directed his attention to the switchboard and Shortreed slipped away. He waited outside for a few minutes and could hear the Major chewing Perine out for listening in on Colonel Breit's conversation with Division.

Prudently Shortreed gave up, returned to his jeep and drove to the ammo dump. Perine's exciting news, whatever it was, would have to wait. After drawing the demo-bag and extra primacord, he started back. On the road he was flagged down by some drunken troopers who refused to let him past until he took a swig of wine.

They were guys he knew, and theirs was a primal need to validate their survival by means of ritual drunkenness. They were comrades-at-arms, and even if Shortreed couldn't get drunk with them, he could at least acknowledge that they and he were survivors. All it took was a drink from the bottle that was going around.

The wine had laid bare thoughts that many of them otherwise would have never acknowledged. The war was winding down and with it, their identity as soldiers. Division, Regiment, Battalion, Company, Section, Squad, Paratrooper. These men were poised on the knife-edge that divides army from civilian life.

Soon there would be handshakes and farewells. Farewell to the army, in all of its greatness and its pettiness. Farewell to warfare and all of its hatefulness and horror. And most terrible of all, farewell to friends, living and dead, the likes of which would never again be found though they searched the wide world over.

These were Shortreed's thoughts. Whether the others shared them or not, he would never know, but they stayed with him as he drove back to Headquarters where he picked up Abbot and Sellers.

It took twenty minutes of picking their way along the rubble-strewn main road into Essen before they came to the part of town surrounding the Krupswerken. There the aerial bombing had been particularly severe due to the strategic importance of the area. The landscape, as Abbot said to the others, was like hell with the fires put out.

They set about reconnoitering the area to decide where to start. Shortreed was careful to keep Abbot and Sellers apart by giving them separate areas to check. There was long-standing bad blood between them. Abbot was in an ebullient end-of-war mood. But Sellers, with his mind on his money, was sullen and withdrawn. Shortreed wanted them concentrating on demolishing walls, not each other.

They began with a two-story building that had been bombed and burned. The four walls were more or less intact, but had serious damage that would make them highly unstable. Working quickly, they collapsed them inward with small charges of TNT.

The dust from the collapsed building still hung in the air as they moved on to the next unstable structure. While they were setting the charges, Sellers began sniping verbally at Abbot. After a little of this, Shortreed moved away from the two men and called Sellers to him.

"Quit fucking with Abbot!" he told him.

"I don't have to kiss your ass, Shortreed," Sellers said defiantly.

"You're not paying attention to what you're doing."

"You're just pissed because I'm after you to do something about the money."

"Right now we're blowing walls and if you don't get your head out of your ass, somebody's going to get hurt."

"I don't have to mind you!"

Shortreed doubled up his fist and waved it in Sellers' face. "You want to bet?"

Sellers changed his mind. "I'm just worried about the money," he said apologetically.

"We'll take care of that when the time comes," Shortreed told him, and they returned to setting the charges. They were almost ready to shoot the next round of explosives, when there came a sudden commotion near-at-hand. After a great deal of yelling, there was a brief flurry of small arms fire.

Abandoning their demolition duties, they grabbed their weapons. Almost immediately a squad of paratroopers marched a group of escaped slave laborers onto the main road where the three demo men waited, sharpset for what might come.

As the prisoners were herded past, Shortreed could see that they were dirty, emaciated and drunk. Incongruously, the most cadaverous of the prisoners wore a stolen and ill-fitting cutaway coat and a Hamburg hat. They had been armed and bent upon laying waste to the neighborhood.

"They ought to shoot the bastards!" Sellers muttered.

Abbot, who was soaring on a wave of end-of-the-war euphoria, was more sympathetic. "Those poor guys had to put with an awful lot of shit."

"So did everybody," Sellers said nastily.

"Knock it off!" Shortreed told them. "We've got work to do."

As they returned to their demolitions, Abbot and Sellers continued to cut and snipe at each other about the marauding slave laborers. This was the excuse they gave themselves. The real reason was that they hated each other's guts and the issue of the slave laborers was a convenient vehicle for that hatred.

Finally, losing all patience with Sellers, Abbot yelled, "Give up, Sellers! The fucking war's over! Relax, will you!"

"Don't tell me what to do!" Sellers snarled back.

When the talking got loud, Shortreed stepped between them. "Knock it off. We can't shoot explosives and screw around like this."

"Then you tell Abbot to keep his fucking mouth off of me!"

"Fuck you too, Sellers!"

"Do you guys want to fight?" Shortreed demanded.

"Abbot doesn't have the balls for a fight," Sellers sneered.

"I don't fight sissies," Abbot retorted.

With a bellow of rage Sellers flung himself blindly at Abbot, and the two of them fell to it. For nearly a minute the fight ebbed and flowed with the honors about even. Then Abbot landed a solid blow to Sellers' jaw and Sellers hit the ground. Abbot stepped closer and aimed a kick at him. Grabbing Abbot roughly, Shortreed pulled him back.

"No kicking!"

Angrily Abbot jerked free and advanced on Shortreed with his fists cocked, threatening, "I'm going to pound your head in!"

Shortreed grinned. "Don't let your mouth overload your ass, Abbot."

For a tense moment, they stood facing each other. Abbot had his fists up, but Shortreed, still smiling, stood easy with his hands at his side. Slowly Abbot relaxed and lowered his guard.

"You're okay, Shortreed," he said and stuck out his hand. As they shook hands Abbot explained apologetically, "I was just hot."

"No hard feelings," Shortreed told him and went to where Sellers sat nursing a bloody nose.

"You okay?"

"Yeah."

Shortreed helped him to his feet. Nearby Abbot was splashing water from his canteen onto his rapidly swelling right eye.

"You feel like walking back to regiment?" Shortreed asked Sellers.

"Why?"

"Me and Abbot can finish here."

"Sure, I'll head back now."

Sellers picked up his M1 and retrieved his musette bag of money. As he started to leave, Shortreed drew nearer and spoke quietly. "When I get back, we'll talk about the money."

"Okay!" Sellers was delighted. "Okay!"

But as Sellers went by Abbot, he couldn't resist the opportunity for one more dig. "That was just a lucky punch."

"Fuck off, Sellers."

"Next time I won't take it easy on you," Sellers taunted.

"Are you threatening me?"

"I'm promising." Sellers turned away and struck out for headquarters.

Shortreed went to take a look at Abbot's condition. After a cursory inspection it was clear that Abbot's right eye would soon be swelled shut.

In the distance, a tank with a bulldozer blade on the front rumbled into the neighborhood and began clearing a major roadblock. The aerial bombing had dropped a four-story brick building across the road and closed it to all but foot traffic. Vehicular traffic had been forced to detour and pick their way through almost a mile of rubble-strewn streets to go around it.

Shortreed and Abbot looked on as the tank began clearing the road. They could see two outside men who seemed to be on the alert for unexploded aerial bombs and another man in the turret. After watching the tank-dozer for a few minutes, Shortreed told Abbot to take it easy. His eye was now swollen shut and it would not have been safe for him to set explosive charges. Shortreed was playing the percentages.

Working carefully and by the book, Shortreed was able to drop two more burned- out buildings by noon, when they stopped for a cigarette and a K-ration. Abbot's high spirits over the war's end were not dampened by his black eye and he daydreamed out loud about the order of business in his early days- soon to come!- in a postwar world.

First, he would spend two full weeks in bed with his girl friend. Then afterwards he'd rehabilitate himself with a few days of drinking and general hell raising. Then back he'd go to his sweetie's arms.

"Hell, it don't get no better 'n that!"

He had no idea that this was more or less the entire regiment's fantasy at that moment.

As for Shortreed, his guard was still up. He was cautiously excited and happy that the war was winding down, but also acutely aware of the multitude of lethal possibilities that still threatened his survival.

While Abbot and Shortreed were eating their K-rations, the tank-dozer finished clearing the rubble of the fallen building and rumbled to another obstacle only a hundred yards from where the two demo men sat. As the tank began moving debris from the road, Shortreed went back to work on what he considered to be the last walls of the day. The tank was already almost too close for him to continue with it.

While he was priming the first charge, the tank-dozer hit and exploded a five hundred pound aerial bomb that lay in the rubble. The shock wave slapped against the wall that Shortreed was working on, and it fell away from him into the street. As it went down, it missed Abbot by only a foot. To their right, another burned out building collapsed rumbling in a cloud of dust.

For a moment, both of the troopers were nailed in place in a state of shock. In the rubble of the street, the wrecked tank-dozer lay on its side. Smoke was already rising from the wreck, and as Shortreed and Abbot sprinted toward the tank, it burst into flames. When they reached the tank, they could hear someone crying out for help from inside. The two outside men had been mangled by the force of the explosion and were dead. Quickly Shortreed crawled in through the open hatchway and pulled a battered tanker out to where Abbot could drag him away from the flames.

Going back into the tank, Shortreed found the other tanker lying against the hull with blood coming from his nose and his ears. A quick examination showed him to be dead. By this time the interior of the tank was burning, forcing Shortreed to beat a hasty retreat to the outside.

He joined Abbot, who stood looking down at the man Shortreed had pulled from the burning tank.

"*Kaput*," Abbot said tonelessly.

"You sure?"

"Yeah."

They walked away from the heat of the burning tank to sit on the doorstep of a collapsed building. They both lit cigarettes. Abbot looked glum and Shortreed thought to himself, "The war ain't over until people quit getting killed."

From back toward Regiment, a figure could be seen jogging doggedly toward them. As it approached, they could see that it was Sellers, who looked about to drop from exhaustion. He got to where the two men sat and stopped before them, gasping for breath.

"What is it, Sellers?" Shortreed asked without much interest.

Sellers panted for a moment, then blurted out between gasps for air, "I talked to Perine! All the old guys are going on furlough!"

'When?"

"Tomorrow!"

Shortreed slumped back against the stairs that went up to a building that was no longer there.

"Whoa!" he said numbly. "The *guerre et* fucking *fini*!"

End of Chapter 9

Chapter 10

The Regiment was still caught up in the delirium of the day before. Colonel Breit had wisely placed a serious guard over the SS commissary and its extensive store of wine. Many troopers nursed hangovers and a few were still drunk.

The excitement continued unabated and those troopers who were considered able-bodied were either put to patrolling the town or to rounding up the escaped slave laborers, the theory being that if the troopers were put to soldiering, things would return to normal. It would have shocked the Colonel had he known that what he called "normal" could never be applied to the Regiment again. With the exception of a few regular army men, the Regiment was looking homeward.

There was another small group of troopers who were not looking eagerly homeward, or at least not now. These were the few remaining troopers who were part of the original cadre of two hundred and eighty men of Headquarters Headquarters who had come over with the 705th to the ETO in December 1943. Now Headquarters Headquarters could only muster thirty-nine of these old timers. The rifle companies were lucky if they could muster half as many. The other originals had either been killed or too seriously wounded in combat to ever return to the regiment or were missing in action or prisoners of war. But the survivors were going on furlough!

At ten in the morning a delousing unit rolled in and set up operations in the Headquarters Headquarters area. The men from the various companies who would be going on furlough were lined up and a roll was called. After this, the men were herded into a large holding tent and told to strip. Their clothing was taken away and piled on a waiting truck to be processed later and their musette bags left in the care of a small guard detail of a corporal and two privates.

Next, delousing personnel started to call the roll. As each man's name was called, he stepped forward and technicians dusted his entire body from head to toe with DDT powder. This was thorough, and included hair, ears, armpits, pubic patch, and even the crack of his ass. When everyone had been dusted, they were told that they must wait for two hours and then take a really hot shower.

The time was spent sitting on benches, wisecracking and daydreaming about the coming furlough. The only other sound was the roar of the burners that were heating up huge amounts of water in the next tent. The purpose of this was, of course, vermin control. But for the troopers, the experience would be one of great pleasure. Most of them had not bathed at all since the jump.

Shortreed and Sellers sat apart from the others and, aside from Sellers' occasional fretting about the possibility of someone going through their musette bags, they were silent.

"I don't trust that corporal."

"Forget it!"

"He had a sneaky look about him," Sellers insisted.

"They're not going to go through our bags."

"I don't trust them!"

"Forget it!"

Finally, a sergeant entered the tent and blew a whistle. "All right, men. The time's up. File into the next tent and shower off. Be careful. The water is very hot and you must stay under it for a full fifteen minutes."

"What about clothes?" someone asked.

"You'll draw clean class A's and new boots as you leave."

The men moved happily into the next tent where the sybaritic joys of a really hot shower awaited them. Ah-h-h-h! Things were improving rapidly.

Fifteen minutes of soaking in a hot shower rid them of the DDT powder and after drying, everyone suited up in the new uniforms and new boots.

Sellers didn't lace his boots all the way up, but instead wrapped the laces around the tops and started out of the tent.

"Hey, where you going?" Shortreed asked.

"For my bag."

"You're calling attention to yourself," Shortreed told him. "Relax, we'll get our bags when everyone else gets theirs."

Later, with everyone dressed and the musettes all back in the hands of their owners, they piled onto the waiting trucks for a trip to Division Headquarters, where they drew two months' pay and got back on the trucks for a two hour drive to an airstrip.

At the airstrip there were four C47's at the edge of the dirt strip with their engines idling. The trucks arrived and disgorged their cargo of freshly deloused furlough-bound troopers.

A sergeant blew a whistle and gave the command, "Line up in a column of fours."

The troopers formed up quickly and waited. Shortreed and Sellers stood side-by-side, with their musette bags on their shoulders.

"It's really happening." Shortreed grinned.

"I'll believe in it when we get there," Sellers was skeptical.

"The DDT convinced me."

Sellers was about to say more, but a jeep drew up and he remained silent. The jeep stopped to one side of the formation and a captain with a field briefcase dismounted. While his driver and the sergeant busied themselves setting up a folding table and a chair, the captain addressed the men.

"Give me your attention, men. When you get your furloughs you will notice that they are written for the town of Nice, France on the French Riviera. Nice is a designated rest area and there will be no officers there except for a small complement whose job it will be to help you enjoy your furlough. Now, pay attention to what comes next. It's very important."

Shortreed and Sellers exchanged glances.

Sellers groaned. "I knew this was too good to be true."

"Wait and see what he says," Shortreed told him.

The captain went on. "In order to discourage black marketing and to stabilize the French franc, the United States government will issue money of a new design. The old francs must be exchanged for new ones on or before the tenth of the month. Soldiers will be able to exchange two months pay and no more."

It was terrible news for Sellers and Shortreed who were dumbfounded by it. They listened, their joy considerably diminished, while the captain opened his briefcase, took out a stack of furloughs and, handing a list of the men to the sergeant, ordered, "As the sergeant calls your name, come forward and get your furlough, then report to the crew chief of the first plane on the left. When that one's full up, you'll be directed to the next plane."

The loading began and Shortreed and Sellers found that they were the last men aboard plane one. They climbed aboard and a crewmember closed the door behind them and fastened it in place. As they settled into their seats, the plane was already taxi-ing. In a few minutes the pilot revved up and began the take-off roll.

Shortreed and Sellers sat side-by-side in the bucket seats that folded down from the wall of the plane. Most of the other troopers were gathering around a poker game that got started as soon as the plane leveled off at cruising altitude. Everyone but Sellers and Shortreed were in soaring spirits. Oddly, their roles had reversed. It was now Shortreed who was the gloomier of the two.

"I knew this was all bullshit."

"Don't be so sure," Sellers told him.

"You can't spend that kind of money on a two-week furlough."

"Who's spending?" Sellers asked. He kept his voice low. "I'm changing mine into Swiss money."

"You still can't take it home," Shortreed protested.

"It can stay in a Swiss bank until I come back for it."

"Um-m." Shortreed looked at Sellers with new respect. "I never thought of that."

"I'll bet you didn't even think to bring a gun either," Sellers said.

"I've got a pistol," Shortreed told him.

Several bott' wine were going from hand to hand in the plane.

"... is dough, it'll be after the fight."

"... anymore."

"... posed to mean?"

"You can't get away with shooting people."

"Anyone tries to take this money is going home in a sack." Sellers clearly meant what he said.

Shortreed took another tack. "If you start trying to change that money into Swiss francs, the CID will be on your tail."

"CID. What's that?"

"Civilian Investigating Department, or something like that. Whatever it is, they're cops."

"I don't like cops,"

"You had better learn to like them," Shortreed warned.

They fell silent. Sellers retreated into his paranoia and Shortreed once again took stock of where he was in time and space. The war was over, and not only was he alive but he was on his way to Nice, France with a bunch of money. Cognac, wine, women, all awaited his pleasure in Nice. For the moment he was blissfully happy and able to ignore his sense of loss and the cloud of war memories that hung over him.

After two and a half hours of flight, an enlisted airman came to the door of the aircrew compartment and called out above the sounds of the engines.

"We'll be landing in ten minutes. Return to your seats and no smoking until we land."

Drunk or sober, the troopers dutifully snuffed out their cigarettes and went back to their seats. They were almost there! Look out Nice, the paratroopers are landing!

Shortreed twisted in his bucket seat so that he could see out the window. The plane was flying at eight thousand feet under an overcast at twelve thousand. Soon the plane flew out from under the overcast into brilliant Mediterranean sunshine that changed the ground below from colors muddied by the overcast into a brilliant palette of idyllic beauty that excited the eye. Some part of Shortreed's inner being started to relax as nerves and muscles knotted since Normandy began untying themselves.

He had a brief twinge of anxiety when he remembered that, although he'd had two combat jumps and sixteen practice jumps, he had only landed once in an airplane. That was when the 705th had landed at night in The Bulge between two rows of gasoline burning in the snow. That had scared the hell out of Shortreed, but now he sought to comfort himself with the thought that the air corps landed in planes every day. Landing in a plane was no big thing.

He went back to looking out the window. In spite of his logic, his anxiety continued to mount. It disappeared only when the plane turned onto the final leg of the landing. Outside his window the intense blue of the Mediterranean Sea leapt up at Shortreed from below. Far out at the horizon, the blue of the sky merged with that of the sea with no line of demarcation. Below and closer at hand, the blue sea lapped against the ribbon of gleaming shingled beach.

What a contrast between this and Germany with its piles of filthy rubble and the stench of combat and death!

This extravagant display of light and colors distracted him utterly from his anxieties, and they were already down before Shortreed became aware that they had landed.

An airman came back into the passenger compartment and unfastened the door and, even though the plane was still taxiing, the paratroopers all left their seats and crowded up to the door. Moments later the plane came to a stop and they were out the door as quickly as if they were on a jump. The airman stood off to the side with the unneeded boarding steps still in his hands. He shook his head and grinned. What a bunch of crazy bastards!

After the troopers hit the ground, a corporal who stood close to several trucks started motioning and calling to them. "Over here! Over here!"

With an exuberant yell, the troopers ran pell mell to the first truck and started piling onto it. It was full in no time and, just as it started to pull away, another C47 landed on the airstrip behind them.

"Hey, here comes some more guys!" one of the troopers announced to no one in particular.

"Tough shit for them," another trooper answered him. "We'll be screwed, brewed and tattooed before they even get to town."

So it was that the advance party of the surviving original members of the 705th Parachute Infantry went on R and R in the town of Nice, France. Nice was an old town that had seen a lot of action and it was getting ready to see a lot more.

The trucks entered town along the Promenade d'Anglais and past the Hotel Negresco. The Promenade went along the oceanfront and a soft breeze was blowing off the sea. The sky was blue, the sea was blue, and the fragrance of flowers vied with the fresh smell of the ocean. As they rolled along, the paratroopers gawked at the beautifully tanned women who strolled along the promenade in various stages of dress and undress.

Some were smartly turned out in unfamiliar but exciting fashions. Others strolled toward the beach in the scantiest of bathing suits, with their street clothes in a bag over their shoulder. It was a tantalizing glimpse of one of the chief attractions of Nice. A bottle of cognac and one of these leggy beauties would go a long way toward healing the psychic wounds that lay just below the threshold of awareness in each of them.

The truck turned off the Promenade and after a short drive stopped before the Hotel Albert. Here they were met by a tech sergeant who explained the arrangement at the hotel.

"All right, men, here's how it is. You'll be assigned a room here. You can stay here or not, as you please. When you run out of money you can come back here and stay for free. First, right now, you must go by the desk and sign in. After that, do as you please. Except, the Old Town on the hill is off limits."

With much good-natured jostling, the troopers lined up before the desk and began signing in. Shortreed and Sellers were assigned a room on the second floor. It had two beds and a balcony that overlooked the street below. After checking out their room, they took their bags of money and headed out for the

Faisan d'Or, which had been recommended by Henri, the desk clerk at the hotel, as the hot spot.

As they walked the few blocks to the bar, night was falling. Shortreed's mind was on the sensual pleasure offered by the night and the town. Seller's mind, racing with excitement, was elsewhere: They had only to the tenth the month to exchange their money!

"We don't have a lot of time," he warned Shortreed.

"For what?"

"To change this money."

Shortreed laughed. "I'm going to spend as much of mine as I can."

"On what? Wine and women?"

"I got a lot of catching up to do," Shortreed told him.

Sellers had bigger ideas. "Get this money back to the states and you can buy something worthwhile with it."

"Like what?"

"Power. Influence."

Shortreed scoffed, "Worthwhile, huh ? You're having a wet dream, Sellers."

Sellers shook his head in disgust and fell silent. A moment later they turned a corner onto the boulevard and arrived at the *Faisan d'Or*. The street was bustling with soldiers and women. Before the bar several pedi-cabs and a horse drawn *fiacre* waited for customers.

From inside came a jumble of voices and a general hubbub of merriment over the sounds of a dance band playing. The tune was Tangerine. Standing out on the sidewalk, a very drunken sergeant, with arms outspread, was singing a parody of the song and making an effort to keep in time with the music from within.

Shortreed and Sellers stood watching him for a moment, along with a few other idlers.

"Tangerine, she's a sex machine," the sergeant sang. "And I've seen skirts of Tangerine raised in every bar across the Argentine."

Everyone laughed as the sergeant sang and danced with an imaginary partner. A whore came up to him and gave him a big come-on, but the sergeant was too drunk and too busy singing to notice her until she pushed herself into his arms and began to caress him. This got his attention at last, and he broke off singing and began to shower her drunkenly with kisses. In triumph she led him off, but not before he stopped to retrieve a bottle from the bushes beside the entrance.

As the whore half-led, half-supported him away, three paratroopers came reeling down the sidewalk. One of them carried a half-empty bottle of cognac and they were singing at the top of their lungs. They marched a little past the bar entrance, then halted, did an about face and lurched noisily inside. As they staggered into the bar, they were fervently singing, "I'd rather be a bulldog in a farmer's backyard than a brigadier general in the National Guard, I'd rather be a pimple on the belly of a whore, than a first class private in the army air corp."

Shortreed shook his head and grinned. He went over to the horse-drawn *fiacre* and started to get in.

"Aren't you coming with me?" Sellers asked.

"Uh-uh."

"How come?" Sellers demanded,

"I know you," Shortreed told him. "You're going to spend your whole furlough trying to get that money changed."

"Suppose I find a way?"

"What's the name of that joint they put us in?"

"The Hotel Albert."

"Leave a message for me there," Shortreed instructed.

"Okay."

Turning away, Sellers entered the bar. Shortreed swung himself up into the *fiacre* and told the driver, "I'm looking for women."

The driver laughed. "The town is full of women."

"Classy women," Shortreed specified. "Can you help me?"

"But of course," the driver said affably. "*Oui.*"

"Just take me where I can find them. I'll do the rest."

"*Pour un mille franc.*"

Shortreed put a fistful of francs into the driver's outstretched hand. The driver took one look and beamed, "*Merci!*"

He shook the reins and the horse pulled the *fiacre* out onto the boulevard, Leaning back luxuriantly, Shortreed grinned in anticipation.

End of Chapter 10

Chapter 11

The next morning, just at the first light of dawn, the shuttered town was sleeping off a night of nonstop revelry. Nothing stirred in the deserted streets, but in the basement of a black-market café the remains of a night of roistering cluttered a table. There were empty champagne bottles, full ashtrays, dirty plates and glasses with cigarette butts floating in half-finished drinks surrounding a platter with the carcass of a well picked-over roast chicken.

The driver of the horse drawn *fiacre* from the night before was passed out in the corner. A brunette who had given her name as Blanche leaned back asleep in a chair with her mouth open. Auburn-haired Elise was sprawled with her head down on the table and Gabrielle, a sharp-featured but pretty blonde was rummaging through an ashtray. At last she succeeded in finding a long cigarette butt which she lit. This done, she began draining the empty champagne bottles until she had most of a glass. There was something absurdly elegant about the way she puffed on the crumpled cigarette and sipped at the flat, stale champagne. The clock on the wall read 5:30.

The owner of the establishment, a large woman in her sixties carrying a picnic basket, came down the stairs into the room. She was followed by a male employee carrying a case of wine. She spoke abruptly to Gabrielle in French. Gabrielle shrugged and, after taking a big swig of the stale champagne, rose and went upstairs with the lit cigarette dangling from her lips.

At the top of the stairs she found her way to a room with a crude pair of parachute wings chalked on the closed door. Beneath the wings, was the letter "S". Gabrielle checked the chalked inscription, then knocked loudly.

"*Il est cinq heures et demi!*"

Suzette answered from inside, "*Du matin?*"

"*Oui!*" Laughing, Gabrielle turned and headed back down to the cellar.

Within the room, Shortreed and Suzette were arising naked from their bed. She was tall and well formed and considerably prettier than the others. After a few caresses that were more the acknowledgement of answered passions than a search for new ones, the two began to put on their clothing. They paused now and again to embrace, but finally they were dressed.

Shortreed took his bag of money and shoved his .45 inside, then closed it. Together he and Suzette moved toward the door where she suddenly threw her arms around him.

"How do you say 'I love you' in French?" Shortreed asked her.

She stopped his words with a passionate kiss on the mouth.

"*Comme ca!*" she told him, giggling, and clung to him as they went out into the hallway. Shortreed turned back to the door to erase the parachute wings and his initial with a rub of his hand. A short distance away, they came to another door with the same wings and initial. This he also removed. On the way to the stairs to the basement, they came on two more such doors. As he erased the last one, Shortreed turned to Suzette and asked, "Which one was that?"

"Forget her!" Suzette told him imperiously.

"She was kind of cute," Shortreed teased.

"Blanche is too old for you, Blondi!" Suzette scolded. "You should have a young girl. Like me. *Vigoureuse!*"

"You sure are." Grinning, he patted her affectionately on the ass, and they went down to join the others in the cellar.

Blanche leaned back in her chair, still sleeping with her mouth open. Elise remained asleep, with her head down on the table and Gabrielle had gone back to nursing her glass of stale champagne. The proprietress stood with arms folded before the picnic basket that rested on the roughly cleared edge of the table. Her employee had placed the case of wine on top of the unlit stove and was standing by, awaiting orders.

Shortreed took in the scene for a moment, then started laughing. "If you don't look like a bunch of recruits."

"*Vous payer*," the proprietress demanded, hand out.

Shortreed looked her over then asked, poker-faced, "Which room were you in?"

One of the girls giggled. The proprietress glared at her sourly, then turned again to Shortreed.

"*Pour le service!*"

"How much?" Shortreed asked. "*Combien?*"

She thrust a check at him. Glancing at it briefly, he dug into his pocket and came out with a big roll of bills. At the sight of so much money, Gabrielle grabbed Elise by the shoulder and shook her awake. They watched wide-eyed as Shortreed counted out twenty one- thousand franc notes.

"Eighteen, nineteen, twenty." He handed the money to the proprietress, who counted it again.

While it was being recounted, Gabrielle held out her hand.

"*Vouz payer moi!*"

Elise's hand was also stretched out "*Pour l'amour.*"

"Wait your turn, girls," Shortreed told them. He turned to the owner. "Put the picnic basket and the wine in the buggy out back."

"*Fiacre,*" she corrected him. "In the *fiacre.*" She spoke in French to the servant and he left with the picnic basket.

Shortreed went in turn to Elise and Gabrielle and gave each several thousand francs. Then he rolled three one thousand franc notes and stuck them in the still sleeping Blanche's open mouth. She roused from her snoring and began to protest, but when she saw what he had shoved into her mouth, she smiled instead.

Shortreed turned to Suzette. "You're staying with me, right?"

"*Oui.*"

"You want me to pay you now or later?" he asked her.

"You paid me last night," she reminded him, then added sweetly, "but money is always nice."

In an extravagant gesture, Shortreed handed her a fistful of thousand franc notes.

The proprietress had been watching in amazement. It came to her finally that Shortreed had bedded each of the women.

"*Formidable!*" she said in awe.

The servant returned and took the case of wine, but not before Shortreed removed a bottle. He handed the bottle to the owner. "Open that for me, *s'il vous plait.*"

While she occupied herself with the bottle, Shortreed went to where the driver was passed out in the corner.

"Hey Jocko! Rise and shine!" He shook him several times by the shoulder. "Come on, let's go!"

The servant returned and spoke to the owner, who told Shortreed "The food and the wine are in the *fiacre.*"

He gave the driver another shake.

"*C'est imposible!* He's drunk." Suzette protested. "What are you going to do?"

Shortreed ignored her and shook the driver again harder. The driver mumbled something unintelligible, then lapsed back in a drunken stupor. With considerable determination Shortreed managed to hoist the unconscious driver over his shoulder.

"All right, girls, let's go!"

They were slow to comprehend.

"Into the buggy!" he ordered, and when they still did not respond, " *Allons!*"

At this they finally rose and hurried through the door. Shortreed followed after, with the driver on his shoulder and his bag of money in his free hand. The proprietress stopped him at the door with the opened bottle of wine.

"What do you wish me to do with this?"

"Suzette!" Shortreed called out the door.

"*Oui?*"

"Come here!"

While they waited for Suzette, the proprietress asked hopefully, "You will come back, *non?*"

Pretending to misunderstand, Shortreed acted as if she were propositioning him.

"Sure I'll come back. And next time I'll leave the girls home." He winked at her. "Just you and me, okay?" Struggling to hold the driver and his bag of money without dropping either, he still managed to pat her on the ass.

Suzette came and took the opened wine bottle and they left. Regretfully, the proprietress watched them go. The crazy American had a lot of money and she would have liked to get more of it.

Outside, Shortreed dumped the driver unceremoniously into the passenger section of the *fiacre*, then boosted Elise, Blanche and Gabrielle in with him. This done, he assisted Suzette to the driver's bench, seated himself beside her and, after a big swig of wine, shook the reins. Obediently, the horse pulled the *fiacre* out of the alleyway and into the street.

Except for an occasional lone figure hurrying to an early morning job, the streets were deserted. They had gone only a short way when, at the Fountain of the Lions, the horse left the street and ignoring all of Shortreed's efforts, went to the catch basin of the fountain. Blocking the sidewalk with the *fiacre*, he drank deeply.

"If the *gendarmes* see us doing this, we will be in *beaucoup* trouble!" Suzette said nervously.

Shortreed shrugged. "The horse is thirsty," he told her. "He needs water. And I need more wine."

He reached for the bottle, but Suzette held it away from him. "You don't want any more for a while."

"I don't?" he asked her incredulously. "Where did you get that idea?"

Once again he reached for the bottle, but Suzette had already passed it back to Gabrielle.

"Let's go to the beach and swim," she suggested.

"Why?"

"If you keep drinking like this, by nightfall you will be *zig-zag* like the driver."

"So?"

"Then who will make love to me?"

"No problem. I can drink all day and make love all night."

"Impossible!"

"What about last night?"

"Last night was wonderful, but you were not *zig-zag*."

Shortreed considered this. Suzette cuddled up against him.

"Let's go swim," she said and kissed him.

The horse finished drinking and Shortreed turned it back to the street. As they started for the ocean, he pulled Suzette even closer. In the rear part of the *fiacre* Elise and Gabrielle passed the wine bottle back and forth between them, while Blanche once more slept with her mouth open.

It was only a short drive to the ocean. Shortreed parked the *fiacre* where the horse would be able to graze on one of the many flowerbeds along the oceanfront. Taking a blanket he went off with Suzette for a dip. In the back of the *fiacre* only Elise remained upright, Gabrielle having joined Blanche and the driver in drunken slumber.

Shortreed and Suzette had been gone less than a half hour, when a bicycle-mounted policeman approached the *fiacre*. Dismounting, he pushed his bicycle to where the horse was grazing on the flowers and confronted Elise with an angry torrent of French.

In response, Elise merely raised the wine bottle in salute. "A *votre sante*," she said and polished off the remaining wine.

The *gendarme* spoke again in irate French.

This time Elise pointed toward the ocean and mumbled unintelligibly.

In the direction of where she had pointed, two piles of clothing adorned the seawall. The policeman pushed his bicycle toward them angrily. As he approached, he could hear Suzette giggling and gallantly halted a few paces away.

"Allo," he called discreetly.

"Allo," Shortreed mimicked.

The *gendarme* broke out in a torrent of abusive French, a tirade about the horse who was eating the flowers. At which

Suzette stood up and retrieved her underpants from where they were lying on the seawall. Only the naked upper part of her body was visible, but that was enough to get the *gendarme*'s undivided attention and he stood gap-mouthed in appreciation of the sea sprite standing there with her hair hanging down in damp ringlets. There was something primal and eternal about the siren call of those magnificent upthrust breasts.

Shortreed stood up and began dressing quickly. The *gendarme* addressed his tirade to Shortreed, but never took his eyes off Suzette. Recognizing a mandate, she took her time in what was a reverse strip tease. Starting naked, she dressed artistically. Shortreed took advantage of this distraction to finish getting dressed. As he was putting on his boots, the policeman came to the end of his complaint about the horse and the flowers and waited with angry expectation for Shortreed's response.

Shortreed did not lace up his boots. Instead, he wrapped the laces around the boots and tied them.

"*Sprechen sie deutsch?*" he asked the policeman.

"*Ja.*"

While the *gendarme* none too patiently presented his complaint once again in German, Suzette pulled herself up onto the seawall and finished putting on her clothes. The policeman continued with his diatribe, but his attention strayed to the occasional flash of Suzette's underpants which she was now wearing, and Shortreed took advantage of the distraction to make a start for the *fiacre*.

But the policeman, finished with his complaint in German, paced along beside him, impatiently waiting for an answer. None was forthcoming.

"*Also?*" he demanded impatiently.

"*Ich nicht verstand Deutsch,*" Shortreed told him playfully, slipping into his shirt.

Suzette caught up with them as they reached the *fiacre*. At a sly signal from Shortreed, she climbed in and waited while Shortreed untied the horse.

"You are an American!" the *gendarme* said accusingly.

Shortreed did not deny it. "What can I do for you?" he asked good-naturedly.

"Your horse is eating the flowers!"

"I'm going to move him right now." Shortreed promised. He mounted up and took the reins in his hand.

"*Non, non*! You must come with me," the policeman ordered.

Unexpectedly, Shortreed whacked the horse on the rump and let out a wild yell. With this, the horse bolted and the *fiacre* pulled away at a breakneck pace. The *gendarme* began to blow his whistle and yelled after them in French. Ignoring his commands, Shortreed continued to urge the horse onwards. With this, the policeman scrambled to his bike and took off after them.

The chase was on! It was much like a high-speed Keystone Cops tour of Nice, for if the cop was unable to overtake the buggy, neither could the buggy outdistance the cop. Two more *flics* on bicycles joined in the chase. From time to time the pursuers would blow the queer little two-tone whistles that were the emblem of the French *flic*. Inside the *fiacre* Suzette had succeeded in opening another bottle of wine, which she and Shortreed passed back and forth as the chase progressed.

They passed a sign that read: "Off Limits to American Servicemen".

"You can't go any further here," Suzette warned him. "It's off limits to Americans."

"Forget it!" Shortreed told her.

"It's against the law!" she insisted.

Shortreed pointed back over his shoulder and the pursuing officers. "We're already breaking the law. So forget it."

This was the old section of town. The buildings were different and older and the street was narrow and uphill. The race slowed noticeably as the hill became steeper. It was clear that the horse did not have much left. On the other hand, neither did the cops. It was a long, steep hill lined with shops and cafes that were still shuttered from last night. Aside from Shortreed and his pursuers, the streets were deserted.

Near the top of the hill, a pair of jump boots stood on the sill of an opened window. Beside the boots sat Yvonne., an attractive brunette who yawned lavishly as she leaned to listen to the sounds of the chase approaching below. The clatter of the horse-drawn *fiacre* was getting louder and the police whistles were drawing closer. At this, Yvonne turned to call out to someone else behind her:

"*Bebe, bebe,* you come! *Tout de suite!*"

Naked and half-asleep, Sellers went to join Yvonne at the window. By now she had become so excited that she had lapsed into a babble of French as she pointed at the approaching buggy and its contingent of pursuing *gendarmerie*.

Sellers, by now fully awake, grinned with enjoyment as Shortreed and his *ménage* in the *fiacre* topped the rise before the pension where Sellers and Yvonne were staying. Strung out behind them were three French *flics* more than a hundred yards further down the hill, pushing their bikes in faltering pursuit.

Shortreed urged the horse onward while Suzette, standing up, peered over the high back of the buggy at their pursuers. The driver and owner of the fiacre was sitting up, swaying unsteadily with the movement of the buggy as he held his head with both hands. Gabrielle and Blanche were suffering various degrees of hangovers. Elise however, was still drunk and felling no pain.

The horse stopped before the pension. Suzette, who was enjoying herself, began to shout, "*Vite*! *Vite*! *Blondi*, why are you stopping?"

Shortreed took another drink from the wine bottle. "This horse is pooped out."

Suzette returned to watching the approach of the *gendarmes* who were still a block away, with a very steep section of the hill to climb before overtaking them.

"Hey, Shortreed!" Sellers called from the open window. Shortreed spotted him and waved.

"How you doing, Sellers?"

"Go to the next corner, turn right and come up the alley in the back," Sellers instructed him.

"That won't help,' Shortreed told him. "I've got to have some place to hide this horse and buggy."

"There's a courtyard in the back with a doorway, "Sellers said.

"How will I know it when I get there?"

"I'll open it for you. Hurry!" Sellers urged.

Shortreed whacked the horse with the reins and they took off again at a jaded trot. Looking in the direction of the pursuit for a moment, Sellers took his boots and disappeared from the window. Yvonne continued to watch the *gendarmes* as they doggedly pushed their bicycles up the hill.

Out in the courtyard Sellers, wearing only his shorts and boots, exited from the house and sprinted to a big double door in the rear wall, barred with a large wooden bar. He listened at the door until he could hear the clatter of horse's hooves coming from the alleyway. Then quickly he unbarred the doors and swung them open.

Shortreed drove in with a clatter and Sellers closed the doors behind him, replacing the wooden bar. Shortreed jumped to the ground and began helping the women from the *fiacre* as Sellers asked, "Why are the cops after you?"

"It's too complicated to explain," Shortreed said.

He helped Elise from the *fiacre*, but she slipped, landing on top of him. He made an effort to catch her, but they both fell to the ground. She landed on top of him, putting her arms around him.

"Man, you're loaded!" Sellers laughed.

"I'm okay," Shortreed grinned. "But these people are all drunk."

Elise began to kiss Shortreed and murmured in his ear. At this, with a screech, Suzette hoisted her skirts and sailed from the *fiacre*. She yanked Elise by the hair with one hand and began pummeling her with the other, while both carried on in an unintelligible flurry of French invectives.

Sellers grabbed Suzette from behind and pulled her off Elise. Shortreed got up and pulled Elise to her feet.

"He's mine!" Suzette screeched. "He's mine!"

Sellers clamped his hand over her mouth, as *Monsieur* Langlois, the proprietor of the pension, hurried from the building to join them.

"You are making too much noise," he warned them. "The *gendarmes* are looking everywhere!"

"Take these girls and put them in a room," Shortreed told Langlois.

"But *Monsieur* Paratrooper -- " Langlois started to protest, but Shortreed overrode him.

"Whatever your price is, I'll pay you double."

Hearing this, Langlois rubbed his hands together and smiled. He addressed the women authoritatively in staccato French and together they started for the back door of the pension.

"Wait a minute!" Shortreed called after them.

Langlois turned back to face Shortreed who pulled the driver from the *fiacre* and lead him unsteadily to Langlois.

"Take him with you."

"But *monsieur*, in the same room?" the proprietor protested.

"Sure." Shortreed grinned. "Why not? Let him live a little."

Langlois shepherded his flock into the rear of the *pension*, and Shortreed returned to the buggy where he removed the case of wine.

"That was dumb getting the cops after you," Sellers said.

"The horse was eating the flowers in the park," Shortreed told him. He began opening a bottle of wine.

"You should have gone with them."

"They would have found this bag of money." Shortreed succeeded in pulling the cork and took a drink from the bottle. "They'll never find me here."

"But they'll be looking," Sellers reminded him.

"So?"

"This happens to be where all the action is." Sellers reached for the bottle and took a big drink.

"What kind of action?"

"The café on the corner is a black market joint."

"So?"

"If you want to deal something, that's the place." Sellers said confidently.

Shortreed laughed. "You want to sell some chocolate bars?"

"I want to buy some Swiss money." He handed the bottle back to Shortreed. "Get the picture?"

From inside the *pension* there came a terrible screeching and shouting in French. It was the upraised voices of Suzette and Elise who had started another fight. At once Shortreed and Sellers turned and sprinted into the *pension* where upstairs they found the two girls rolling around the floor, pulling hair, screeching and biting. Langlois flustered about trying to stop them. The other girls and the driver stood watching with expressions ranging from bemused to befuddled.

At the other end of the hall Seller's girl Yvonne stood in a doorway, watching the fight without emotion. Giving up his vain effort at intervention, Langlois dashed into a nearby room and came back with a pitcher of water which he flung on the combatants.

It was at this moment that Shortreed and Sellers burst into the fray. They grabbed the still screeching girls from behind and clapped their hands over their mouths. Shortreed held onto Suzette and Sellers to Elise. Except for needing to avoid getting clawed themselves, the two troopers had no trouble holding them.

Suddenly, from downstairs there came the sound of heavy pounding on the front door. Langlois hurried to the window at the end of the hallway and cautiously peered out onto the street. Silently he motioned to Shortreed and Sellers. Without turning loose of Suzette, Shortreed joined him. Through the window they could see a *Gendarme* standing at the front door. He hammered on the door once again and called out in French.

Shortreed released his hold on Suzette, telling her, "Keep your mouth shut. One word from you, and you'll be sorry."

"What shall I do?" Langlois asked.

"Get rid of him," Shortreed ordered.

"How?"

Instead of answering, Shortreed began unbuttoning Langlois' shirt and went on to remove his shoes and pull off his socks. When he began to muss up Langlois' hair, the puzzled proprietor flinched back. "What's this all about?" he asked Shortreed plaintively.

Down below, the *Gendarme* knocked again.

"Tell him that he is making too much noise," Shortreed instructed. "That he woke you up."

"But *monsieur*--"

Shortreed gave him a nudge toward the stairs and told him, "Act mad."

Reluctantly Langlois followed his instructions. As he descended the stairs, the *Gendarme* could be heard pounding again loudly on the door. Sellers moved to the window with Elise. Suzette spat at her and the fight almost began again, but Shortreed clapped his hand over her mouth and held her firmly.

Down below Langlois and the *Gendarme* engaged in a spirited discussion. Clad only in his trousers Langlois looked ridiculous, but the officer seemed to be going along with his claim of having been awakened.

"You're going to have to ditch these broads," Sellers told Shortreed.

"I'm keeping this one." Shortreed nodded at Suzette.

"Okay. But get rid of the rest of them."

Shortreed shrugged and yawned. "I'm going to bed. Get rid of them for me."

"How?" Seller sounded pissed.

"As soon as the cops quit nosing around, load them in the buggy and send them back to town."

"They're not my girls," Sellers protested.

"The cops will be looking for me,"

"So?"

" I might as well be sleeping."

"Who's going to pay for the buggy and the driver?"

"I bought the buggy last night," Shortreed told him.

"OK, I'll do it, I guess." Sellers assented.

"Tell the driver to pick me up tomorrow at the Hotel Albert about 10 in the morning."

Down at the door Langlois suddenly pointed off uphill and shouted.

"Look! Look!"

The *Gendarme* followed his gesture with his eyes and Langlois insisted that he had seen an American soldier run across the intersection. There was another quick exchange between the two men, then the *Gendarme* was on his bicycle, pedaling off furiously in the direction Langlois had indicated.

Closing the door with an audible sigh of relief, Langlois started back up the stairs. Shortreed and Sellers relaxed and Suzette began to caress Shortreed kittenishly.

"What time are you going to get up?" Sellers asked

"About eight this evening."

"I'll be in the Café Tam Tam."

"Where's that?"

" On the corner down there."

Wiggling back into his shirt, Langlois joined them. Shortreed opened the door to one of the rooms and peered in. "This one's empty."

Pulling Suzette close, he bellied up to her. "We'll take it."

Automatically Langlois started to protest, but stopped as Shortreed shoved a bunch of francs into his hand.

Sellers released Elise, who promptly screeched, "Pig! American pig!" He clamped his hand quickly back over her mouth .

Grinning, Shortreed wagged his finger at her and said, "Behave yourself or I'll turn Suzette loose on you again."

As Shortreed led her into the room, Suzette smiled in victory and flounced her hair at her defeated rival. Before he could close the door, Sellers called after him, "Shortreed!" and added as Shortreed turned back to face him, "We've got business at the Tam Tam. Be there."

End of Chapter 11

Chapter 12

Out in the streets the day was dusking. Inside the Café Tam Tam the night was getting off to a slow start. Sellers and Yvonne sat at a table in the back. Near the front a Senegalese soldier sat drinking a glass of wine and the bartender was polishing glasses at the bar, which ran along one wall of the café. At another table near the front a waiter was setting the table for a sumptuous meal.

Antoine, the proprietor of the Tam Tam, came from the kitchen and made his way to where the waiter was carefully arranging a snowy napkin on top of the single dinner plate. Slight of build, he looked to be in his mid-thirties and walked with a pronounced limp. Seating himself at the table, he began a quiet conversation with the waiter, during which he glanced over several times at Sellers and Yvonne. It was obvious that they were of great interest to him.

At Sellers' table, Yvonne, lost in some private daydream, appeared to be drunk. She caressed Sellers' arm absently while he nursed a snifter of brandy and gave his attention to watching Antoine.

"Who's the guy at that table?" he asked her softly.

Yvonne shrugged. "Nobody."

At this point, the waiter left the table and went to where the Senegalese soldier sat. He said a few words to the soldier, who gulped his drink and left. Clearly, he had been told to do so.

Sellers drained his glass and said suspiciously, "He don't act like he was nobody."

The waiter appeared at their table. "*Encore, monsieur?*"

"Yeah."

"*Ma'mselle?*"

"*Non.*"

The waiter returned to the bar and spoke to the bartender who deftly poured a small amount of clear liquid into the bottom of the snifter before filling it with cognac. The bartender nodded to the waiter and, satisfied that this had been unobserved, he brought the glass back to the table where Yvonne appeared to be passed out with her head cradled in her arms on the tabletop. Ignoring her, Sellers shoved a few francs at the waiter with a curt "*Merci.*"

The waiter turned to leave.

"Not so fast, jocko!" Sellers told him.

The waiter turned back obediently to face him. "*Oui?*"

"You drink it!" Sellers ordered.

The bartender and Antoine were watching intently.

"But *Monsieur*-- " the waiter protested.

"I said drink it!" Sellers snarled.

The waiter patted his stomach. "*Mon ulcere—*"

"Fuck your ulcer!" Sellers pulled aside his shirt so that the waiter could see the .45 automatic shoved in his waistband.

The waiter looked frantically to Antoine for help. None came.

"What's the matter?" Sellers demanded. "Is there something in my drink?

"*Non, non*!" the waiter pleaded. "I have *l'ulcere*--"

"You're going to have something a lot worse than that if you don't drink."

Finally, in almost tearful desperation, the waiter drained the snifter of cognac in one gulp.

Sellers relaxed slightly. "Now bring me another one."

As the waiter returned to the bar, Antoine smiled sardonically at him over his wineglass.

While this was happening, doors away from the café Shortreed sat on the edge of his bed, wearing only his pants. Suzette lay on the bed watching him while he laced his boots. Shortreed finished and went to the washbasin, on a stand near the window. He splashed water into the basin and began washing his face. There was a knock at the door and he returned quickly to the bed and took up his army .45 from the nightstand beside it.

"Allo," Langlois called through the door.

"Answer him," Shortreed whispered.

"*Oui?*" she said cautiously.

"You ordered champagne. *Il est ici.*"

"Bravo!" Shortreed said. "And goodbye. *Adieu.*"

"*Adieu.*" Langlois echoed him and left.

Shortreed put the pistol back on the nightstand and stretched luxuriously. Then he sat beside Suzette and tousled her playfully.

"Why don't you get the booze."

"Booze?" She was puzzled.

Shortreed grinned. "The champagne."

"*Non,*" she said, pouting prettily. "You get it, Shawtreed."

"How did you know my name?"

"The other soldier called you Shawtreed."

"Shortreed," he corrected her. "Not Shawtreed."

Suzette tried to pronounce his name several times with little success. There was something endearing and intimate about her efforts. The moment was as unaffectedly real as either of them had known for a long time. Were they able to forget all of their grim yesterdays, the door to genuine affection stood open. Even to love.

Shortreed laughed. "No, no. Short-Reed."

Suzette tried again. She did a little better this time, but she was still giving his name the wrong inflection."

"No. Short-Reed, " he pronounced with exaggerated care.

"Shh--ort—reed," she tried experimentally.

"Repeat after me, Shortreed."

This time she was very close and Shortreed laughed.

"Good! Very good. Now once more, and I will go for the champagne."

Moving up close, she cuddled her body against him, kissed him and said playfully, "You will get the champagne, Shortreed, *non?*"

He tousled her again. Laughingly she returned his caress, telling him, "If you get the champagne, I'll be very nice to you."

"You'll be very nice to me anyway, won't you," he said.

There was nothing playful in his voice. No longer kittenish, she released him, rolled away him and lay on her back. To Shortreed, studying her as she stared silently at the ceiling, she seemed thoughtful and sad.

"What's the matter?" Shortreed asked.

This was greeted with silence.

"Relax, baby," he told her. 'I'll get the champagne."

She continued to stare at the ceiling, ignoring Shortreed while he went to the door, brought the champagne back into the room and busied himself uncorking the bottle. He found two glasses in the ice bucket and filled them. When he offered one glass to her she refused it.

Shortreed shrugged and began to drink from his own glass. He waited, expecting her to say something, but she remained silent. He finished his glass and held hers out to her again, but she shook her head and turned away.

It pissed him off and he drained her glass in one gulp and poured himself another, telling her angrily, "I can't stand moody people. If there's something on your mind, say it. Don't play games with me."

After another moment of silence, she said with feeling, "You're cruel!"

"Get off my back!" he told her and drank off most of his second glass. He could feel there was a fence between them and it was growing higher, but he told himself that he didn't care.

"You knew I would be nice to you anyway."

There was something tragic about her voice. Shortreed recognized this, but only said, "That's what I'm paying you for."

"This afternoon you said you loved me."

"I was pretending," he told her.

"So you pay me to pretend with you, but you keep telling yourself that we're only pretending. Why?"

"I don't have to answer that," he told her belligerently.

"If two lonely people choose to pretend, what's wrong with that?" she asked him.

He shrugged. "It's not love."

"Pretend for a week and it is an *affair de coeur*," Suzette countered.

"Let's drop the subject!"

"Pretend for twenty years and it's a marriage. Maybe even a happy marriage."

"Shut up!"

"Don't you know it is all pretend," she told him. "There is no love."

"I'm warning you!" he threatened.

"Oh, *mon gallant*," she taunted him. "You are looking for love?"

"One more fucking word from you and you're going to be damned sorry!" he threatened.

"Of course people fall in love," she told him and he relaxed slightly, until she almost shouted at him, "Once! After that they pretend."

It was obvious that somehow Suzette had managed to strike a raw nerve in Shortreed's psyche. He took the champagne from the ice and, without bothering with the glass, gulped directly from the bottle.

"You don't know nothin' about me," he told her defiantly.

"You pretend with…ah…" She could not find the right English words and switched to French, "*Avec ferocite*," and added sadly, "The same as me."

Shortreed gave her a quick look and drank again from the bottle. There was a silence, as both of them were entangled in memories of unhappy love affairs.

Suzette broke the silence, telling him haltingly, "The first time… it was for me like the Garden of Eden…All things were shiny…The world was bright and clean…"

Although she was speaking directly to Shortreed, he avoided eye contact with her.

"I was Eve and my Adam was *tres gallant*." She paused for a moment, then continued, her voice tinged with bitterness, "Now the world is *sale, sordide*…and there are too many Adams."

Shortreed said, trying to convince himself, "People can fall in love more than once."

"Impossible!" Suzette rejected this defiantly.

He drew back his hand as if to slap her, but controlled the impulse. Instead he rose and grabbed his shirt. Fiercely he pulled it on and began buttoning it. Suzette, on the verge of tears, watched Shortreed mutely, while he stuffed the shirt into his trousers, took up the .45, and shoved it into the bag of money and grabbed his jacket.

He stopped at the door and, returning to the bed, dug in his pocket for a large roll of franc notes which he threw down on the bed beside Suzette.

"Don't be here when I come back."

She began to weep softly. "I'm sorry, Shortreed, I didn't mean to--"

She stopped when, without another word, Shortreed returned to the door and left the room.

Taking up the roll of money, Suzette stared at it for a moment then, with a cry of anguish, hurled it across the room. She rolled over on her belly and began to weep in earnest, reaching after a moment for the pillow from Shortreed's side of the bed and pulling it to her. She hugged the pillow, embracing it as if it was Shortreed, and buried her face in it.

"I love you," she wept in a small voice, crying alone.

At the café Tam Tam, the waiter who had been forced by Sellers into drinking the doctored cognac, sprawled comatose at the bar. At Sellers' table, Yvonne still went through the pretense of being passed out drunk. But covertly, she kept a watchful eye on Antoine and the bartender, who polished a glass while he kept his attention on Sellers.

The second shot of cognac had also been dosed and Sellers, his face flushed and his eyes unfocused, was visibly on the verge of collapse. Finally his head sagged down on the table. But some part of him was still functioning. His survival instinct, honed by a hundred and thirty days of combat, kicked in and forced him upright.

Unsteadily he surveyed the room. Things went in and out of focus and, when he turned his head, the room spun crazily. It was only his superb physical condition that kept him going and still upright.

He was vaguely aware that the waiter was passed out at the bar, and that the bartender was staring at him, sphinx-like, with a half-polished glass in his hand. The room dissolved into a whirling maelstrom of converging angles and fragmented images that went in and out of focus. Then, with great effort, his focus came to rest on Antoine, who continued to savor his food, but with something sinister in the sardonic attention that he kept on Sellers.

Unsteadily, but with deadly purpose, Sellers opened his bag of money and took the .45 automatic from the bag. With considerable difficulty he managed to cock the hammer. He rose unsteadily and took up the bag of money. Waving the gun threateningly, he made a wobbly path toward the door and the street beyond.

Antoine and the bartender watched him and wondered if Sellers was going to escape. But halfway to the door, he stumbled and fell. With a ferocious singleness of purpose, he pulled the bag of money beneath him and aimed the automatic in the general direction of Antoine. But he was unable to hold the pistol up and he collapsed. He made a few further efforts to drag himself back into consciousness, but it was no use and he fell face downward.

Antoine and the bartender watched silently as Sellers made one last attempt to rise. He could not and finally passed out. At a signal from Antoine, the bartender came from behind the bar and went to where Sellers lay on the floor. Quickly he removed the gun from Sellers' hand and then, without ceremony, rolled him onto his back, exposing the musette bag of money. Under Antoine's watchful stare, he scooped it up and started back behind the bar.

So intent were both of them on this, that neither was aware of Shortreed's entrance, until they heard his voice, flat and deadly, telling them, "Drop it!"

The two Frenchmen stared at him, totally nonplussed. Shortreed had his .45 automatic ready and the look on his face told them that he would shoot if necessary. He strode to where the bartender stood and took the money and the gun from him without ceremony. Then, with one swift motion, he shoved the gun against the bartender's belly.

"Motherfucker!" He shoved the terrified bartender back against the bar.

"It was only for safekeeping!" The bartender lied frantically. "You can see he's drunk."

Shortreed cocked the .45 and pushed with it a little harder. The bartender looked as if he was going to faint.

"Please, *monsieur*," he pleaded.

"I got a feeling you're just the corporal," Shortreed said grimly. "Who's in charge?"

He followed the bartender's quick glance over toward Antoine, and moved a little so that he could cover them both.

"Okay, jocko," he told Antoine. "Over here."

Antoine shrugged, wiped his lips deliberately with a napkin and walked to where they stood, again limping noticeably.

"Your friend is drunk," he told Shortreed in good English.

"You put something in his drink!"

Antoine shrugged noncommittally.

With a sudden gesture, Shortreed prodded the gun against Antoine's belly.

"Didn't you?"

Antoine smiled disarmingly. "Of course."

"You're a cool one," Shortreed said in surprise.

Again Antoine shrugged. "It seemed so easy."

Out in the street a pedicab was passing the door. Shortreed whistled and the driver stopped. He was obviously tired and wanting to be through for the day.

Shoving the gun out of sight in his bag, Shortreed motioned him over. Reluctantly the driver dismounted and came over to them.

"*Oui, monsieur.*"

Shortreed indicated Sellers and said, "Take him out and put him on your tricycle."

"*Non, monsieur*," the driver told him. "I am tired."

Fishing out a handful of franc notes, Shortreed tossed them to the driver. He seemed revitalized by the sight of that much money, but nevertheless looked covertly to Antoine for permission. Antoine gave him a slight nod, and together Shortreed and the driver half-dragged, half-carried Sellers to the pedicab. Shortreed stowed the two bags of money beside Sellers, then climbed in himself. Antoine, who had limped along beside them, tugged at Shortreed's sleeve.

"Your friend wanted to buy Swiss francs."

"So?"

"I'll make you a proposition."

"Like you made him?" Shortreed asked.

Antoine laughed. "You have no choice but to deal with me."

"Then I won't deal."

"Your money won't be good for long,"

"Knock it off!" Shortreed told him harshly.

"Your government is going to issue new money."

"I said I'm not going to deal with you!"

"You have no choice," Antoine said again.

"If you can trade old francs for Swiss money why can't I?"

"You can." Antoine smiled. "If you know where to go."

"What's your proposition?"

"Swiss francs at sixty per cent of the face value of the French francs."

"Fuck you, jocko!" Shortreed said. He ordered the pedicab driver, "Take off."

The driver took his time, giving Antoine the opportunity to continue insistently, "The other bag, *Monsieur*. It has money also. *Non*?"

"Get moving!" Shortreed yelled at the driver.

As they started off, Antoine grabbed Shortreed's arm. 'When you're ready to deal, I'll be here."

"I'm not going to deal with you," Shortreed told him flatly.

"But *Monsieur*, I am the only one who can get Swiss francs."

"Get moving!" Shortreed snarled, rapping the pedicab driver on the back of the head, and they pulled away.

Antoine yelled after them. "I will need two days notice. Don't forget. Two days!"

As the pedicab moved away, he limped back into the bar, where the bartender still sagged weakly against the bar top.

"Jacques!" Antoine shouted. "Jacques, come! "

An aproned man came from the kitchen and was immediately ordered in staccato French to follow the pedicab. Stripping off his apron, he went to where his bike was parked, mounted it and took off, peddling at full speed after the pedicab.

Antoine returned to his table, but before he sat back down, he noticed that the woman who had been with Sellers and who had appeared to be passed out drunk, was no longer there. He gestured to the bartender, who came over to him."

"Where is the soldier's woman?"

"She left by the back door."

Scowling his displeasure, Antoine seated himself and turned his attention to the remains of his meal.

By the time night fell fully, the streets of Nice teemed once more with soldiers bent on another night of revelry. Shortreed's pedicab pulled up before the Hotel Albert. On the sidewalk, a scattering of soldiers loitered about, smoking and passing bottles around. The more enterprising were already away on a night's career of whoring and public drunkenness.

As Shortreed and the driver struggled to get the semi-conscious Sellers from the pedicab, Jacques peddled up on his bicycle and stopped nearby to watch. Shortreed was unaware that he had been followed, and neither he nor Jacques realized that Seller's brunette girl Yvonne had pulled up behind them in another pedicab and was watching them from the shadows.

'Hey Shortreed!" A voice called from the sidewalk. It was Cardone, the machine gunner from H Company. "You need some help?"

"Yeah, gimme a hand."

Together they maneuvered Sellers out of the pedicab and onto the sidewalk. Shortreed leaned back in to retrieve the two bags, and paid the pedicab driver while Cardone held Sellers upright. The pedicab pulled away.

"Boy," Cardone said. "Has he ever got a load on."

"Help me get him to our room," Shortreed told him.

"Boy, he's fucking drunk."

Together they took Sellers inside the hotel and past the desk. In a corner beside the stairwell, they found the sergeant from A Company completely drunk. He had a case of wine beside him and apparently intended to spend his furlough right there. Drunk.

"What a jerk," Cardone said. "That's no way to spend a furlough."

"Maybe he's got more to forget than we have," Shortreed told him.

Arriving at the room, they opened the door, dragged Sellers to his bed and dumped him down. Anxiously, Shortreed checked Sellers' pulse. Watching him, Cardone began to have doubts about what was wrong with Sellers.

"He's just drunk. Aint he?"

"That too," Shortreed said.

"What do you mean?"

"Knockout drops."

"You know who gave them to him?"

"Yeah."

"Let's take some guys and go clean the place out."

"I'll take care of it," Shortreed said.

"I got rolled last night myself," Cardone told him.

"You know who did it?"

"I wish."

"You broke?" Shortreed asked.

"Yeah."

Shortreed took out a roll of thousand franc notes, peeled off five of them and handed them to Cardone. "There you are. Five thousand francs."

"What's the catch?"

Shortreed nodded at Sellers. "Stay with him until he comes out of it."

"Okay. But why?"

"This bag's full of G.I. chocolate," Shortreed lied.

"What am I supposed to do?" Cardone asked.

"If anyone comes prowling rooms, run them off."

"You got it," Cardone assured him.

Sellers muttered and tried to rise from the bed. Shortreed took Seller's musette bag to him and shoved it under his head.

"Sellers! Can you hear me?"

Sellers mumbled unintelligibly.

"Come on!" Shortreed demanded. "Can you hear me?"

"Yeah," Sellers said. Mumble, mumble "Yeah."

"Your bag is under your head. Okay?"

"Yeah, yeah."

Shortreed went back to where Cardone was standing.

"When he comes out of it, tell him to meet me at the *Faison d'Or.*"

"Okay."

Shortreed took his own bag. He said to Cardone, "Keep your hands out of that bag," and left.

Except for a few paratroopers who wandered around the lobby, it was empty and at the desk, the clerk was alone. Shortreed went to him and asked, "Do you speak English?"

"*Oui.*"

"Do you see that sergeant over there by the stairs?"

"What about him?"

"Keep an eye on him."

"Why?" The clerk wanted to know.

"If anyone tries to go through his pockets or steal his wine, run them off."

"I'm not a policeman," the Frenchman protested,

"You are now." Shortreed peeled off a thousand franc note and handed it to him. "Here's your pay."

The clerk was impressed. "*Merci, merci*! You have my word. I will keep a good eye on the sergeant."

Shortreed glanced about. After assuring himself that he and the clerk were more or less alone he leaned over and said confidentially, " Someone told me that this money was all going to be taken up soon."

The clerk nodded. "The tenth day of this month will be the last day for exchanging it."

"What's wrong with it?"

"The *Boche* printed it and it's inflated."

"What good does it do to take it up?"

"Your government is putting American dollars behind the new money."

Satisfied that Antoine had not been lying, Shortreed asked, "Is there a limit to how much a solder can exchange?"

"For soldiers, two months pay."

"What about civilians?"

"I don't understand."

"Is there a limit to how much a civilian can exchange?"

'The CID and our own French police are investigating anyone who tries to exchange large sums."

Shortreed turned to leave.

"*Monsieur.*"

"Yeah."

The clerk spoke cautiously. "You have more than two month's pay?"

"I know someone who might."

They fell silent as two drunken troopers stumbled boisterously from the street to the desk.

"Hey Frenchy! What room are we in? Kirkwood and Cooper."

The clerk checked his list. "Room 24, second floor."

But, instead of going upstairs, they left again, one telling the other, "You see? You dumb shit! I told you it was twenty-four."

When they were gone, the clerk resumed the conversation. "If you have a lot of money, it is possible that something could be arranged."

"Keep talking."

"There's a certain person who for a price can –"

"I want to buy Swiss francs," Shortreed overrode.

The clerk beamed. "It can be arranged."

"Tell your man I want to see him."

"Come with me tomorrow morning."

"Bring him here."

"Impossible."

"Okay, the deal's off."

"Please understand. I cannot--"

Shortreed cut him short. "I'll find someone else."

He turned and started for the door. The clerk came from behind the desk and followed him, saying, "There's only one person who can do what you want."

"Yeah well if he won't come here, you can forget the whole thing."

"On the tenth day of this month your money will be worthless," the clerk reminded him.

"I'll have Swiss francs before then."

"Not unless you buy them from the person of whom I speak."

"Tell him to meet me here."

The clerk shrugged. "I can try."

As Shortreed started to open the door, the clerk stopped him. "If you have money, be careful of making a display."

Without comment, Shortreed continued out the door.

"The CID is everywhere," the clerk offered him a final warning. He returned to the desk and took up the phone.

Outside the hotel, Shortreed hailed a pedicab. As he climbed in, Jacques who had waited patiently in the shadows nearby, mounted his bicycle and pedaled after him.

End Of Chapter 12

Chapter 13

On the sidewalk before the Faison d'Or there was light foot traffic, consisting mostly of soldiers and their girls, with a sprinkling of others. Shortreed's pedicab pulled up before the club. As he was paying the driver, Jacques pulled in and parked his bicycle unobtrusively in the shadows. Shortreed took notice and saw also that the Frenchman was working too hard at trying to appear casual. A warning flag went up in his mind, but he pretended to be unaware of this and continued inside the club.

The American Bar was in the main part of Nice and was one of the better clubs in town. In one corner, almost out of sight, Monique sat nursing an *aperitif*. She was keeping a close eye on the entrance and watched with interest as Shortreed entered and sat at the bar away from the other patrons. The bartender approached Shortreed.

"*Oui monsieur?*"

"You speak English?"

"*Oui.*"

"Is the owner here?"

"I'm sorry, *Monsieur*." The bartender shook his head.

"I want to see him."

"He's busy."

Shortreed peeled a thousand franc note from the roll he took from his pocket and handed it to the bartender, who examined it and smiled.

"What shall I tell him?"

"I want to talk to him."

"About what, *Monsieur*?"

"Something confidential."

After a moment the bartender nodded and left by the door at the end of the bar. Looking about, Shortreed spotted Monique who had been studying him casually. Now she looked away quickly. He continued to look at her, liking what he saw, and waited for her to turn once more and meet his glance. When she did, he smiled at her. Clearly she was tempted to return the smile, but when the bartender returned, she looked away.

"Take the door at the end of the bar," the bartender instructed Shortreed. "Then it's the second door on the left."

Shortreed took his musette bag of money. Monique followed with her eyes, as he went through the door that the bartender had indicated.

In contrast to the nightclub, the office was without glamour or excitement, a place to do business and nothing more. There was a desk, several file cabinets and, near the desk, a small table at which Henri, the owner of the club, was seated. He was a rotund little man as fat and sleek as a boar rat. The meal before him would have made a generous repast for two. He eyed Shortreed for a moment and Shortreed looked back at him expressionlessly.

Finally Henri asked, "What is it you wish to talk about?"

"I want to buy some Swiss francs."

Henri returned to his food. "Impossible."

"That's not what I heard."

"The risk is too great."

"You got to play big to win big," Shortreed said.

Henri took a chunk of bread and wiped at the sauce on his plate. "How much money do you have?"

"A lot."

"Twenty or thirty thousand francs?" Henri asked deprecatingly.

"Several million," Shortreed told him flatly.

Henri tossed the piece of bread down on his plate. "Goodbye!" he said with finality.

"What do you mean, 'Goodbye'?"

"I have no time for jokes," Henri told him severely and reached again for the bread. Clearly he considered the matter closed.

Taking the musette bag from his shoulder, Shortreed opened it. He strode to Henri's side and grabbing him by the collar, shoved his face almost into the bag.

"Does that look like a fucking joke?"

Henri's eyes bulged out, partly from the rough treatment, but also from the sight of so much money.

"*Formidable*! "

Shortreed released him and watched as Henri took a sheaf of bills from the bag and fanned through it.

"How much is here?" he asked.

"I don't know."

"What?" Henri's voice was incredulous.

"There are fifty bills to a packet and you can see the bag is full," Shortreed said.

Henri was transported. "Beautiful," he murmured. He was moved.

"After the tenth," Shortreed said, "they'll just be so many ass wipes."

"The new issue French francs will be impossible," Henri told him.

"I want Swiss francs."

Henri rose from the table, wiping his mouth. He went to the phone and guardedly gave a number in French. As he waited, Shortreed said, "My friend also has a bag of thousand franc notes."

"The same size?"

"Yeah."

Henri returned his attention to the phone and held a rapid conversation in French with someone at the other end of the line. Shortreed watched, sharpset and alert.

Henri hung up from the conversation and went for his coat. "Come," he told Shortreed.

"Slow down," Shortreed said. "I'm not going anywhere.'

"But *Monsieur* Paratrooper-" Henri protested.

"I'm not going anywhere," Shortreed repeated.

"But it's all arranged."

"Tell your friend to meet me here in about an hour."

"He won't come here."

"For this much money he will."

Henri shook his head. "You do not understand-"

"What is it I don't understand?" Shortreed countered belligerently.

"He is a very important personage."

"If he's too important to come here, then fuck him." Shortreed would not be swerved.

"You can trust him," Henri assured.

Shortreed raised his jacket so that the .45 could be seen. "This is the only thing I trust."

"He hasn't seen the money."

"Tell him he can look at it here. Nowhere else."

Henri shrugged philosophically. " I will do my best." He returned to the phone, adding, "But even so, he won't bring the Swiss francs."

"Why?"

"Certain arrangements would have to be made."

"Tell him to come by himself."

Again Henri spoke into the phone in rapid French. Shortreed watched for a moment then, closing the musette bag and rearranging his jacket over the pistol, he left the room, telling Henri, "I'll be back in an hour."

At the bar he ordered a cognac and took it to Monique's table. As he approached, she turned her head away and tried to ignore him.

"Mind if I join you?"

Not meeting his glance, she shook her head emphatically.

"Dinner together?"

"*Non.*"

"A walk along the promenade?"

"Please Monsieur-"

Shortreed sat down at her table and for the first time she looked directly at him. He met her glance and grinned disarmingly.

Ignoring the grin, she said, "I'm sorry, I wish to be alone."

Shortreed's attitude changed. She was acting oddly and he sensed that this was not the standard brush-off. Something serious was bothering her and it had nothing to do with him.

"Are you in some kind of trouble, lady?" he asked.

She shook her head, seeming strangely defeated.

"Can I help?"

She showed surprise at the offer, but again shook her head.

At the end of the bar near the door, an American sergeant and a whore entered noisily from the street. Both were very drunk, as they made their way boisterously and unsteadily to the bar where they loudly demanded drinks.

Rising from Monique's table, Shortreed shouldered the musette bag and picked up his cognac.

"I'm sorry I bothered you," he told her honestly and crossed back to the bar. Draining his cognac at a gulp, he started toward the far end of the bar and the door, but something made him look back. To his surprise, he discovered that Monique was following him with her eyes. She looked despairing, so vulnerable and alone that he almost went back to her. But then he recalled how definite she had been in her rejection. She didn't want him there. Whatever was bothering her, it was not something she wanted to share with him. His mind was conflicted by this as he continued toward the front door.

As he passed the sergeant and his whore, the sergeant called out to him, "Hey Trooper!"

Shortreed paused near him and said, "Looks like you're doing all right, Sarge." He was aware of the whore's glance, regarding him blearily.

"Have a drink," the sergeant urged him.

"Thanks," Shortreed said, "but I'm in a hurry."

"Come on, one drink won't take that long."

"I got to see a guy," Shortreed told him.

The sergeant grabbed him insistently by the arm, and tried to press him down onto a barstool. With a good-natured laugh, Shortreed pulled loose. "Okay I'll buy the first round."

He tossed a couple of hundred franc notes onto the bar and ordered, "I'll have what they're having."

"That's better." The belligerence had faded from the sergeant's manner, but as he and the whore turned to order, Shortreed slipped quietly out the door.

On the street he stood for a moment, wondering what to do. He had an hour to kill and no intention of drinking any more before the moneyman showed up. He started to walk, more or less aimlessly. Almost immediately he became aware that Jacques had mounted his bicycle and was once again following him.

As Shortreed and his shadow moved away from the entrance to the American Bar a pedicab pulled up and a man dismounted. Charles was tall for a Frenchman and although his suit coat did not match his trousers, he was neatly dressed. Pinned conspicuously on the front of his coat were several French military medals.

Inside the club, nothing had changed. Not even the drunken sergeant, who still wanted someone to drink with him. When Charles entered, he spotted him immediately and called, "Hey Frenchy! Come have a drink!"

The tall Frenchman shook his head curtly and searched the room with his eyes. His gaze found Monique who was still at her table, and she flinched as she recognized him. It was clear that she feared him. He started for her, but the drunken American sergeant grabbed at him, urging again, "Come on, Frenchy! Come have a drink!"

"*Non!*"

The sergeant was undeterred. "Don't be an asshole!"

"I do not wish to drink with you!" Charles said angrily.

"Drink, or I'm going to pound your head in," the sergeant threatened.

Charles tried to get away, but the sergeant held him fast, in a drunken bear hug. While they struggled, Monique seized the opportunity and, reaching under the table for a cheap suitcase, she started with it toward the back door.

Out on the street, Shortreed, with Jacques still following him at a discreet distance, was nearing the alleyway. It was poorly lit and, as Shortreed passed two soldiers headed in the other direction, he used them for cover and ducked quickly into the alley. With a burst of speed he sprinted down the alley and concealed himself in a doorway. From the vantage of his hiding place, he watched as Jacques pedaled obliviously past the entrance to the alley.

Satisfied that he had managed to give Jacques the slip, Shortreed relaxed. He'd wait a bit to give Jacques a chance to move on, and then he would be on his way. A few doors behind Shortreed, Monique stepped quietly from the back door of the American Bar. She backed away a few steps cautiously, turned to run, but bumped into Shortreed who still peered toward the mouth of the alley. At the moment of contact he wheeled and, in an unbelievably fast burst of motion, grabbed Monique by the throat and slammed the terrified girl against the wall. He almost hit her but managed to stop the chain reaction she had triggered by bumping into him from behind. Her suitcase fell to the ground and ruptured open, spilling its contents.

Monique was wide-eyed in fear.

"You took me by surprise," Shortreed said apologetically.

She was unable to reply, still rattled by his explosive reaction.

Then, behind them, Charles came rushing out of the back door of the American Bar. When he spotted Monique with Shortreed, he stopped in his tracks.

"Do you know this guy?" Shortreed asked her quietly.

"*Non*! No. I have never seen him before in my life!" There was fear in her voice. She was obviously lying.

Shortreed gave the Frenchman a hard look, but he continued to glare at Monique.

"You got a problem, mister?" Shortreed asked belligerently.

Charles ignored this and lit a cigarette.

"Well?" Shortreed demanded.

"I thought I knew the lady," Charles said.

Shortreed strode to him belligerently.

"But I was mistaken," Charles added quickly.

"Then fuck off!"

Charles turned and stalked away angrily toward the alley. They watched him as he disappeared back into the shadowed alleyway. Then, stooping, Monique began to gather her scattered clothing back into the suitcase. Shortreed bent to help her.

"What's your name?" he asked.

"Monique."

"I'm Leroy Shortreed. Everyone calls me Shortreed."

Soon they had all of her things back in the suitcase. As she straightened to her feet, he offered, "Will you have dinner with me?"

She hesitated for a moment, then smiled at him. "*Oui.*"

With Shortreed carrying her suitcase, they went around the corner back onto the street. Shortreed gestured at a sidewalk cafe and when she made no objection, he escorted her over to sit at a table on the sidewalk. It afforded a very good view of the entrance to the *Faison d'Or*.

Back up on the hill in a storeroom in the old town a pimp, a petty criminal from the Riviera underworld, sharpened a mean-looking stiletto against a whetstone, giving it his full attention. On the table at which he worked there was an open suitcase. It was filled almost to overflowing with American cigarettes that had recently been part of the American chain of supply. Lying beside the suitcase was a small .32 automatic.

Maurice ran his finger experimentally along the cutting edge of the stiletto. Dissatisfied, he went back to rubbing it against the whetstone until he was interrupted by a knock at the door. Taking up the pistol, he went quietly to the door and waited. When the knock came again, he slid open a peephole in the door and squinted through it for a moment. Satisfied, he unlocked the door and a girl entered quickly. It was Yvonne.

He locked the door behind her, sat back down and resumed sharpening the stiletto.

"You're going to get shot one of these days if you don't start knocking the way I taught you," he told her.

Ignoring his complaint, Yvonne reached over to take a cigarette from his shirt pocket. Inhaling, she blew out the smoke, extracted a packet of thousand franc notes from the cleavage of her brassiere, and tossed it on the table before him.

Maurice stopped sharpening and examined the packet of bills. He was visibly impressed.

"Where did you get this?" he asked.

"From the American soldier I spent the night with. He had a bag full of these packages."

"Why didn't you take all of it?" Maurice demanded.

She shrugged. "I would have, but they drugged him at the Tam Tam."

"They got the bag of money?" he questioned.

'*Non*, as they were taking it from him, his friend came in and rescued him."

"Where is he now?"

"At the Hotel Albert."

Maurice rose and thrust the stiletto into a scabbard inside his waistband.

"Both soldiers have large pistols," Yvonne told him.

He laughed and shoved the .32 into his trouser pocket.

"They'll never have the chance to use them," he said confidently and they left together.

At the sidewalk café, Shortreed sipped a glass of wine. Most of his dinner lay untouched on the plate before him as he enjoyed this moment with Monique, watching her. She ate with good manners but very hungrily.

This was not lost on Shortreed and he asked her bluntly, ""How long has it been since you had a full meal?"

She looked up at him startled, as if about to blurt out the truth. Then she changed her mind and lied," This morning."

He made eye contact with her and prodded gently, "Yesterday? The day before?"

She looked back at him in a silent plea for him to change the subject, then dropped her eyes to her plate and went back to eating.

After a moment she asked him, "Are you here on furlough?"

"Yeah."

"Are you enjoying yourself?"

"I'm pretending."

"I don't understand."

"I'm doing all the things that soldiers dream about but…" He left the sentence unfinished.

"It can't be because you're shy," she challenged him roguishly.

Shortreed laughed. "No. And the town is full of girls."

"You don't like girls?"

"I'm crazy about them. It's just..." He fell silent again.

She sipped her wine, waiting for him to continue. When he did not, she prompted him, "It's just what?"

"You don't get to know much about a girl on a furlough."

"Most soldiers don't want to."

"I'm not most soldiers."

She returned to her meal and ate in silence while Shortreed stared moodily at his wine. The waiter came over to the table and started to remove some of the empty dishes.

"Bring us the check," Shortreed ordered.

"*Oui, Monsieur.*"

When the check was presented, Shortreed put some franc notes on the plate. He waited until the waiter left with the money, then told Monique, "We're going to spend the rest of the evening together."

"*Non,*" she said.

"Why?"

"I don't want you to be disappointed when the evening is over."

Shortreed was puzzled. "What do you mean?"

Monique glanced at a nearby table, where a whore coquetted blatantly with an American soldier. "I'm not like her."

Shortreed followed her eyes. "I know that."

With this understood, the thought of spending the evening with Shortreed was not displeasing. "I like you," she admitted.

Shortreed grinned. "I'm falling in like with you too."

He reacted as across the street a pedicab arrived before the Faison d'Or and Sellers dismounted. It was only a moment until, as he was paying his fare, a second pedicab with Maurice and Yvonne pulled up into a more dimly lit area off to the side. Sellers seemed unaware of their presence. Shortreed watched all of this unfold and, getting up from the table, told Monique, "Don't go anywhere. I'll be right back."

He dashed across to catch Sellers before he could go into the bar. Yvonne had left Maurice behind in the second pedicab and gone to intercept Sellers, but when she saw Shortreed, she faded back quickly.

Sellers seemed much better than when Shortreed had last seen him, but he was still unsteady on his feet and looked sick.

"I'm across the street," Shortreed told him, and led Sellers back to the café table.

"That's the one who rescued him," Yvonne told Maurice.

"He too has a bag of money."

"How can you be sure?" she asked.

"If it didn't have something important in it, he would have left it with the girl at the table," he told her.

"You really know your business, don't you," she said with genuine admiration.

"You can tell by how they carry the bags."

"What will we do now?"

"Wait."

As they started for the table, Shortreed stopped Sellers. "Wait until you sit down, then look to the right of the entrance to the Golden Pheasant."

"Why?" Sellers wanted to know.

"The girl you had with you at the Tam Tam is there in a pedicab with a Frenchman."

"So?"

"She knows you have that bag of money."

"Bullshit! How would she know that?"

"While I was rescuing you at the Tam Tam, she was watching it all. Then she slipped out the back door."

"Let's get them!" Sellers' voice was pissed.

"No," Shortreed said. "Just remember that they're following you."

"Who's the broad?" Sellers wanted to know as they approached the table.

"Her name is Monique."

"Hi ya, Monique."

She looked up from her dessert questioningly.

"This is Sellers," Shortreed told her.

Monique nodded acknowledgement. "*Monsieur* Sellers."

"She understands English," Shortreed warned.

"Did you do any good?" Sellers asked him quietly.

"I'm supposed to meet a guy across the street."

"When?"

"Pretty soon."

"Let's wait over there."

"We're supposed to be there at eight o'clock."

Monique kept up with their conversation which was mystifying and of no particular concern to her. But she was aware of the contrast between the two troopers. Sellers was twitchy and impulsive, while Shortreed was like a coiled spring. There was a lot there, but Shortreed was clearly more controlled and conscious of what he was doing than the other American soldier.

Sellers reached over for the wine bottle and took a big drink from it. As he set it back down, Shortreed moved it away from him.

"What the hell is going on here, Shortreed!" Sellers protested.

They made eye contact and Shortreed said softly and levelly, "You were drugged this morning while drunk. The woman who was with you when that happened is following you now. They know what's in that bag."

"Maybe." Sellers took back the bottle and drank from it again.

"If you don't keep your head out of your ass," Shortreed told him, "they'll take you for everything you've got."

As they were talking, a pedicab pulled up across the street from the *Faison d'Or* and Antoine got out and limped his way toward the entrance. Shortreed nudged Sellers who was in the middle of taking another swig from the bottle.

"See what I see?"

Monique, sipping her wine, followed his glance. Something was happening and she was beginning to feel interest.

Sellers was incredulous. "Is that your man?"

"Could be."

Angrily Sellers pushed to his feet and would have gone after Antoine, had Shortreed not grabbed him and shoved him back down at an empty table nearby.

"Where in hell do you think you're going!"

"He's one of the guys who tried to poison me!" Sellers was enraged. He pulled free and made another effort to leave, but again Shortreed pushed him back down at the table.

"Don't stir shit!"

"Why?"

"We've got less than ten days left to change this dough."

"Is that all?"

They were sitting too far away for Monique to hear, but the tension was obvious. She tried to make sense of what was going on.

"Ten days," Shortreed said again. "That's all."

"I'm going to desert!" Sellers decided.

"You fool!"

"Come with me!"

"Knock it off."

"We can make it to Switzerland with no sweat," Sellers insisted.

Shortreed shook his head. "If you go, you're going by yourself."

"If we don't get this money exchanged soon, I'm going!" There was no doubt in Sellers' mind. He was definite.

"Count me out."

"Okay, you're out."

"You know you can't go to Switzerland and just walk in."

"You want to bet?"

"You're going to need a passport. Identification."

"I'll bribe someone."

"You're having another wet dream," Shortreed said with contempt. "Your best chance is right here."

"Then we ought to get on the ball!"

"Go back to the Hotel Albert and wait."

"Wait! For what?" Sellers protested angrily. "I need to get moving on changing this money!"

"The desk clerk is going to bring someone up to our room to talk about it."

"When?"

"This evening."

"How come you're not going to be there too?" Sellers asked suspiciously.

"He's not going to bring money. He's just going to talk about a deal."

"So how do we hook up again?"

"Leave a message for me at the desk."

"You ought to come with me," Sellers insisted.

"I'm busy."

Sellers cut his eye over at Monique. "That's all you ever think about."

"You need to rest."

"Yeah, it wouldn't hurt." Sellers put his hand to his forehead. "What a fucking headache!"

"Take off, Sellers."

Seller started to protest, then reached a decision. He rose from the table. "See you."

"Don't forget." Shortreed looked across the street at Maurice and Monique. "Those two are following you."

"Fuck them," Sellers said like he meant it, and hailed a pedicab.

As Shortreed went back to Monique, it was no surprise for him to see the pedicab carrying Maurice and Yvonne make a u-turn and follow after Sellers. Monique looked up at him with a smile from the last lingering bite of her dessert, and he smiled back. He offered her a cigarette and, lighting it for her, asked, "What would you like to do next?"

"It's a nice evening. Let's take a walk," she suggested.

"Sounds good to me." He reached a hand to pull her to her feet.

With Shortreed carrying her suitcase, they walked together along the middle of the street. It was early evening, and people on foot shared the street with the pedicabs. The bars were going full blast and many couples were moving between them and strolling about.

At first Monique seemed to be enjoying herself. But then she became nervous and turned inward, barely giving Shortreed the most cursory attention. He started to get angry but then became aware that the bemedalled Frenchman he had run off earlier was again following them at a safe distance. He stopped and turned Monique to face him.

"That guy is back and he's following us," he said. " Not that this is news to you."

She tried to make little of it. "It's not important."

"I can see that from the way you're acting," Shortreed said sarcastically.

She was silent.

"It's real easy," he told her. "We'll lead him down a side street and - "

"No, no." She was adamant.

"What is the guy to you?"

"Nothing."

"Then let me comb him out of your hair."

"I don't want you to get in trouble over me," Monique insisted.

"Well I'm going to kick his ass anyway."

Setting the suitcase down, he started back toward the Frenchman. It was plain that he intended to fight.

"Don't, Shortreed!" she called after him.

He ignored her.

"I won't be here when you get back."

She picked up her suitcase and began to walk away quickly. Shortreed stopped, caught between wanting to get rid of the Frenchman and the prospect of losing Monique.

To her relief, he turned and ran after her. Pulling the suitcase from her hand, he tossed it into a pedicab that was parked nearby,

"Come on, Monique!"

"No!" she told him. "If you stay with me you'll just get in trouble."

Undeterred, Shortreed scooped her up in his arms and deposited her in the pedicab.

"Will you take us up to the Old Quarter?" he asked the driver.

"*Oui*."

As the driver pulled away from the curb, Shortreed handed him a thousand franc note.

"*Tout suite*?"

"*Oui, Oui!*" the driver agreed and pedaled away briskly. A moment after their departure Charles hurried up and jumped into a pedicab. At once it pulled away, following after Shortreed and Monique.

<u>End of Chapter 13</u>

Chapter 14

The Criminal Investigation Division of the U.S. armed services was charged with investigating crimes committed by American servicemen or civilians trafficking in stolen U.S. property. In Nice the CID had its headquarters in the basement of one of the better hotels in the city. Locally most of their investigations involved stolen American cigarettes and army rations as well as the black market network that trafficked in such items.

Captain Walters was the officer in charge of field operations. His father had been a minor official in the American diplomatic corps and he had been raised in Paris. As a result of his upbringing, his French language skills were extensive and his accent convincing. Walters was no desk jockey. He reveled in undercover work and, when dressed in hand-me-down civilian clothing, was a believable copy of a low level black marketer, equally convincing to Frenchmen and American servicemen alike.

It was eight-thirty P.M., and Captain Walters was prepping his surveillance detail for the evening assignment. There were three enlisted men in uniform, one of whom was Staff Sergeant Wilson who was armed with a .45 automatic.

As he put the finishing touches to his civilian costume, Walters advised the sergeant, "Don't stay so close tonight with the backup."

"Sir, we had to stay close last night. There was a dead space for the radio where we should've been."

"If you have the same problem tonight, find a good spot further away from me, not closer." He put on a worn beret. "That's an order."

"Yes, sir." Wilson said and added, " Have you read the report from the day watch?"

"It was the same old thing."

"Sir, the word on the street is that some soldier on leave in town has a big bag of French francs."

Walters paused in adjusting the angle of the beret. "Who told you that?"

"Bouchard, sir."

"The pimp?"

"Yes, sir."

"He's usually full of shit," Walters said matter-of-factly. Finished with the beret, he picked up a small automatic, shoved it into a holster inside his waistband and ordered, "Let's roll."

Together Walters and the three enlisted men went out to the alley where a jeep waited. The enlisted men got into the jeep, while the Captain took a bicycle from a nearby rack.

"I'll make my first stop at the Café Tam Tam," he told Wilson. "When I leave I want to know if I'm being followed."

"Yes, sir."

"Then I'll wait at the bottom of the hill and if Antoine leaves we'll tail him."

"What if he's not there, sir?" the sergeant asked, handing Walters a battered briefcase.

"We'll look for him." Walters took a walkie-talkie from the briefcase.

"Did you check the batteries?"

"Yes, sir. There's a new battery in your set and ours."

"All right, let's move out."

The driver started the jeep and, as it moved away, Walters pedaled off into the darkness.

Walters was not the only one pedaling on the main street that led uphill to the Old Quarter. Shortreed had taken over from the pedicab driver and was pumping the pedals as hard as he could.

The exhausted driver sat beside Monique in a state of near collapse. Monique was frightened and trying to ignore their headlong flight, but Shortreed was in his element. He stood on the pedals, pumping his legs furiously as he moved in and out through the uphill traffic. He was certain that somewhere on the hill behind them the Frenchman was tailing along, doing his best to keep them in sight. Well, let him! Unless he was in better condition than Shortreed, he was doomed to be an also-ran.

At last Shortreed felt they had enough of a lead that he could give the Frenchman the slip by turning off onto one of the side streets that ran at a right angle to the main street. Turning the corner, Shortreed flogged himself to a maximum effort until he came to another street that ran uphill toward the old part of the city. Here he stopped and looked back the way they had come. Satisfied that they had lost Charles, he dismounted and helped Monique from the pedicab.

"This looks like a pension," Shortreed indicated a nearby building. "Let's spend the night here."

"No."

"Why?"

"I don't want to go to bed with you," she told him.

Shortreed gently turned her face to look at him. "If you say no, that's the way it will be."

"No," she said again and walked away with her suitcase.

Shortreed caught up with her. "I really meant what I said."

"I'll find my own pension," she told him and would have walked away, but Shortreed held onto her.

"You don't have any money."

"I have enough."

Before she could stop him, he took her purse and opened it, revealing that it contained only a single twenty franc note.

"Twenty francs." He shook his head. "You couldn't rent a park bench for that."

He gave her back the purse. For a moment she remained resolute but she began to wilt under the stress of what he had said. Shortreed waited patiently for her to face up to the truth of her reality.

Finally she sighed. "I don't even know you." She sounded alone and defeated.

Shortreed spoke gently and from the heart. "We'll take the time to get acquainted first."

Monique closed her eyes in misery. "No."

"The truth is you've got no money," he told her.

She hung her head in shame and defeat.

"And no place to go."

After a long moment, she consented tonelessly, "All right."

Shortreed put his arm around her and, carrying his musette bag and her suitcase in his other hand, he took her into the pension where he paid the *concierge* for what she promised him was her best room. In the daytime there would be a view of the ocean.

After the *concierge* left, Shortreed set the bags down. Monique opened hers and took a few things from it. She was silent and withdrawn. He tried to start a conversation, but the awkwardness between them made it limited and strained.

"Where are you from?" Shortreed asked.

"Marseilles."

She stood with a dress in her hands and finally put it over a hangar. Shortreed took it from her and hung it in the closet. She simply stood and looked at him. But when he turned from her to close her suitcase and put it on the floor of the closet, she turned out the single light. It left the room in darkness, except for the spill from a streetlight outside near their window.

In this semi-darkness, Monique stood rigidly with her back to him. There was an awkward moment then Monique, as if determined to get it over with, began to unbutton her dress.

Shortreed stood behind her and watched her without comment. Burdened down with shame and defeat, she finished with the last of the buttons and let the dress fall to the floor. She started to remove her slip, but Shortreed stopped her.

"Monique."

"Yes."

He turned her to face him so that their eyes met.

"You misunderstood me," he said.

"How?" She was faintly sarcastic.

"I do want to get acquainted first."

Monique was puzzled but relieved.

She looked at him for a long moment, then they both smiled.

"You're a very strange man."

Shortreed went and took a blanket from the bed. He spread it on the floor near the window.

"You can sleep on the bed and I'll bunk here on the floor."

She went and lay on the bed without covering up, and watched the lights of the city far below. After several moments, she felt a pressure on the mattress as Shortreed sat down beside her. She tensed, but he was careful not to touch her.

"Do you like Nice?" he asked."

"I came here from Cannes yesterday." She was silent for a moment, then went on, "Marseilles, Cannes, Nice, after a while they're all the same."

"It's okay to run. As long as you're running to something," Shortreed commented.

Monique looked puzzled. "What do you mean?"

"I can get that guy off your back with no sweat," he told her.

She did not respond. Instead she looked away for a moment at the lights below, then change the subject.

"See those lights down there?"

"What about them?"

"That's the promenade."

"It's so full of soldiers it might as well be an army camp."

"I think it's beautiful from here."

"It's the fanciest sewer in the world," he said with disgust. "It comes from nowhere and it goes nowhere. And it's full of people, all doing the same thing."

"Down there, they are enjoying themselves," she contradicted.

"They're pretending!"

Her voice was faintly teasing. "But you never pretend."

Shortreed was silent for a moment, then answered. "That's the first thing you learn in the army."

"What does a soldier pretend?"

"That you're not afraid." He spoke with some difficulty. "That seven days furlough goes on forever." He did not speak for a moment, but it was clear there would be more coming and she waited.

Finally, she prodded him gently, "And?"

"That your friends aren't all dead."

He stopped abruptly and stared moodily at the lights below. His mind was somewhere else, perhaps in some private hell. Instinctively, Monique moved closer to him, sensible to his inner turmoil.

"Shortreed." She spoke softly.

"Yeah."

"What about women?"

He answered somberly but without bitterness. "Women? They're all beautiful, and true and in love. For a thousand francs a night or a fancy car. Or just because they're bored."

"We're not all like that," she countered.

Shortreed shrugged. "Maybe."

He got up from the bed and went to where the blanket was spread on the floor. Picking up the musette bag stuffed with money, he put it against the wall, then lay down beside it. After a moment he said, "There's two kinds of women in this world. The ones like those in the streets down there and…"

He stopped there, then pulled the blanket over him. Monique watched from the bed as he took the pistol from the bag then shoved the bag under his head as a pillow.

"And what?" she demanded.

"And the others." He pulled the blanket up under his chin and shut his eyes. As far as he was concerned, the subject was closed.

Not so with Monique. She propped her chin in her hand, considered him for a moment, then spoke. "Shortreed."

He opened his eyes and looked at her.

"Someday, if you are lucky, you will learn to tell us apart."

Her eyes met his defiantly. Then she smiled sweetly and said, "Good night, Shortreed."

For a long time he lay awake, thinking about her. Monique was different from the others and the difference was exciting and alluring. Perhaps it was because they hadn't jumped into bed together at the first opportunity, Nah, it wasn't that, it was more, something mysterious that he couldn't place. One thing was sure, whatever the attraction was, he could feel it tugging at him and he resolved that he would not let himself fall in love. Then why was he playing such an elaborate game with her? Or with himself? Or was it a game? He fell asleep with no answers.

Down below in the city, the night's revelry was going full blast. By this hour almost everyone who wanted a woman had one, and those who found better solace in booze were roaring drunk. The town was jumping as these survivors of countless firefights and artillery barrages submerged their battle jangles in an orgiastic revel of women and alcohol.

Sergeant Wilson and his crew had parked their jeep inconspicuously in the shadows. Now Wilson spoke into the walkie-talkie, "Surveillance one to surveillance two."

He repeated this several times before there was a crackle from the radio and Captain Walters' voice responded, "Surveillance two to surveillance one, come in."

"We've lost contact," Wilson said.

"Subject is proceeding in a pedicab south along Rue Andre Theirau," Walter told him.

"I read you. Over and out." The sergeant released the talk button and nodded to the driver who put the jeep in gear, and they eased back out onto the street.

On the side street where the Hotel Albert was located, things were much the same. The only difference was that the density levels were lower. The soldiers were just as wild and just as drunk, but there were fewer of them. There were a few pedicabs moving along with amorous couples.

Across the street from the hotel, Captain Walters sat astride his bicycle in a patch of shadow. He was watching as Antoine alighted awkwardly from a pedicab and began to limp toward the hotel entrance. Walters slipped the walkie-talkie from his battered briefcase.

"Surveillance two to surveillance one," he said softly as he followed Antoine's progress.

The response was immediate. "Surveillance two, we have you loud and clear. Come in."

"Subject entering Hotel Albert. Do not contact me until further notice. Over and out."

"Roger, out," Surveillance One replied tersely and there was silence.

Walters slid his radio back into the briefcase under some loose packs of American cigarettes and, leaving his bike in the shadows, strode across the street to the hotel entrance.

In his hotel room upstairs, Sellers sat near the window smoking edgily, with an open bottle of wine on the windowsill beside him, and his .45 automatic lying beside the wine bottle. At a soft knock, he stubbed out the cigarette, grabbed the .45 and went to the door. He opened it cautiously to see Antoine, who smiled at him sardonically and said, "*Monsieur*. We meet again."

Sellers widened the crack in the door, allowing Antoine to enter. Then he slammed it shut and wheeled to face the still smiling Frenchman. Shoving the automatic into Antoine's belly, he snarled, "I ought to blow your guts out!"

"But you won't," Antoine said calmly.

"Motherfucker!"

Savagely Sellers kicked Antoine's legs from under him, sending him sprawling in an ungainly heap on the floor. Antoine cried out in pain as the fall twisted his prosthetic leg at an ungainly and unnatural angle. Sellers aimed a second kick at Antoine's head, stopping only as he heard, "The money, *Monsieu*r. Please think of your money."

Desperately Antoine told the outraged and half-drunken trooper, "I have made all the arrangements."

"Fuck you!" Sellers snarled.

"In two days, you can have Swiss francs!"

"You doped me!" Sellers would not be appeased

"You can have all the Swiss francs you want!" Antoine pleaded.

"Keep talking."

Still in pain, the Frenchman tried to rise but was unable to. He tried again without success.

"Help me."

Instead Sellers asked him, "What's your proposition?"

"Your money exchanged at sixty percent of the face value."

"For Swiss francs."

"*Oui.*"

"That don't sound like much." Sellers was unimpressed.

"It is the standard price."

Sellers reached for the wine bottle and took a big drink. "What are you making out of it?"

"I buy at sixty percent face value and I sell at seventy-five."

"How do I know you won't try to steal it again?" Sellers wanted to know.

Antoine had regained some of his composure. "You don't. But it's a chance we both take."

After a thoughtful moment, Sellers nodded. "Okay, it's a deal."

"First you must show me the money."

Sellers took his musette bag from the bed and dumped it in Antoine's lap. Visibly impressed, the Frenchman grabbed a sheaf of bills and began counting.

"It's all thousand franc notes," Sellers told him.

"How many?"

"Fifteen or twenty thousand."

Sellers laid his gun on the floor where it would be handy, and began replacing the packages of money in the bag.

"Your friend," Antoine asked, watching him. "Does he have money also?"

Sellers took the bag and his gun and laid them on the bed.

"He's got about the same amount."

"*Bien*. Come to the Tam Tam at three o'clock this Thursday."

"Fuck that!" Sellers told him. "You bring the money here."

"Impossible."

"Why?"

Antoine laughed. "You might be tempted to steal it."

Their eyes met, then Antoine continued. "The people with the Swiss francs are known criminals who would attract the attention of the police if they came to this part of town."

"I'll have to talk to my partner."

"You'll be there." Antoine said confidently.

Taking up the .45, Sellers cocked the pistol and put it against Antoine's head. "You know something, Jocko? If you think you're going to steal this money, you got another think coming."

Clearly he was not bluffing. Thoroughly intimidated, Antoine did his best to maintain his composure. "Now that we have a deal, you can trust me."

Sellers took the gun from Antoine's head, uncocked it and shoved it inside his waistband. While the American was lighting a cigarette, Antoine crawled to the bed and pulled himself to his feet with difficulty. With his prosthetic leg at an odd angle, he presented an ungainly and pathetic picture. Sellers watched without emotion as Antoine made his painful way to the door and paused there.

"Thursday at three o'clock in the afternoon?" Sellers asked.

"At the Tam Tam," Antoine added.

Sellers went to the door as if to open it, but instead aimed another kick at Antoine's legs.

His eyes blazing with fury, Antoine yelled at him, "Stop! We're even now! If you have any sense, you will leave it that way!"

Equally enraged, Sellers glared back at him and for a moment the two were locked in a silent confrontation. Then Antoine broke the spell. "Think of your money."

Sellers took a big swig from the wine bottle. "I'll see you Thursday,"

"At three o'clock," Antoine reminded as he left, closing the door behind him.

Sellers stared at the closed door, then grinned drunkenly. "Senator Sellers. Don't that sound nice."

Below in the lobby, Captain Walters still in his guise as a shabby civilian black marketer, stood near the entrance door haggling with two paratroopers over the price of a carton of cigarettes. Stalling for time, he was purposely offering them a very low price for their cigarettes. The troopers referred to Walters as "Frenchie" and were loudly condescending and abusive. In the middle of their diatribe, Antoine came slowly down the stairs and made his way around them, his lips tightly held against the pain from the stump of his leg.

Walters watched covertly as Antoine limped past them and left. Quickly agreeing to the price the troopers were demanding for their cigarettes, he paid them, took the carton and went out the door. The troopers also left, and the lobby of the hotel was empty except for the room clerk nodding at his desk and the drunken sergeant in the corner.

At midmorning the next day Shortreed and Monique arrived by pedicab at the Hotel Albert. The town and the streets were beginning to show signs of life as soldiers moved along in small groups, laughing, drinking, ogling girls and nursing hangovers. Near the entrance to the hotel, the horse drawn *fiacre* and its driver waited. Paying off the pedicab operator, Shortreed transferred Monique to the *fiacre*. The hung-over driver was visibly nursing a morning-after headache but, ignoring this, Shortreed greeted him breezily, *"Bonjour."*

The driver acknowledged this with a glance and retreated into his misery.

"I'm going to leave Monique with you and go get my friend. Wait here," Shortreed told him.

The driver nodded. As Shortreed started to leave, Monique spoke.

"Shortreed."

He turned back to her. "What?"

She started to say something, but stopped. After a moment she touched him on the shoulder and smiled. "Hurry back."

Something in her manner hinted at an intimacy that was growing unbidden between them. There was a brief electric moment of eye contact that silently acknowledged their mutual need to love and to be loved.

"Hurry back," she urged him again warmly. She watched until he disappeared into the hotel, smiling until she was approached by a soldier who shoved his way to her from the crowded sidewalk.

"Hello baby."

She turned away and tried to ignore him. But he was insistent.

"Are you waiting for someone?"

"*Je ne parle pas l'anglais.*"

Grinning, the soldier moved closer. "Let me teach you."

Again she tried to ignore him. "*Non.*"

"Then you can teach me some French." The soldier put his foot on a step of the *fiacre* as if preparing to mount up and sit beside her.

At this moment Shortreed and Sellers emerged from the hotel and started for the *fiacre.* When Shortreed caught sight of the intruder, he exploded into action. Striding to the *fiacre,* he grabbed the soldier by the collar and yanked him back to the sidewalk. The soldier whirled to face Shortreed.

"Oh," the soldier said as he measured Shortreed. "She's waiting for you."

"That's right, buddy," Shortreed told him, then added, "Goodbye."

Glaring back at Shortreed, the soldier made no effort to leave and stood his ground. Seemingly casually and without braggadocio, Shortreed dropped his musette bag to the sidewalk. The soldier got the picture. He shrugged and grinned.

"You can't blame a feller for trying."

"Okay, you tried," Shortreed told him. "Now beat it."

When he took off, Shortreed retrieved his bag of money from the sidewalk and climbed in beside Monique. As Sellers joined them, she moved closer to Shortreed.

"Is there a bank in this town?" Shortreed wanted to know.

"There must be."

"Where is it?"

"Ask the driver," she told him.

Sellers was alarmed at this exchange. He asked Shortreed suspiciously, "What do you want with a bank?"

"I want to make a deposit. Two months' pay."

"Man, I told you the deal was set!"

"I like to have an ace in the hole."

"If you start messing around with a bank, you could fuck up the whole deal."

"Relax, Sellers," Shortreed said. "You worry too much."

Sellers said fiercely but quietly for Shortreed's hearing alone, "I can't understand a guy with as much money as you have, worrying about a few thousand francs."

"Shut up," Shortreed said, then called out to the driver, "Take us to a bank."

"*Oui, monsieur.*"

The driver shook his reins and the *fiacre* pulled away from the curb.

As they rode the short distance to the bank, Sellers smoldered silently. This going to the bank seemed stupid to him. Why risk close to half a million dollars in order to be sure of having a few thousand?

When the driver brought the *fiacre* to a halt before the bank, they could see that the sidewalk in front of the bank was teeming with soldiers, girls and hustlers of every type. Sellers watched with disapproval as Shortreed handed Monique a packet of thousand franc notes. She took them gingerly.

"What's this for?"

"Go inside and open an account in your name," Shortreed instructed her.

"I don't understand."

"Just do like I tell you."

She still hesitated.

"I'll explain later."

Still puzzled, Monique got down from the *fiacre* and went inside the bank.

Sellers continued to scowl. "Are you falling in love, Shortreed?"

"Nah."

"Did she know you had all that money before she went to bed with you?" Sellers wanted to know. His tone of voice was derisive.

"She hasn't gone to bed with me," Shortreed said defensively, knowing in his heart of hearts that he had already fallen in like with her, and like could turn into love with no warning.

"Sounds like love to me," Sellers persisted.

"Shut up!" Shortreed said angrily.

Sellers laughed nastily. "I watched you do this once before."

"Yeah, when?"

"You don't remember?"

"Let's drop the subject."

"What about Helen?"

"I didn't love her."

"You thought you did."

"She was nobody to me!"

"You know, Shortreed, for a guy as smart as you are about some things, you sure are dumb about broads."

"Get off my back!" Shortreed snarled.

"Helen didn't marry you because you were Roy Shortreed."

"Why then?"

"Because you were a paratrooper. A prize she could show off."

"That doesn't have anything to do with Monique!"

"You wish."

"I know!"

"She's working you for all you're worth," Sellers said with conviction.

"She doesn't know about the money."

Sellers laughed nastily. "She does now."

"What do you know about women?" Shortreed challenged.

"I've had as many as you had."

"What did you pay them?"

"Money! The same as you paid the girls you had when the cops were chasing you."

"That was a one shot."

"Everyone says that."

Suddenly, like a snake striking, Shortreed grabbed Sellers by the necktie and pulled him close until they were face-to-face, eye-to-eye.

"Knock this shit off! If you don't quit lecturing me, I'm going to pound your fucking head in!"

"Forgot this woman, Shortreed!" Sellers pleaded. "Antoine's the one we have to worry about!"

Slowly Shortreed released him.

"There's nothing we can do about Antoine."

"I got a plan," Sellers told him. "We're supposed to be at the Tam Tam at three o'clock tomorrow."

"So?"

"We'll show up when they open at eleven."

"Why?"

"We'll take over till the money comes."

"Suit yourself."

"Don't you see? If he's running a game, we'll bust it up."

"I'll be busy until three."

"With that broad," Sellers said disgustedly.

Monique came out of the bank. With difficulty she made her way across the crowded sidewalk toward the *fiacre*.

"When we get this money changed, you'll have enough to buy any woman in the world."

Shortreed saw Monique approaching and told Sellers contemptuously, "You were born a two bit hustler and you'll die one!" Dismounting, he helped her back into the *fiacre*.

"Because I like money?" Sellers challenged.

"Because you like it too much."

"There are other things?" Sellers asked sarcastically.

Shortreed glanced at Monique. "Yeah."

"Whatever those things are, " Sellers told him nastily, "I can get them for you wholesale."

"Knock it off, Sellers," Shortreed warned.

"You want power?" Sellers asked him loudly. "You want people to bow and scrape? You want broads falling all over you?"

"You're pissing me off, Sellers!" Shortreed warned.

"All it takes is money."

"Bail out, Sellers!" Shortreed's voice was flat and deadly. "Now!"

Sellers jumped to the street and turned back to face Shortreed. For a moment, the two glared at each other. Monique watched this clash of wills and values with interest.

It was Shortreed who put a stop to the confrontation. "Tomorrow at three o'clock. I'll see you there."

Sellers looked Monique over with open contempt. "So long, chump."

He stalked off angrily and disappeared into the crowd on the sidewalk. Shortreed leaned forward to tap the driver of the *fiacre* on the arm and gestured for him to drive away.

"Did they ask you a bunch of questions in the bank?" Shortreed asked Monique.

She was troubled and did not answer him immediately. "No." After a moment, she inquired, "The money. Was it stolen?"

"Not exactly."

"Why did you give it to me?"

"How much did you have last night?"

"Twenty francs."

"You stayed with me last night because you had no place to go. Right?"

She nodded mutely.

"If you stay with me tonight it will be because that's what you want to do."

"Shortreed, don't build your dreams around me," she pleaded.

"Why?"

"I'm not what you think I am."

"Let me make up my own mind, will you."

"Take your money back," she said unhappily, "and let's say goodbye."

Her eyes were fixed on the floor of the *fiacre*. The tragedy of her life and memories of the war weighed heavily on her.

Gently, Shortreed tilted her face up. "You really want to say goodbye?"

"I'm afraid of you, Shortreed."

"Why?"

"The gun. The money."

"That's not what's bothering you," he challenged her.

"No?"

"You're afraid of getting involved."

"Aren't you?" she asked him shyly.

"I'm willing to take a chance if you are."

For a moment she looked at him silently, asking herself, did she really want to get involved with this strange man? He was dangerous, tender, exciting, and wounded in so many ways.

As they passed a flower stand, Shortreed grabbed a bouquet of flowers and tossed the attendant a hundred francs. He handed the bouquet to Monique and she buried her nose in their fragrance.

"Well?" Shortreed prodded her.

"Well what?"

"You feel like taking a chance?"

She smiled at him. "I'm not sure."

But after a moment she cuddled closer to him and Shortreed put his arm around her.

<u>End of Chapter 14</u>

Chapter 15

Later Sellers picked up Celeste along the street. She was a dyed blonde with a great body and a vacant face, which bothered him not at all. He wasn't looking for a life partner, but just a quick fix and a pleasant way to kill time until eleven o'clock tomorrow.

Tailing along discretely behind him were Yvonne and Maurice in a pedicab operated by Pierre, who worked often with Maurice. Yvonne was wearing slacks and looked very different from the way she had looked at the Tam Tam. She had on a minimum of makeup and a hat slouched over her face and was fairly certain that she would be unrecognizable to Sellers if he saw her only at a distance.

The two in the pedicab were silent and deliberate, with all of their attention focused on following Sellers and his new lady of the evening. At last Sellers and Celeste came to the *pension* that was her base of operations and went inside.

"They'll be there a long time," Yvonne said with assurance.

Maurice looked at her questioningly and she explained, "He kept me busy all night."

"What do you know about her?" he asked Pierre.

"She's an amateur from Marseilles," Pierre said.

"Amateur?"

"She doesn't even have a pimp."

Maurice considered this in silence.

"What now?" Yvonne asked him.

"Stay here with Jacques," he ordered and started to get out of the pedicab.

She grabbed at his arm. He shook it free, telling her, " I have other business to attend to."

"*Non!*" she protested. "Do you think I am going to sit here all day while he and that little bitch from Marseilles are tearing up her bed together?"

"If you go with me, there is nothing for you to do," Maurice told her.

"And if I stay here there is less than nothing!"

He shrugged.

"Suit yourself."

She got out of the pedicab. Maurice instructed Pierre to follow the soldier if he left the *pension*, and they took another pedicab to the building where Maurice kept his contraband. There was a horse-drawn wagon tethered nearby, but the driver was nowhere to be seen.

Maurice paid off the pedicab and waited with Yvonne in silence until it had disappeared around a corner. Then he gave a low whistle. The driver of the wagon hurried from hiding and climbed to the driver's bench.

Quickly Maurice swung the gate open and the wagon drove into the small courtyard. Just as quickly he and Yvonne entered and barred the gate behind them. The wagon was piled high with lawn keeper's equipment and what appeared to be grass clippings covered with a tarp.

In reality, beneath the tarp were cases of stolen G.I. chocolate. They were worth a small fortune on the black market.

"How many?" Maurice asked the driver.

"Twenty four cases," he replied.

"You know where they go."

As the driver began unloading, Maurice and Yvonne went inside and sat at the table. Maurice poured himself a large drink of cognac and she lit a cigarette, then kicked off her shoes. She watched as the driver passed through the hallway beyond the room with his arms full of boxes, then said, " I want some new clothes."

"Don't start that again." Maurice took a generous swallow of his cognac.

"But you promised."

"If we start spending that kind of money it will attract too much attention."

"We could go to Paris."

'Not now. We're too busy."

"Money!" she said fiercely. "That's all you ever think about. You never think about me!"

Suddenly, the driver ran into the room in a panic. "Soldiers! Everywhere! It's a raid!"

Outside there was a loud crash as the raiding party broke through the barred gate with an armored halftrack. It stopped inside the courtyard with its .50 caliber machinegun menacing the front entrance. A detail of armed soldiers ran into the courtyard and from there into the house.

When the raid started, Maurice drew his automatic and raced to the back door, only to find the alleyway filled with soldiers. Desperately he sprinted to the stairwell that led to the upper stories. He reached the stairwell just ahead of the American sergeant, Wilson. As Maurice lunged up the stairs, Wilson shouted in French, "Stop or I'll shoot!"

Maurice replied with two quick shots of his automatic and disappeared up the stairs. Not intimidated, the sergeant took the stairs two at a time in pursuit. Near the fourth level he began gaining on Maurice and called once more for him to surrender. Again Maurice responded with gunfire. Sergeant Wilson replied in kind, and the wall-rattling boom of his .45 panicked Maurice, who fled to the roof with the sergeant at his heels.

The roof was four stories above ground level and was in the middle of a large group of similar four-story buildings. Each was separated from its neighbor by a narrow passageway. By taking a slight run across the roof, Maurice could leap across the gap to the next building. By the time the sergeant had reached the roof, Maurice was already on the roof of the adjoining building and was preparing to jump to the next one.

On the top of each roof the stairs terminated in a telephone booth-like structure. Maurice would jump from one roof to the next, then dodge behind the booth-like structure and keep running to his next leap. This enabled him to keep the sergeant's line of sight blocked except for the few seconds when he actually made his leap.

Wilson took advantage of these moments of exposure to fire at the fleeing Frenchman. One of his rounds came so close to Maurice that he dove for cover behind a stair terminal. From this cover he emptied his automatic at his pursuer in a vain effort to stop him. The sergeant responded with rapid fire but after three rounds his clip was empty. When he reached to his web belt for another clip, Maurice seized the opportunity and dashed into the stair terminal, seeing a chance to make his way to the street and freedom.

But *merde*! He discovered the door was locked!

Frantically, he turned and ran toward the next building. As he ran, he could hear the sergeant shoving a fresh clip in place and the sound of the slide slamming a live round into the chamber of the sergeant's .45. Spurred on by these sounds, Maurice made a desperate last-chance dash for freedom.

He made it to the jump before the sergeant could fire, but all this exertion had weakened him and he jumped short, failing to land on the next roof. The best he could do was to grab the cornice with his hands. This left him dangling four stories above the ground without enough strength to pull himself up onto the roof.

A moment later when the sergeant got there, he found himself staring across the gap at a terrified man who was about to fall to his death and begging desperately for help. Wilson backed off for a running jump. If Maurice could hang on until he got across, he would rescue him. But as the sergeant leapt to the other building Maurice's grip failed and, with a cry of anguish, he plummeted the four stories to the cobblestones below.

This all flashed across Wilson's vision while he was still in the air. Landing, he twisted back to look at the crumpled figure awkwardly sprawled on the ground below. The sergeant was no philosopher and would never understand the dynamics of how he could be willing to blow someone's ass off one minute and end up crushed because he couldn't rescue him a minute later. For a moment he desperately wished he was out of the war, out of the army, and home again with his wife and kids.

Back where the raid was taking place, the raiding party was busy mopping up. Two army trucks were now parked near the shattered gate to the courtyard, and a steady line of soldiers were loading Maurice's store of contraband into the waiting vehicles.

In the main room Yvonne sat at a table under the watchful eye of a corporal with an M-1 slung over his shoulder. The skirt of her dress was pushed above her knees, displaying her shapely legs to the best advantage. The corporal was well aware that she was after something, but he couldn't help being a little titillated by the sight of so much leg.

She spoke suddenly. "*Monsieur* Corporal, I would like to make you an offer."

"What is it?"

"Captain Walters was in the hall a moment ago."

"So?" His voice was wary.

"I want to talk to him."

"That's not an offer."

"If you get him for me, you can spend a night with me free."

"Why do you want to talk to him?" the corporal challenged.

"I have information he would like to have."

"I don't know," he said doubtfully.

Slowly she inched her dress even higher.

"I usually get a thousand francs."

This was too much for the corporal. He unslung his M1 and held it ready.

"Okay, let's go find the captain."

Captain Walters was overseeing the loading of the last of the contraband when the corporal marched Yvonne up to where he stood.

"What's this all about, corporal?" he asked.

"She says that she has important information for you."

Walters looked Yvonne over for a moment, then said, "I know you. I've seen you before."

"I'm not a criminal. I'm a licensed working girl," she told him.

"What's the information?"

'There's an American paratrooper in town who has a large bag of money.'

"We've already heard that rumor."

The captain turned away from her. But Yvonne called after him.

"Do you know his name and where he's staying?"

The captain showed interest and turned back to her. "Do you?"

"Let me go and I'll tell you," she offered.

"If you're lying, we can always pick you up again."

"I know that."

"Okay," he decided. "What's his name and where is he staying?"

"His name is Sellers and he's at the Hotel Albert."

"Anything else?"

"He's good in bed."

The captain laughed. "Get out of here."

She exchanged a quick glance with the corporal, acknowledging her debt, then went out hastily onto the darkening street, still unaware that Maurice had died in his fall from the roof. Her fury at the American pigs would await that discovery.

It was after dark when Shortreed and Monique returned to their *pension* after what had been a frustrating day of subtle and at times less than subtle probing of each other's inner being. Both were hag-ridden by memories of past disastrous relationships that had mangled their willingness to become involved in the vulnerability of real love.

Chance encounters were part of the wartime mindset. They brightened a night, a week, a furlough, and were gone. Such moments were incomplete, and they left behind an emptiness that ached for fulfillment.

Both Shortreed and Monique felt this, but neither could overcome the fear of disillusionment and reach out fully to the other. The promise was there, and both were aware of it. The prize was the great jewel of human existence – love. Yet the sparring continued.

With the coming of nightfall they had pushed such considerations aside, and had taken refuge in small talk and inconsequential conversations over a bottle of cognac.

Now Shortreed dismissed the driver of the *fiacre* with instructions to pick them up next morning, and, to bring a picnic basket. They went on into the *pension*.

Monique kicked off her shoes and lay down on the bed fully dressed. Shortreed sat down on the end of the bed, pulled the cork from the cognac and held it out to her. She shook her head. He shrugged and took a big drink from the bottle.

"Why did you order the picnic basket?" she asked.

"In the morning we're going on a picnic," he told her.

"Your friend wanted you to meet him someplace at eleven."

"The appointment is for three o'clock in the afternoon and he's not my friend."

After a moment of silence she rolled over on her side.

"I'm going to sleep."

He watched in silence until finally she was breathing deeply and sound asleep. Then he returned to his pallet by the window, where he made himself comfortable on the floor and began drinking in earnest.

If they had been going to make love tonight, he would have bought wine, the lover's friend. But love wasn't in the cards, and cognac was the drink for forgetting. God knows, Shortreed told himself, he had a lot to forget.

But this line of thought brought up the image of the sergeant lying drunk in the corner of the lobby of the Hotel Albert. He didn't want to get that drunk. Resolutely he corked the bottle and set it aside. For a long time he struggled to resolve the conflict he felt in his mind about the girl asleep on the bed.

She was beautiful, exciting, magical, and when she smiled she seemed to shine a light on him, a light that illuminated forgotten places in his inner being. Places that had been walled off by the war, with its blood and anger, and its anguish. Why should he not seize the opportunity to open the door to that space by pulling her into his arms and making himself whole again?

But mixed with this was a cynicism that had been born of the same blood and disillusionment and anguish. After all the shit that had been heaped on him by his wife, why should he stick his neck out for more wounds? Memories of his wife Helen flooded into his mind. What a trashy bitch! Angrily he reached again for the cognac, uncorked it and drank deeply. Soon, he lay back on his pillow and fell asleep, leaving his problems and his anger temporarily held at bay by the cognac.

Toward morning there was a great upwelling from Shortreed's subconscious. It overwhelmed the flimsy cognac barrier and intruded into that area of awareness between sleep and waking, where the subconscious mind speaks to the conscious mind in symbols and playlets. It is here that broken icons parade across the stage of dreams to reveal hidden faces of unsuspected beauty or new and abject terrors that winnow the very gristle of the human soul.

On this stage of dreams, the subconscious speaks. "Here are your realities. Some are clothed in mystery. Some are puzzles to be solved. Others are blatant and obvious. But they are all your realities, and they won't go away until you have dealt with them."

Strangely, it was the memory of the uncritical, unquestioning love of Peso, the Border collie, that sprang first and unbidden from the abyss of anger and loss and grief that was his subconscious. Peso had abandoned his sheepherding chores to take up with Shortreed while the regiment had been on maneuvers near Tidworth in England. As soldiers and dogs have done since time immemorial, they bonded quickly to each other and became fast friends.

When the regiment moved out on Christmas Eve to go to the Bulge, Shortreed had decided reluctantly to leave Peso behind. They were not going to jump, and would land to offload the troopers, but no one knew what kind of shit they would be getting into. So Peso was left behind in England. At least that was his home turf.

It turned out that the fighting had been fierce, and the artillery had been more or less constant and heavy. Shortreed had missed his dog, but more than once had given thanks that Peso had been left behind.

Turk, his buddy, had been in the hospital when the regiment left for the Bulge. A week later, after he was released from the hospital, Turk came through the regimental area in England on his way to rejoin the regiment. Peso ran to him and greeted him eagerly and, when Turk left for Belgium, he brought Peso on the plane with him. They deplaned at a forward landing strip in Belgium and boarded a truck together for the combat zone. But when they got close enough to the action that Turk could hear U.S. artillery firing, Turk had a change of heart. Why take the dog into the hell of combat?

After some soul-searching, he had put Peso out of the truck near an artillery unit where at least he would be in the rear and a little safer than he would be further forward. To Turk's dismay, Peso followed the truck for almost ten miles in the snow before stopping in a state of near-collapse.

Turk was scarred by this, as was Shortreed. Turk, because of the part he had played in this sad event, and Shortreed because he and Peso had soldiered together for a long time. The feeling of abandonment Peso must have felt, along with his valiant, futile effort to keep up with the truck left a knotted place in Shortreed's heart, a place that would always belong to Peso.

These thoughts were crowded from Shortreed's mind by a string of images that appeared to him in rapid-fire dream sequences. Flies on the faces of dead friends in Normandy. The desolation and devastation left behind when the Krauts hit the Second Battalion with a ten minute screaming-meemie rocket attack; the twenty-three troopers burned to a crisp on the Rhine jump, when their burning plane got too low for them to jump and crashed into a stone barn. That was the day after Shortreed's twenty-second birthday but shit, that was an old man in combat, and then there was Skidmore looking up at him from the floor of the plane while shrapnel rattled and thumped on the fuselage, "Help me, Shortreed!" and there was Byrnes yelling from the door, "See you in hell, Shortreed!" Byrnes and Turk went out the door in close sequence. Byrnes knew he was jumping into eternity. Turk did not know. A few minutes later Turk was dead and Byrnes was missing forever.

With a cry of despair Shortreed half awakened and reached for the cognac, only to find Monique at his side. She had heard him wrestling with his subconscious and had gone to him out of instinctive compassion to comfort him.

"What are you doing here?" he demanded.

"Ssshh – you were having a nightmare."

"Yeah."

"Everything's all right now," she murmured in his ear and held him. "Go back to sleep."

For a long time they lay together in an embrace that reached beyond lovemaking, an embrace that assured them that someone cared and that they were not alone in the night.

Finally Shortreed fell into a peaceful sleep, and after a time Monique returned to her bed.

<u>End of Chapter 15</u>

Chapter 16

There may have been some ambivalence between Shortreed and Monique, but there was none between Sellers and his goal of changing his money to Swiss francs. Not only that, but he wasn't going to let that one-legged son-of-a-bitch run the show. His plan was to surprise them by getting to the Tam Tam early and taking over. If Antoine thought he was going to fuck Sellers out of his money, he'd better think again.

At eleven-twenty in the morning, the Café Tam Tam had just opened its doors. The tables and chairs were in place on the sidewalk, and the bartender was behind the bar polishing the glassware. Otherwise the place was empty.

The first inkling the bartender had that something was amiss came when Sellers and Antoine entered from the kitchen. Antoine's right pant leg was empty, and he hopped unsteadily on one leg. Sellers brought up the rear with his bag of money over his right shoulder and his .45 in his right hand. On the other shoulder he carried Antoine's prosthetic leg. It was an ugly and awkward looking thing, with the necessary straps dangling untidily.

Antoine made it to the nearest table where he sat heavily. Sellers dumped the leg onto the table with a thud. Then he pointed his gun at the bartender.

"Come here."

Silently, and with great misgivings, the bartender joined them.

"Sit down," Sellers ordered.

The bartender sat down at the table next to Antoine. Sellers kept them covered with his gun while he went behind the bar.

"Help yourself," Antoine said, hoping to distract him.

Sellers ignored Antoine and carefully searched the back bar area.

"Bring a bottle and let us drink to success," Antoine urged.

"Shut up!" Sellers snapped as he continued his search. At last, lifting a bar towel innocently lying to one side, he found a small .32 automatic concealed beneath it.

"Ah-h! Here we are." He held up the gun and displayed it for the other two men to see.

"But Monsieur-" Antoine started to protest, but Sellers cut him short.

"Fuck you!" He shoved the automatic into his back pocket.

"Calm yourself." Antoine tried to explain, " With so much money at stake, it's better to be safe, *non*?"

Sellers waved his .45. " Don't worry, I'll keep us safe." He grinned nastily and took a corked bottle of cognac from the back bar which he carried back to the table. He handed it to the bartender.

"Open it."

While the bartender obeyed, Sellers continued, "When you're through with that, close this joint."

"*Non*!" Antoine protested vehemently.

"I said close it!" Sellers repeated.

"We do not wish to act as if anything different was going on here." Antoine argued.

'What if someone comes in off the street?"

Antoine indicated the bartender. "He will tell them to come back later."

"Nah," Sellers said uncertainly. "I think we ought to close it."

"This is not a good neighborhood," Antoine told him.

"So?"

"Everyone here is a thief, a criminal, and carries a gun."

"Tough shit for them." Sellers waved the .45.

"*Monsieur* Paratrooper, for this much money, they would kill their mother."

The bartender finished opening the bottle and placed it in front of Sellers.

"I'll bring glasses."

"Forget the glasses," Seller snapped. "Get behind the bar and stay there!"

The bartender went behind the bar again and resumed polishing the glasses.

Sellers tilted the cognac bottle and took a big drink, then held it out to Antoine.

"*Non, merci.*"

"Drink!" Sellers ordered him.

Antoine shook his head, but Sellers waved the .45 in his face. He shrugged philosophically, accepted the cognac bottle and drank from it.

"I don't like to drink alone," Sellers said hostilely.

Antoine reacted to his tone. "Why do you hate me?"

"Why? You doped me and tried to steal my money!"

"You can trust me now."

Sellers took the bottle back. "I'll bet." He took another swig.

"There is too much at stake here," Antoine argued. "I promise-"

"Fuck you!" Sellers exploded. "Promise till you're blue in the face, but if you make one funny move, I'll blow your ass off!"

During the silence that followed this outburst, Sellers idly began examining Antoine's prosthetic leg.

"How did you lose it?" he wanted to know.

"*Le Boche.*"

"The Krauts got it, huh?" Sellers stood the leg up on the table and flexed the knee joint experimentally.

"Give it back to me please," Antoine pleaded.

"Forget it."

Still in the nondescript second-hand clothing that was his disguise as a French black marketer, Captain Walters parked his bicycle and entered the Tam Tam. He was carrying the battered briefcase that completed his disguise.

"The bar is not open," the bartender told him immediately.

Walters ignored him and went directly to the table where Sellers sat with Antoine.

"What do you want?" Sellers asked nastily.

"You have cigarettes? Chocolate?"

"Take off!" Sellers told him.

"But *Monsieur* Paratrooper--" Walters offered the standard protest.

"This is a private conversation."

Walters accepted this with a shrug and, after a cursory glance at the prosthetic leg and the half-concealed .45, he went back outside to his bicycle. Through the door they watched him toss his briefcase into the basket and pedal away.

"Who was that guy?" Sellers wanted to know.

"Forget him." Antoine shrugged. "He's nobody."

Sellers took another drink from the bottle and held it out again to Antoine, who shook his head.

"Drink!"

As Antoine drank from the cognac, Sellers started laughing. "We might as well party a little while we wait."

In spite of his drinking, Sellers had lost none of his single-mindedness of purpose. With the deadline only two days away, he was in headlong pursuit of his goal of changing his money into Swiss francs. Had anyone suggested to him that his destiny was entangled in all of this, or that his goal and his destiny were one and the same, he would have said, "Fuck destiny! The money is what I want!" And that too, was a part of his destiny.

Shortreed was in no way headlong. In fact, for the first time in his life, he was nonplussed by a woman. There was an emotional vortex that centered on Monique. From time to time he would dip into the upper reaches of that vortex. Only to break off and withdraw when the pull threatened to entrain him and deliver him defenseless to Monique, who was for him at the center of these swirling and sometimes conflicting emotions. It never occurred to him that she also found herself at the center of a similar vortex of feelings, and that Monique's emotions were almost exactly parallel to his own.

They were on a blanket in the shade of a large oak tree. Monique was tidying up the remains of a picnic lunch and returning things to a large basket. Shortreed lay on his back with his head cradled on his musette bag of money.

"Your friend Sellers frightens me, " Monique said.

"He's not my friend," Shortreed told her emphatically.

She was puzzled by this. "But you're together. You...you--"

"In the army," he explained, "everything is alphabetical."

He was thoughtful for a moment, then added, "We're the last of the S's."

She smiled in relief. "I'm glad you're not friends. He's a bad person."

"How am I doing?" he asked.

"What do you mean?"

He sat up and ticked each question off on his fingers.

"Did I steal the money? Did I shoot prisoners during the war? Do I go to church? Do I have a girl in every town?"

Embarrassed, she lowered her eyes. Shortreed put his hand under her chin and lifted it, forcing eye contact. .

He teased her, "Look, I'm nice to my mother and I don't kick little doggies."

Monique was flustered. "I didn't mean to annoy you."

"Who's annoyed?" he said with a big grin. "I'll give you one more question. Then we'll quit talking about me."

She smiled fleetingly at this, then turned pensive. It was obvious that she did have another question, and that it was important to her.

Finally she asked, "Who is Helen?"

Shortreed was momentarily stunned, then angry.

"Did Sellers tell you about her?" he demanded.

"You were cursing her in your sleep last night," she told him softly.

The smile went from Shortreed's face. After an awkward moment, he answered her, "She's my wife."

"Your wife?" Monique's voice was shocked.

Shortreed looked at her, but she avoided eye contacted and seemed as if she were about to weep. After studying her for a moment, he opened his shirt, removed his money belt and took out a letter which he handed to her.

"Read it."

Puzzled, she accepted the letter and began to read it. Quickly finished with it, she continued to stare at the piece of paper.

"That's what they call a 'Dear John'," he told her.

"Did you know the man?"

"Nah." He shrugged. "Some 4-F."

She looked at the letter again and read the date aloud, "May 28, 1944."

"We came back from Normandy in July. It was on my bunk when we got there."

She returned the letter to him and he sat staring at it, hung up in thought.

Summoning the courage, Monique asked, "What was she like?"

"Like a cheap radio. High frequency, low fidelity," he told her with bitter sarcasm.

"What do you intend to do about her?"

"I've done it. But you have to wait a year before a divorce is final. That year will be up in July."

"Did you love her?"

Shortreed shrugged. "She was beautiful, exciting, vain… and empty."

He put a cigarette between his lips but did not light it. Instead, he continued to stare moodily at the letter.

"I'm surprised that you have kept it so long."

"It's to remind me never to fall in love again," he said flatly.

He struck a match and lit the cigarette. On impulse, Monique suddenly took the letter from him and held it in the flame of the match. As it caught fire, she laid it on the ground and added the envelope. Together they watched in silent fascination as flame consumed the letter and the envelope, crumbling them into ashes.

Slowly they turned until their eyes met.

"That was yesterday," she told him.

They embraced and Shortreed gently laid her back on the ground.

"Monique," he murmured, "I'm glad I found you."

He sought her lips with his and they kissed hungrily. The embrace warmed as they gave themselves to the moment.

The driver of the *fiacre* approached, then stopped, when he found them entwined. He cleared his throat, "*Monsieur.*"

Shortreed reacted in a blur of motion. He rolled away from Monique and came up to one knee, with his .45 covering the driver. The motion was defensive, but the speed of it was frightening. There was an awkward silence as Shortreed lowered the gun.

"*Monsieur*, we must leave soon," the driver said apologetically. "If you wish to be at the Tam Tam by three o'clock."

"Okay. We'll be with you in just a little."

But the moment had been destroyed. In silence they went about the business of getting everything back into the picnic basket. This done, they folded the blanket and started for the *fiacre.* Suddenly Shortreed dropped the blanket and set the basket down. He gathered Monique to him in a passionate embrace, and they kissed hungrily. It was a long moment before they pulled apart.

"Shortreed, you wonderful man," Monique told him happily. "I love you!"

He showered her throat, her face, and her lips with kisses, all the while murmuring, "I love you."

Reluctantly, he allowed reality to intrude and stopped kissing her. "We better get rolling."

But Monique kept her body pressed tightly against him.

"Get rid of the gun," she pleaded. "Please!"

He patted the bag of money that hung over his shoulder. "I'm trading this for Swiss francs."

"Why?"

"In a few days, this money will be worthless paper. If I get it changed to Swiss francs, it will still be good."

"Do you need a gun for that?"

"Suppose someone tries to rob me?"

"Forget the money, please," she pleaded.

He patted the bag of money. "Tonight we'll be rich."

"Not if you're in prison," she said. "Or dead."

He kissed her again, then promised, "I'll be careful."

Together they took up the basket and the blanket and made their way to the *fiacre*. As they walked toward it, Shortreed was in a lyrical mood. He no longer resisted the thought but freely admitted to himself that he was in love and it felt good. Even better, she was in love with him.

Up on the hill in the Old Quarter of Nice, a raiding party of CID soldiers was using an obscure alleyway as a staging area. This was not like going into combat, but there was an element of danger and excitement here that was reflected in the way the men acted. Some of them complained about being ordered to wait until the moneyman showed up. Why not grab the underlings first and then wait for the big shot? It would be easier that way.

But in spite of their bitching, the final consensus was that the moneyman was indeed the prize and a premature raid might scare him off.

At the mouth of the alleyway Captain Walters, still disguised as a French black marketer, pedaled his bicycle into the alley. He stopped beside the communications jeep and ordered, "Get me the second squad, sergeant."

"Yes Sir." Wilson switched on the transmission button. "Blue one to blue two, come in."

The radio sputtered into life. "Blue two to blue one, over."

Wilson held out the hand set to the captain, who spoke into it. "This is Walters. I checked the back door. It's locked, but I want the second squad there just the same."

"Yes Sir."

"And no shooting unless it's absolutely necessary. Got that?"

"Roger Wilco."

"Don't move into position until you get our signal," Walters ordered.

"Anything else, sir?"

"That's all. Over and out."

Walters returned the handset to Wilson, who asked, "Do you think they're armed, sir?"

"The paratrooper has a .45. Who's on lookout?"

"Smith, sir."

"Shake him up and see what's happening."

Wilson took the handset but, before he could speak, a voice began on the radio.

"Surveillance One to Blue One. Come in."

"Surveillance One, we have you loud and clear."

"Subject crossing *Rue* St. Francois de Paulo heading in your direction."

"It's Smith, sir," Wilson held out the handset to the captain. "Do you want to talk to him?"

Walters shook his head. "That's all I needed to know."

Wilson spoke once more into the handset. "Message received. Over and out."

Captain Walters lit a cigarette. His mind was on the paratrooper at the Tam Tam. He was armed, drinking heavily, and fresh out of combat. Such men were always dangerous. Hopefully he would be too drunk to fight by the time they made their move.

At the Tam Tam nothing had changed, except that the cognac bottle was half-empty. Both Antoine and Sellers were showing signs of drunkenness. Sellers took another generous swig from the bottle, then once more examined the prosthetic leg.

After flexing the knee several times, he got up from the table and held the prosthetic against his own leg. He regarded it solemnly for a moment, then laid it on the table before Antoine and sat back down.

"You can have it back, Frenchy. It doesn't fit me."

"It doesn't fit me either," Antoine said.

"No?"

"It hurts. It's heavy."

"You ought to be proud of it," Sellers said nastily. "It makes you a hero. A one-legged hero."

Antoine fingered the straps thoughtfully. "I'm ashamed of it."

"How come?"

Antoine hesitated a moment, then from the depths of his own misery, he spoke. "I should've done more."

"You lost a leg. How much more can you do?"

"The others are dead."

"That ain't your fault."

"Think," Antoine said accusingly, "at some time in the war did you not hang back a split second that saved your life and caused someone else to lose theirs?"

Sellers experienced a brief spasm of guilt as he remembered removing the grenade launcher from his rifle and throwing it away. This was followed by a memory of Sanford lying dead on the battlefield. Had he kept the grenade launcher, it would have been him lying there, not Augie Sanford.

After this brief pang of guilt, Sellers recovered quickly. Dramatically he tore the decorations bar from his uniform and tossed it down before Antoine.

"Look at that!" Sellers demanded.

"So?"

"Purple heart with oak leaf cluster. Bronze star with oak leaf cluster, four battle stars, one invasion arrowhead, and the combat infantry badge. Does that look like I spent my time hanging back?"

Antoine fingered the decorations bar for a moment, then pushed it back to Sellers.

"You didn't answer my question," Antoine said.

"Those other guys, the dead ones, they hung back too," Sellers told him. "They just didn't do it at the right time."

"Don't you feel bad that so many people died and you didn't?"

Furious at this, Sellers pointed the .45 at Antoine. "Get off my back, you crippled son-of-a-bitch, or I'll blow your fucking head off!"

It was at this moment that a pedicab pulled up before the café and Marcel dismounted and went inside. He carried a bulging satchel and at this Sellers and Antoine broke off their confrontation and watched silently as Marcel came to join them at the table.

Suddenly there was the roar of a jeep motor outside and a jeep screeched to a halt before the café. Captain Walters and his men jumped from the vehicle and rushed into the café, with their guns covering the three men at the table and the bartender. Sergeant Wilson carried a tommy gun. The others had .45 automatics. Outside more soldiers were arriving on the double.

"Everyone stay put!" Walters yelled. "This is a raid!"

Sellers lurched up from the table and fired at Walters, who collapsed to the floor wounded. Marcel dropped his money satchel to the floor and stood with his hands in the air. There was a brief flurry of gunfire, and Sellers fell to the floor dead. At the same time, Antoine took a burst from the sergeant's tommy gun that killed him instantly.

While two soldiers hustled Marcel and the bartender outside to the jeep, Sergeant Wilson went to the table where he examined Sellers and Antoine. Satisfied that both men were dead, he went immediately to Wilson. The captain sat on the floor, clutching his bloody shoulder.

"You hit bad?" the sergeant asked.

"Bad enough."

"Do you want to wait for an ambulance or do you think you can make it in the jeep?"

"Take me in the jeep. I'm bleeding all over."

"Evans! Smith! On the double!" Wilson yelled. When they came quickly, he ordered, " Put the captain in the jeep and get him to the hospital."

Carefully they got Walters to his feet and loaded him into the jeep between them. The driver revved his engine and burned rubber as they took off.

Thus, in the spring of 1945, Sellers' story ended..

<u>End of Chapter 16</u>

Chapter 17

As things were winding down at the Tam Tam, Shortreed late for his rendezvous, was riding uphill toward the café. He was alone except for the driver. As they approached the top of the hill, the jeep carrying Captain Walters came tearing past them, going in the opposite direction. The jeep driver was honking his horn furiously as he wove in and out through the light traffic.

In the back seat, the two soldiers held Captain Walters erect between them. He was a bloody mess, and only the efforts of the two enlisted men kept him from collapsing as he swayed to and fro with the movement of the jeep.

The driver of the *fiacre* pulled his horse over to the curb and stopped. He and Shortreed both stared after the jeep as it continued its breakneck pace down the hill.

"Do you wish to continue?" the driver asked.

"No," Shortreed told him, "wait for me here."

Taking his musette bag of money, Shortreed jumped to the ground and disappeared down a side street. Downhill, the wail of a siren could be heard approaching. Striding rapidly, Shortreed turned from the side street onto one that ran parallel to the main boulevard. From there he continued uphill until he was even with the Tam Tam. He moved cautiously between buildings until he found a vantage point that gave him a clear view of the entrance to the Tam Tam and the action taking place there.

The second jeep was still parked before the café. The only soldiers present were members of the raiding party and they were busy controlling the crowd that had continued to gather. Finally the ambulance arrived and the crowd opened up to allow it to back up and stop before the café entrance. Two soldiers got out, opened the back door of the ambulance and took out the stretcher. The crowd fell silent as they carried the stretcher into the Tam Tam.

Shortreed knew in his heart that this was going to be bad news. Sellers was somehow connected with all this excitement. He had either wounded or killed someone, or someone had done it to him. Either way the prospects were not good.

Suddenly there was a gasp from the crowd as the stretcher-bearers came from the café with a blanket-covered body on the stretcher. As they were loading it into the ambulance, Shortreed could see Antoine's artificial leg lying on top of the blanket.

"Well, at least it wasn't Sellers," Shortreed told himself.

The two soldiers took another stretcher and went back into the café. After a long wait they came out again with a second blanket-covered body. Shortreed flinched when he saw a pair of jump boots sticking out from beneath the blanket. Undoubtedly they belonged to Sellers and he was dead.

They had not really been friends, but nonetheless Shortreed was shocked by Sellers' death. Sellers had survived all the hell that the 705th had gone through, only to die like this. The war and the *Wehrmacht* had been unable to get him, but his mindless pursuit of money and power had laid him low. It was almost as if he had died by his own hand.

Ultimately the realization came to Shortreed that if he had not tarried with Monique, it might have been he who was carried from the Tam Tam under a blanket. He shuddered at the thought and gave silent thanks for Monique.

"Ps-s-s-t!"

It was Suzette tugging at his sleeve. She had spotted him from the crowd and joined him.

"What happened here?" he asked her quietly.

"Your friend Sellers is dead."

"How did he die?"

"The CID shot him."

'Why?"

"He shot first."

Shortreed fell silent as he considered this. Suzette took advantage of this moment to press herself against him and put her arms around him.

"You spend the night with me, *non?*" she invited.

Shortreed shook his head. "No."

"Please, Blondi."

"I got to go."

He pulled free of her embrace and moved away between the buildings. He made his way back to the *fiacre* and rode to the *pension* in deep thought. In his mind Shortreed knew that his story was still unfolding and that Monique was looming large in it.

At the *pension* he instructed the driver to wait. Shortreed dismounted from the *fiacre* but did not go inside directly. He sat instead on the steps out front, his mind still struggling with the incongruities of Sellers' death and with the reminder of his own mortality.

It was late afternoon of a spring day in Nice. Far out toward Africa, the blue of the sky and of the Mediterranean merged imperceptibly and a soft breeze ruffled the hairs on his arm. Small wonder that he was able to shrug off his concerns about life and death. The sea and the sky and the sunlight were sovereign against such somber thoughts. What the hell? He was still alive and in one piece, he was in love and it was spring, and the war was yesterday. Thus revitalized he entered the *pension* and took the stairs two at a time in his eagerness to take Monique in his arms.

At the top of the stairs, Shortreed stopped in surprise. Two Frenchmen and the old harridan who was the *concierge* stood in the doorway to his room, peering in. Mystified, Shortreed approached quietly and looked over their shoulders.

Within the room, Monique sat on a stool in the middle of the room, submitting while Charles, the decorated French veteran stood over her with a pair of hair clippers. She was almost bald, and Charles was just cutting the last lock of hair from her head. Her long beautiful hair lay around her in piles on the floor.

Monique stared straight ahead, her face an expressionless mask. As he worked over her, Charles had an air of triumphant self-righteousness.

One of the Frenchmen at the door half-turned, saw Shortreed and reacted. This alerted the others, but by then they found themselves covered by Shortreed's .45. With a motion of the gun he herded them into the room and entered after them, closing the door behind him.

They waited apprehensively for Shortreed's next move. Monique continued to stare before her without expression.

"Monsieur," Charles began nervously, "the *Mam'selle* was what you call a *collaboratrice*."

Without taking his eyes from Charles' face, Shortreed spoke to Monique.

"Get up, Monique," he told her. His voice was flat, emotionless and intimidating.

She obeyed silently and as she moved aside, Shortreed motioned to Charles with the gun. Reluctantly Charles sat on the stool.

Shortreed turned to Monique and ordered her, "Cut his hair."

"I'm not a collaborator!" Charles protested.

"Fuck you!" Shortreed told him. "Go ahead, Monique."

The others watched in fascination as she took the clippers and approached Charles. She started to cut his hair but stopped abruptly.

"*Non!* I cannot! I cannot!"

"How come?" Shortreed demanded.

"It's true," she said, in little more than a whisper, and closed her eyes in misery.

The others looked with relief at Shortreed as he shoved the gun inside his belt. Charles rose from the stool and went to him.

"You must understand, Monsieur," he told the trooper self-righteously "She earned this. It was no more than her due."

Without warning, Shortreed punched him savagely in the gut. "Now get out of here."

He watched the other two Frenchmen help Charles to his feet. Silently they filed out of the room and Shortreed closed the door behind them. Alone with Monique, he turned to face her, but she would not meet his eyes.

"I'm sorry," she said quietly.

Shortreed took no notice of her. Instead he went over to the closet, took her hat, and jammed it down on her head. Without her hair, the hat was too big and came down over her ears.

She caught a glimpse of herself in the mirror and winced at her reflection. "Shortreed, let me explain," she begged.

"There's nothing to explain."

Monique was anguished. "It was not what you think it was."

"Look," Shortreed said to her. "We've got a bag full of money."

"Shortreed, listen to me please!"

She looked at him pleadingly and for a moment it seemed that he might relent. But then he went back to the money. "We've got only a few days to spend it."

He reached for her hand.

She pulled it back. "I'm not going!"

Shortreed pulled her to him roughly.

"Yes you are."

His tone of voice did not invite argument, and she did not resist as he led her to the door and out.

They spent the rest of the day with the issue of Monique's shaved pathetic head and her German lover lying between them. Shortreed was appalled by the thought that she had, by her own admission, been a *collaboratrice*, and furthermore, what did that word mean?

Was it simply that she had gone to bed with an enemy soldier? Or had she given away information to the enemy? The way he used the word 'collaborator' seemed to be different from the way the French used it.

Somehow neither of them was able to address this issue, even though both made tentative efforts. They spent the time being polite to each other and uncommunicative.

Earlier Shortreed had given up on the idea of buying Swiss francs with his money. There were a few days left in which the money could be spent. He resolved to spend as much as possible during that time. The remainder he would return to the French people. The SS had stolen it from them, and in his view they were entitled to get it back. As for Shortreed himself, he felt that he was entitled to a finder's fee.

Foremost in his mind was the thought of throwing a giant party, one that would be a memory-maker for everyone involved. To that end Shortreed, with Monique in tow, had rented one of the better nightclubs in town and arranged for an enormous quantity of champagne. Now, with the day dusking, Cardone, armed with money, was scouting the town for women. Two other troopers were going through the town, inviting every paratrooper they encountered to come to the party.

When night fell, Shortreed and Monique sat side by side at a table near the front of the rented nightclub. The garishly lit club was empty except for the band and a bunch of paratroopers. The band was tuning, and the troopers were drinking at the bar. A few waiters were moving tables and chairs to the wall in order to provide more room for dancing. Behind the bar, three bartenders were making preparations for a monumental party.

One of the troopers looked toward the street and let out a wolf whistle. Shortreed watched with a sardonic smile as the other troopers looked and joined in the whistling. On the street before the club, a string of pedicabs were drawing up before the entrance. The front one held Cardone, who was grinning from ear to ear, and the madam of the fanciest whorehouse in town. Strung out behind them, each pedicab held two whores. They all climbed down and with Cardone and the madam leading the way, went in procession into the club.

The whores, dressed in their finery, swished past the troopers at the bar and seated themselves at the other side of the club from the men. One of the troopers immediately left the bar and crossed the room to make a grab for one of the girls.

"Knock it off!" Shortreed ordered. "The party hasn't started yet."

Respectfully Cardone escorted the madam to a table where a glass and a bottle of champagne awaited her, then went to report to Shortreed.

"We're two short," he told Shortreed. "They'll be along later."

Shortreed got up and went over to the troopers lining the bar.

"All right, you guys," he told them. "Here's the story. The booze is paid for and so are the girls!"

"Yippee!" a trooper yelled. "Let's go!"

"Not so fast," Shortreed corrected him. "You all have to leave now--"

"Hey what about the party?" someone shouted.

"It's like this. The party starts when each of you come back with a French man or a French woman--"

"I don't get it," one of the troopers complained.

"Tell them I'll give them money," Shortreed said. "But first they have to tell me what they're going to buy with it."

"Is that all?"

"That's all," Shortreed told them. "Now take off!"

As they started to leave, Cardone joined Shortreed and asked, "Am I supposed to go with them?"

"No," Shortreed said. "I've got another job for you."

"What is it?"

"The fat bartender will give you the address of a wig salesman. Go get him."

"What do you want with a wig salesman?" a trooper asked incredulously.

"Never mind," Shortreed said. "Just tell him to bring all of his samples."

"Suppose he won't come?"

"Show him this." Shortreed handed him a stack of franc notes. Cardone took the money, waved a salute with an almost empty bottle of champagne and left.

Returning to the table, Shortreed sat down again beside Monique who stared straight ahead and took no notice of his presence. Aware of the chasm that had opened between them, he had no idea of how he felt about his broken dream that she was The Girl who somehow would heal him of his mistrust. Now it had begun to seem that she only aggravated it.

He lit a cigarette and made another effort to make eye contact with Monique, but she was cocooned within her anger and her misery. One of the waiters brought a magnum of champagne in a bucket of ice. He opened it with a flourish and poured them each a glass. As he left the table, Shortreed raised his glass to Monique.

"*Vive l'amour*," he said bitterly.

Outwardly she ignored him. Inwardly they were equally consumed with thoughts of the other and anger at all that had happened. Shortreed swallowed his champagne at a gulp, then retreated back into his isolation.

First he, then she, would make a tentative but heartfelt overture to the other, but to no avail. Back and forth it went between them until it was almost midnight and there was a world-class bacchanal going on around them. The nightclub was a throbbing mass of paratroopers and whores, dancing and reveling in various degrees of drunken abandonment.

Along one side of the room several husky troopers maintained control over a line of French civilians that stretched from the table where Shortreed sat with Monique to the side door. Shortreed's musette bag of money was at his elbow and a Frenchman stood before him reciting a sorrowful tale of woe that was replete with numerous Gallic shrugs and gestures. The man finished his story and waited expectantly.

"What did he say?" Shortreed asked.

"His wife left him," Monique said. "He wants to get her back."

Shortreed laughed uproariously, then stopped in mid laugh to stare at the Frenchman solemnly for a long moment.

"He wants ten thousand francs," Monique added.

Shortreed counted out twenty thousand francs and gave them to her.

"Tell him to forget his wife and get a girl friend."

She handed the money to the man and repeated Shortreed's advice in French

Shortreed said, "Tel him that he must go to the bank tomorrow and trade it for new francs."

"*Merci*! *Merci beaucoup*!" He was beside himself with joy at this largesse and continued to babble his effusive thanks, until Shortreed nodded to one of the troopers.

"Get this guy outta here."

The trooper shrugged and grabbed the Frenchman by the collar and the seat of his pants. He high-stepped him out the side door, still waving his fistful of francs and shouting encouragement to those waiting in line. While this was happening, another trooper led a giggling whore to the table.

"Hey Shortreed, I thought you said these girls were paid for."

"They are."

"She says she won't go to bed with me."

"She doesn't have to unless she wants to," Shortreed told him. "That's part of the deal."

"So what do I do?"

"Romance her," Shortreed advised, laughing. "It'll be good for both of you."

Looking baffled, the trooper led the whore back to the bar, where he offered her another glass of champagne with an effort at gallantry.

Shortreed turned away from watching them and regarded Monique soberly for a moment.

"This German. What was his name?"

Monique looked wretched. But she managed to reply, "Kurt."

"You want to tell me about him?"

She was silent and he continued to stare at her solemnly for a long time.

"Well?"

She made eye contact with him before she spoke. "I loved him."

This was interrupted as Cardone bulled his way through the crowd with a pudgy little man in tow. He was very neatly dressed and carried a large leather sample case.

"Here you are, Shortreed." Cardone gestured at the little man. "I want you to meet Lucky Pierre, the phantom wig salesman. I haven't paid him yet, but I showed him the money and made a lot of promises."

"Good job, Cardone." Shortreed pointed to a very pretty girl who sat alone against the wall. "That one's yours."

With a big grin, Cardone handed back the money he had taken as bait for the wig salesman, and hurried over eagerly to join the girl. Shortreed turned to Pierre.

"Do you speak English?"

"*Oui, Monsieur.*"

"What's in the bag?"

"Samples."

Shortreed reached over and removed the hat from around Monique's freshly shaven head. She flinched and the salesman raised an eyebrow.

"*Collaboratrice?*" He seemed genuinely shocked and about to refuse. But before he could speak, Shortreed held up a packet of bills and riffled them.

"There are fifty one-thousand-franc notes in this package." He threw the packet down on the table before Pierre, who stared at it, then overrode his principles and opened the sample case. He removed a mirror on a stand and set it before Monique. Then he selected a wig from the case and held it next to her face. He studied the effect for a moment, then shook his head and took another from the bag.

As this went on Shortreed turned away from them and called out loudly, "Next case!"

One of the troopers herding the line led another Frenchman to the table. He was not young and was poorly dressed, but managed somehow to look dapper in spite of his shabby clothing. There was something birdlike and precise about him, and he made his pitch for the money in a torrent of French. It took no knowledge of the language to catch on to the fact this man was a con artist and what he was saying was the purest flim flam.

He finished his spiel with a flourish and an expectant smile. Pierre still flustered back and forth with his selection of wigs and Monique was so engrossed in this that Shortreed had to prompt her.

"Well, what did he say?"

Pierre was just setting a different wig in place. Monique somehow seemed to be changing personality to suit it.

Without taking her eyes from the mirror, she answered Shortreed, "He wants five thousand francs. He has worked out a gambling system. He wants to break the bank at Monte Carlo."

"Suppose he breaks the bank," Shortreed demanded. "What's he going to do with his winnings?"

Monique asked the man in French and he told her, gesturing expansively, of all he planned to do with his winnings. As he finished rattling on and became silent, Pierre made the final adjustment on the new wig, and Monique turned hopefully to Shortreed for his approval.

Ignoring the wig, he asked brusquely, "What did he say?"

"He will buy his mother a house, pay his debts, contribute to charity, and only then will he buy new clothes and other things badly needed."

"Bullshit!" Shortreed mocked and spoke to the man directly. "You know what? You'll always be a lousy tinhorn gambler, whatever you do!"

The gambler flinched at Shortreed's tone, but brightened when he counted five one thousand franc notes into his hand. He was effusively grateful. Shortreed fished a fifty-franc note from his pocket and held it out to him.

"*Cinquante franc? Pourquoi?*"

Shortreed said to Monique, "Tell him it's for bus fare home."

When she translated this for the gambler he started to protest. But the look on Shortreed's face warned him and he left quietly.

Shortreed watched as Pierre tried still another wig on Monique. Again, there was the suggestion of a personality change. Each wig seemed to resonate, but incompletely, with some facet of her personality.

The first wig had stamped her as a flirt. The next had made her look motherly. This one? He wasn't sure exactly. But she looked different.

The next client in the line, a woman, approached Shortreed. Some casual spectators had noticed the show taking place with Monique and the wigs and were crowding closer to the table, while the bacchanal of troopers and whores continued with drunken abandon in the background.

The current supplicant might have been pretty when younger, but now was overripe and had been used and abused. She had a worn face and the lines around her mouth somehow validated her tearful recital of the woes that had beset her life.

As before Shortreed made a pretense of listening attentively to every word of her narrative, but his mind was on Monique. He spoke without turning to her.

"Did you love him more than you do me?"

"I don't know," she told him honestly.

"What kind of an answer is that?" Shortreed demanded in frustration. But instead of saying any more, Monique retreated into the wigs and the mirror.

Getting no response, the Frenchwoman pressed on with her weepy narrative of a ruined life that could only be mended by a liberal application of money. The crowd of onlookers was growing, and moved closer as the parallel dramas of free money and blighted love unfolded before them.

To Shortreed, even with his very limited understanding of French, the woman's narrative had the ring of cant. Certain rhythms of inflection came more or less sequentially, and the rise and fall of her voice sounded faintly as if the whole story had been memorized. Long before she had reached the end of it, Shortreed grew bored.

"Tell her to get to the point," Shortreed said brusquely to Monique.

"She wants to visit her mother's grave," Monique told him, as she made a small adjustment to the wig Pierre had just put in place.

"Tell the truth!" Shortreed exploded. "Whatever the truth is, tell her I'll give her money for it, but she gets nothing for lies!"

Monique repeated this to her in French. Relieved of the burden of concealing her true desires, the woman rose to the occasion. She wanted finery and a new hairdo, cosmetics from the best salons, a *haute couture* gown from a *boutique.* And with all of this, *certainment*, a young man, a new admirer.

Monique suppressed a faint, not entirely unsympathetic smile as she translated this catalogue of desires for Shortreed.

While the woman waited expectantly, something about her connected with Shortreed's inner humanity. She and the others seeking money became real to him. They were the flotsam and jetsam of the war, noncombatants whose lives had been shattered by the endless insanity and dislocations of the times.

He tossed the woman several packets of francs, a few more than he had originally intended. She took the money and continued to thank him over and over until he dismissed her with a wave of his hand.

"Next case," Shortreed called, and an elderly man left the line and stood before him.

"*M'sieur*, if you please, I need money." His voice was heavily accented.

"How much?"

"*Beaucoup.*"

"How much is *beaucoup*? *Combien*?"

"Twenty thousand francs."

"That much?"

"I have two horses who, like me, are too old to work. For twenty thousand francs I can move them back to where they can live out their lives on pasture."

"How long have you had them?" Shortreed wanted to know.

"Together we delivered milk for more than twenty years," the old man said. "They are my friends."

The old man waited nervously while Shortreed considered his request. He relaxed as Shortreed counted out twenty thousand-franc notes, then looked incredulous as Shortreed, on impulse, added a full pack of fifty one-thousand franc notes to the stack.

"Merci!" he gasped.

"The extra fifty thousand is to help you find pasture for yourself," Shortreed told him seriously.

The old man, beyond words, broke into tears, Some of the onlookers' eyes were wet as the old man made his way to the door in a daze.

Shortreed turned back to Monique and asked abruptly, " "What exactly did you do that made them cut your hair off?"

"I had a German boyfriend," she said as she turned away from the mirror to face him. "Half of our government got in bed with the Nazis for personal gain – greed! Who shaved their heads? My crime was love!"

"You didn't do anything else?"

"Like what?"

"Like give them secrets?"

"What secrets? I was a secretary for a company that shipped farm produce to the big cities. I had no secrets!"

Standing behind her, Pierre settled another wig gently on her head and held out the mirror with a flourish. For the first time she showed some real interest and rearranged a lock of hair. It made her look much more as she had before her head was shaved. She was no longer psychically naked.

Unnoticed by the two estranged lovers, the number of spectators around the table had continued to grow and the area around their table was crowded. The band still played, but few couples danced. What was happening between Shortreed and Monique had become the center of attention.

Shortreed's attention was completely on the now hopeful Monique. He grinned affectionately and bent over to kiss her. At this, one drunken paratrooper began to applaud and, as others joined in, the troopers guarding the door turned to see what was happening. With this, the French civilians whom they had been holding at bay streamed past them into the club, looking as if they would overwhelm everything.

Shortreed and Monique continued to kiss until they could no longer ignore the crowd. They broke off the kiss and Shortreed began ripping open the packets of franc notes, and flinging loose bills into the crowd. Immediately there was a frantic scramble for the fluttering shower of franc notes.

As Shortreed continued to rip open the packets and throw the money, he was yelling, " The Nazis took it away from you guys and I took it back from them. So here's your piece!" Finally the money bag was empty. Shortreed flung the empty musette bag into the crowd. He caught Monique by the hand and together they fought their way out of the club to the sidewalk, leaving behind them a mad saturnalia, as people continued to jostle for the money. In the background the band played on, but no one danced. Instead the civilians swirled and eddied around little islands of paratroopers, who ignored them and continued to drink and fondle their women. It was Dante-esque, a *tableaux vivant* of drinking, whoring, grabbing, greed, and lust , a *dans macabre* that was all too human, yet somehow poignant

Shortreed and Monique took a pedicab back to the *pension* on the hill. As he paid the driver, there was a great shout that rose up from the town.

"*La Guerre est fini! La Guerre est fini!* The war is over!" It was a joyous cry.

Later, they stood at the window of their room and listened to the pandemonium of celebration that rose from long-suffering survivors of a terrible war.

With Shortreed's arm around her Monique continued to stare down through the window. She still wore the last wig, the one she had chosen, and was in a pensive mood.

"Shortreed."

He stopped nuzzling her neck long enough to say teasingly, "Don't bother me. I'm busy."

She persisted, "What you said about there being two kinds of women -- You were wrong."

He stopped nuzzling. "How?"

"Beside the ones in the street, and the ones you called 'the others', there is also the one in your head."

He turned her gently to face him. "Don't complicate things."

"The woman in your head is a statue," she told him. "Cold, impossible, unreal."

"What does that make you?" he asked.

"A human being."

She faced away from him to the window and once more he embraced her from behind.

"Let's not talk about it," he pleaded with her softly.

He turned her toward him and started to kiss her, but she resisted and shook her head. "You're still trying to pretend I'm a statue."

She pulled off the wig. "This is who I am."

For a long moment Shortreed regarded her silently. Then, pulling her to him, he enfolded her in an embrace and began to shower her with kisses, stopping only long enough to tell her, "And this is who I am."

With a little cry of joy, she returned his embrace passionately. "Oh Shortreed, I love you!"

"Monique," Shortreed murmured, with a deep feeling of joy and release.

She turned her face to his and they kissed hungrily, cheeks, eyes, face, mouth, in a rapture of human understanding and animal love.

Outside, the clamor of delirious celebration continued. The War was over.

The End